Clenched Fists,
Burning Crosses

RADICAL
SOUTHS ▼

MICHAEL P. BIBLER and **JAIME HARKER**, editors

Radical Souths reclaims and reprints some of the most revolutionary works of Southern literature from the twentieth century. The fight for racial, sexual, economic, and political justice in the South has always been a homegrown struggle led by Southerners themselves, and Southern writers have always turned to the power of literature to bring those ideals to life. This series makes key texts from this radical tradition available to a wider audience, giving these voices of antiracist, queer, feminist, and socialist protest renewed urgency and authority.

A complete list of books published in Radical Souths is available at https://uncpress.org/series/radical-souths/.

A NOTE TO READERS

Some of the books in the Radical Souths series may contain racist, misogynist, queerphobic, or transphobic language, as well as graphic descriptions of sexual or racial violence, including assault, lynching, rape, and murder. But we the editors believe these scenes are never gratuitous. These books attempt to imagine ways to confront, challenge, and change these patterns of language and violence. And we feel that when the authors of these books choose to include graphic scenes, they do so to remind us exactly what is at stake in fighting the forces of domination and oppression. We invite our readers to approach these books with care but also with an open mind and a willingness to turn any potential shock and anger into action.

Clenched Fists, Burning Crosses

A NOVEL

▼

Cris South

AFTERWORD BY JAIME HARKER

The University of North Carolina Press
CHAPEL HILL

Originally published by the Crossing Press Feminist Series.
First published by the University of North Carolina Press in 2025.

Designed by Lindsay Starr
Set in Sentinel by codeMantra

Manufactured in the United States of America

Cover art: Woman using a linotype machine, Chicago, IL, 1941.
Photograph by Russell Lee, courtesy Library of Congress Prints
and Photographs Division.

Library of Congress Cataloging-in-Publication Data
Names: South, Cris, author. | Harker, Jaime, writer of afterword.
Title: Clenched fists, burning crosses : a novel /
Cris South ; afterword by Jaime Harker.
Other titles: Radical Souths.
Description: Chapel Hill : The University of North
Carolina Press, [2025] | Series: Radical Souths
Identifiers: LCCN 2025025186 | ISBN 9781469691145 (cloth) |
ISBN 9781469691152 (paperback) |
ISBN 9781469691169 (epub) | ISBN 9781469691176 (pdf)
Subjects: LCSH: Ku Klux Klan (1915-)—Fiction. | Feminists—Fiction. |
Lesbians—Fiction. | Anti-racism—Fiction. | Rape—Fiction. | Southern
States—Fiction. | BISAC: FICTION / Historical / General | HISTORY /
United States / State & Local / South (AL, AR, FL, GA, KY, LA, MS, NC, SC,
TN, VA, WV) | LCGFT: Novels. | Lesbian fiction. | Autobiographical fiction.
Classification: LCC PS3569.O74 C4 2025 |
DDC 813/.54—dc23/eng/20250606
LC record available at https://lccn.loc.gov/2025025186

For product safety concerns under the European Union's
General Product Safety Regulation (EU GPSR), please
contact gpsr@mare-nostrum.co.uk or write to
the University of North Carolina Press and
Mare Nostrum Group B.V., Mauritskade 21D,
1091 GC Amsterdam, The Netherlands.

For Jennifer,

with love

The Klan and the Nazis are our enemies and must be stopped, but to simply mobilize around stopping them is not enough. They are functionaries, tools of this governmental system. They serve in the same way as our armed forces and police. To end Klan or Nazi activity doesn't end imperialism. It doesn't end institutional racism; it doesn't end sexism; it does not bring this monster down, and we must not forget what our goals are and who our enemies are. To simply label these people as lunatic fringes and not accurately assess their roles as a part of this system is a dangerous error.

—From "Revolution: It's Not Neat or Pretty or Quick"
by Pat Parker in *This Bridge Called My Back*
(Kitchen Table: Women of Color Press)

Acknowledgments

THANKING THOSE WOMEN who read, believed, critiqued, suggested, argued, cared, cried, fought, and supported the process of this book, and me, seems like an impossibility. The book probably would have happened eventually, but it would have been longer in coming. Although it was a long, hard process, their encouragement made it a positive experience and, often, an exciting one.

So I would like to thank Diana Rivers, Maureen Brady, Boone, Ayana, Robin Divine, Patricia, Judith McDaniel, Sue Brown, Liz Snow, Helen Langa, Eleanor Holland, Tia Cross, Candace Burt, Susan Waldrop, Barbara Bradford, Jane Ollenberger, Merryl Sloan, and Jennifer Mayo for their readings and reactions, not to mention invaluable suggestions. Some of these women read along constantly; some read periodically; some read only once. But they all kept me believing in myself.

Then there was Elly Bulkin, who kept telling me to write (and to send her a copy of) a manuscript she had never seen. I want to thank one woman who asked not to be named, who believed in what I was doing and sent money to help the project along. Special love and thanks to Mab Segrest for re-treating to the beach with me for a month to write and heal.

Very, very special thanks go to Catherine Risingflame Moirai, Merril Harris, and Minnie Bruce Pratt for their tre-mendous belief in what I was writing, in me as a writer, and for their constant willingness to go through each line, word by word, over and over and ...

Last of all, thanks to Nancy K. Bereano for establishing a warm working relationship between editor and author, and for being a friend in the middle of the crises. And there is a special hug and kiss for Dorothy Allison and Barbara Kerr for making me laugh as I finished this book.

All those wonderful women.

—CRIS SOUTH

Clenched Fists, Burning Crosses

1

"THE KLAN RALLY was attended by an estimated one hundred twenty men, women and children. Many of the men wore T-shirts with the words WHITE POWER imprinted on them. There were guards posted around the site of the rally, supposedly to keep out troublemakers and undesirables. When asked who these undesirables were, the guards refused to comment.

"David Burke, leader of the American Nazi Party in this area, was quoted today in an interview as saying that his party is in complete support of this latest rise in Klan visibility and mobilization.

"Also in the news today, teachers talk strike in Boston. We'll be back with that story after . . ."

Jessie turned off the television set with one hand and gently pushed the cat out of her lap with the other. The Klan, the Klan. They were certainly getting into the news a lot these days. She stood up and stretched her stocky, muscular body, groaning softly as joints popped and cracked. Glancing at the ceiling, she tried to envision a thirty-foot-tall burning cross. She shook her head. Maybe it would all die down. Surely no one in this day and time would take them seriously. They were a bunch of clowns, trying to get attention. They were like little kids playing dress-up: robes, hoods, and dramatic crosses burning. Jessie snorted. The less said about them, the better.

She walked to the front door and into the yard. Kelly ran in tight circles in front of her, eager for a walk. Jessie grinned as she rubbed the setter's head.

"Later," she promised the dog. "I've got to hoe the garden."

Clouds were building on the horizon, grey and black thunderheads which promised rain soon. Jessie picked up the hoe and started around the house.

"How're you, Jessie?" Mrs. Carpenter approached laboriously, leaning heavily on her walking stick, her white hair standing on end in the wind.

"I'll do. How are you?"

Dorothy Carpenter stopped a few feet from Jessie and wiped her face with a tissue. "Hotter'n hell today."

"That it is," Jessie agreed. "Been to the mailbox?"

"Yeah. Nothing there."

"Well, no news is good news."

"I suppose." Jessie smiled. It was like talking in code. She leaned on the handle of her hoe and waited, watching Dorothy as she scanned the sky suspiciously.

"It's gonna rain cats and dogs," she said. "Can't rain enough. The well's gonna run dry for sure if it don't. Dry as a bone, that's what it'll be."

"It's held up pretty well so far this summer."

The old woman eyed Jessie. "So far. Lots of summer to go yet. You fix that leak? I been hearin' the pump runnin' some today."

"I fixed it. I washed dishes. That's probably why you heard the pump."

"I told Ben to get himself down here and fix that for you, but he said you could manage."

"He was right. Just a washer. Only took a couple of minutes to fix."

"Can't understand for the life of me why a girl like you'd want to live in an old, broke-down place like this anyway. And all by yourself, too. Don't you git scared stayin' in this house and nobody with you?"

Jessie looked at her and shrugged her shoulders. "I haven't yet. You just worry too much."

Dorothy Carpenter's eyes narrowed quickly at the mild reproof. "You should, too. Lotsa meanness. Ain't safe for a woman to be livin' alone."

"You and Mr. Carpenter are just up the hill."

"Shoot," she snorted. "Somebody yell fire and I'd burn up 'fore I could get to my feet. And Ben'd burn 'fore he heard you. You keep that dog of yours in the house nights?"

"Sure do," Jessie answered, nodding her head.

"That's good. Guess she'd bite, wouldn't she?"

"She probably would."

"You just remember to keep that old gun loaded and your doors locked. Y'know, I used to be a good shot in my time, but I cain't see good enough these days to hit the broad side of the barn. Pretty useless, I guess. And Ben, he don't see no better than he hears. Not much good for nothing either. You're smart not to have nobody hangin' on you. Well, I guess I'd better get on back home, or he'll come lookin' for me to make him some dinner. You'd think he could at least make himself a sandwich when he gets hungry. Useless old man. My hip's killin' me today. You come and set later if you got time. Gets lonesome up there with nobody to talk to."

"Maybe later," Jessie agreed. She watched Mrs. Carpenter begin the long, slow trip back to her house at the end of the driveway. The elderly landlady reminded Jessie of her own grandmother. She picked up the hoe and headed towards the garden.

JESSIE FLOPPED DOWN on the grass and rolled over on her back, lifting her T-shirt to catch the breeze and dry the sweat that ran down her chest. She wished the garden were further from the road so she wouldn't have to wear a shirt at all. But it was too close to risk it, much as she was tempted to try on days like this one. And Ben Carpenter, it wouldn't do to forget about him. In spite of being elderly and slow, he could move his large body very silently and had sneaked up on Jessie more than once. Jessie didn't trust him. He had hugged her too many times for Jessie to believe his "grandfather" claim.

Clouds were still building in the sky, but so far there had been no rain. The young plants in the garden were growing too slowly in the dry heat, and the ground was beginning to crack like clay pottery around the edges of the large plot. She might have to start hauling water from the creek, bucket by bucket, if the weather didn't turn soon. Already she was saving her bath water and bringing it out, a panful at a time, and pouring it around the tender plants. Not nearly enough to do much good though. The leaves were yellowing and beginning to go limp. The hay around the plants and between the rows helped keep in some moisture, but the ground was being baked completely dry by the steady July heat. There had been no rain to amount to anything since early in May. She leaned on an elbow and broke off a brittle grass blade and stuck it in her mouth. She could see the tree line along the bank of the creek, on the other side of the pasture. A long damned way to haul water.

The sound of the car in the driveway broke her reverie. Jessie rolled onto her stomach and lifted her head so she could see over the tall unmown grass. Kelly dashed by her with an excited yip, tail wagging madly. She could see Denny holding out her hands to fend off the leaping dog while she tried to make her way into the house. Jessie rose to her knees and waved her hand in the air.

"I'm by the garden," she called out, and then sat down again. It was too hot, too hot to do anything except sit and think about the heat.

" . . . c'mon, Kelly. That's enough." Denny's voice grew louder as she approached. "Dammit, Kelly! You're drooling on me again! I hate it when you do that. Stop it!" Denny sat down beside Jessie, a disgusted expression on her face. "I can't take it when she drools all over me."

"Setters drool. That's a fact."

"Yeah, I know," Denny answered flatly as she pulled some dry grass and tried to wipe her bare legs, "but I wish she'd turn her head or something. Look at me!"

Jessie laughed outright. "Any time you want to try to teach her that, you have my blessing."

Denny tossed the grass aside. "I came out to work in the garden. I've been spending too many hours over books and behind the cash register. I turned it all over to Dianne this morning and told her not to look for me again until Monday. Hell, by the time I get back, she'll have everything right, the books balanced, and an order ready for me to call in. She knows more about that restaurant than I do, and I'm the manager."

"And she probably figured most of it out by trying to cope with things when you were away."

"Probably. Some good news came through last week though. Janice, you know, the woman who owns The Food Patch? She is definitely going to open another place this fall, and she wants Dianne to manage it for her."

"That's great."

"Diane is thrilled. It means a lot more money for her, which I know will help since she has a child to support. I feel happy for her and sad for me. I like working with her and hate to see her go."

"But she deserves better than what she's got working for you, Denny."

"I couldn't agree more. Waiting tables is shit work no matter how you cut it. I think she'll do great. She's much better at it than I am, that's for sure."

Jessie glanced again at the sky. The thunderheads were close now and building quickly overhead. She slid the hoe across the grass to Denny and then rose to her feet, relieved by the cool wind preceding the oncoming storm. "I didn't hoe the last two rows, but that's about all I left. If you feel real industrious and it doesn't pour on you, you can always mulch with the hay. I'm going inside and taking a fast bath before the storm gets here."

Denny nodded absently as she stepped over the rows of plants and began to hoe near the fence. Jessie, glad for the break, headed into the house. A bath would feel good. Then maybe she could talk Denny into staying for dinner. Most women didn't want to drive so far out into the country, even for a meal. She hadn't had any company in a long time.

BEN CARPENTER SPIT a stream of tobacco juice on the ground. Dorothy shifted her position in the cane-bottomed chair, lifting her hair off the back of her neck with one swollen hand.

'Think it'll rain?" Ben asked his wife.

"Yep," she answered as she pulled the sticky cotton fabric of her dress away from her damp body.

"Huh?" he persisted, cupping one hand to his ear and leaning his head in her direction.

Dorothy sighed. It hurt her throat to have to yell so much. "I said yep, I think it'll rain." She frowned in disgust. Wisht he'd buy himself a hearin' aid, she thought silently.

"Whose car's that down there?"

"One of Jessie's girlfriends," she hollered back at him. He nodded and was quiet for a moment.

"I cain't figure it out," he said finally, his words accompanied by wheezing sounds as he spoke. "She lives down there all by herself and only some girls comin' to see her. Never talks about no man. Think maybe she just don't have no boyfriends?"

"Ain't nobody been to see her lately." Dorothy struggled to her feet. "Maybe not. But you're the one what told her not to be havin' men hangin' around the place. Reckon if she does have boyfriends, she ain't about to let us see 'em."

"Huh?" Ben cupped his ear once more.

Dorothy snorted as she reached for her walking stick and headed towards the house. "I said I'm gonna start supper cookin'!" She walked away, swaying from side to side as she coaxed her lame hip along. "Ain't good for a blessed thing," she muttered to herself as she reached up to open the screen door. "Not one blessed thing. Cain't hear, cain't see. Just a pack of trouble, him wantin' to be waited on and me with my bad hip!"

With a grunt of effort, she pulled herself up the two steps and disappeared inside the house.

JESSIE SLID THE CUE STICK gently through her fingers until it bumped the ball. For a moment she thought perhaps Laura had been wrong. Just because this style worked for her. . . . The white ball glided smoothly over the green felt and touched the side of the eight ball. Corner pocket. C'mon. She held her breath. The black eight teetered on the edge for a long moment. Then, almost in slow motion, it dropped into the pocket. Laura laughed from her perch on the barstool, a deep sound that seemed to rise up from her toes. She nodded her head emphatically.

"I told you. You just have to relax and kiss that ball. Just like loving a woman. Works every time," Laura said, her brown eyes dancing delightedly. Denny laughed as she leaned her stick against the side of the pool table.

"I guess this means I buy the beer," she said, pulling a crumpled bill from her pocket.

"I guess you do," Jessie answered, smiling. It was the first game she had ever won, and she did not attempt to disguise her smugness.

As Denny passed she patted Jessie on the shoulder. "I expect another game. A tiebreaker. I'll be back in a minute."

Jessie put quarters in the slot and waited for the balls to drop. She racked them slowly, arranging their order inside the blue plastic triangle, alternating high and low numbers, eight ball in the middle. Laura stood up, stretching her arms over her head. "I could have sworn you weren't paying any attention to what I was telling you the other night," she said to Jessie, "but you are doing all right. My money's on you for this next game."

Laura winked and walked away.

Denny reappeared with two beers and set them on a nearby table. Picking up her cue stick, she chalked the rubber tip carefully, her face set in concentration.

This time Denny played seriously, and the game moved faster. When Denny sank the eight ball, Jessie still had four balls left on the table. She shook her head ruefully and put her stick back in the wall rack.

"That does it for me. I owe you a beer," Jessie promised.

"I won't forget," Denny laughed. She dropped her arm around Jessie's shoulders and led her to an empty table. "Let's sit down and finish our drinks. I haven't really seen you in a couple of weeks. What's going on in your life these days?"

Jessie sat down and lit a cigarette, ignoring Denny's look of distaste. "Mostly, I've been working to get everything together at the shop."

"How's all that going?"

"I've drummed up some small accounts. I don't think I could do it all by myself, and I'm sure glad I didn't try. With Laura handling graphics, design, and scheduling, and me running the presses and hustling, it's still almost more than we can deal with."

"Well, the word is definitely around. A lot of liberal and left-wing political groups are looking for printers like you who they can trust not to botch their work and miss their deadlines. I think you'll do okay. Just takes a little time."

"I hope so. I'm sure nervous enough about it." Jessie studied her beer for a moment. "Denny, do you know Kate Robbins?"

Denny was startled by the abrupt change in the topic, and she peered at her friend in surprise. "I know who she is. Why?"

"Just wondering," Jessie answered with a casual shrug of her shoulders. "I'm supposed to have dinner with her."

Jessie's tone caught Denny's full attention as she tried to decipher the meaning behind the words. "Yeah? Where'd you meet her?"

"At a battered women's shelter meeting a few weeks ago. We've had lunch a couple of times, and she asked me to dinner."

"At her house?"

"At her apartment." Jessie glanced at her. "Why?"

"Just curious," she answered with an enigmatic smile. Denny tried to be casual as she adjusted her glasses, pushing them back up her nose with one finger. "Want to tell me about it?" she asked.

"What's to tell? I'm just having dinner with her."

Denny grinned and moved the conversation closer to home. "Are you attracted to her? You're acting awfully cool about this."

Jessie shifted uneasily in her chair. "Yeah, well, a little bit. But that doesn't mean ..."

"Is she attracted to you?" Denny's grin was spreading even wider as she waited for Jessie's answer.

"Hell, I don't know. Maybe. I didn't ask her."

"There are signs, y'know, Jess, certain signals that let you know ..."

"Well, I don't know very much about that," Jessie answered defensively, feeling she was definitely losing control of the conversation.

"Calm down. I'm not attacking your virginal lesbian self, sugar. Just making an observation." Denny looked as though she might burst with delight over the unexpected turn the evening had taken. She leaned back in her chair and draped an arm over the back, her gaze never leaving Jessie's face.

"Cut it out, Denny. This is the very first time I've ever been attracted enough to consider doing something about it, and I think I have the right to be a little uptight. Tell me what I'm supposed to do!"

"About what?"

"About Kate Robbins!"

Denny laughed out loud. "Just relax and go have dinner with her. You can't plan these things. They never go right if you plan them. Have dinner and enjoy. What will be and all that." Denny shrugged and grinned. "Then I want to hear every detail."

JESSIE GLANCED AROUND the room trying to find some part into which she could fit comfortably. Finally, she sat down on the floor by the fireplace and leaned her elbow on the edge of the wood coffee table. The space around her was totally foreign to her, crowded with plants, mismatched furniture, canvasses in various stages of completion leaning against the walls. In one corner there was a tall work table which was covered with tubes of paint, jars, brushes, and cloths. Jessie twisted her head in an attempt to see the paintings better. She didn't think she could just look through them without Kate's permission, but she didn't want to ask. What if she hated Kate's art work? What would she say then? Besides, she didn't know anything about art. She didn't know how to talk about it, what to comment on if asked. She wondered if Kate ever showed her work.

When Kate came back into the room, Jessie busied herself with staring at the contents of her wine glass. She was very ill at ease, even after nearly two hours alone with Kate. It had not occurred to her, as she had readied herself for this evening, that she might not be able to think of anything to say. Now she found herself wishing she had suggested they go out for dinner. Perhaps some neutral territory would have made talking less difficult. At the very least, there would have been some distractions to fill the long silences. She shifted her position a bit, her crossed legs rapidly growing numb from lack of circulation. She was afraid to move around too much, not wanting Kate to notice her uneasiness.

Kate was puzzled. She eased her lanky body down as close to Jessie as she dared place herself. She was a little afraid that if she got too close, the younger woman might bolt from the room. She helped herself to some more wine and tried to refrain from looking at Jessie. The evening was certainly proving to be a surprise, she thought silently. She was baffled, remembering how easily Jessie had talked when they had had lunch together. Had she done something to put her off? Kate didn't think so.

Kate leaned back and sipped her wine, watching Jessie covertly. The warmth she felt spreading through her body had little to do with the alcohol she was taking in. She wanted this woman, and she had thought Jessie felt the same way. Maybe Jessie was simply very shy.

"You said you are a writer," Kate said. "What sort of writing do you do?"

Jessie glanced at her quickly, then looked away. "Not very much these days. I'm too busy trying to get the business on its feet."

"Well then, what sorts of things do you write when you have the time for it?" Kate patiently rephrased the question.

Jessie shrugged. "Some poetry, but mostly fiction. It takes a lot of time to write. At least, for me, it takes blocks of uninterrupted time. I haven't had very much of that lately."

"What kind of fiction?" Kate leaned over and refilled Jessie's glass. She wanted to touch her.

"I've done some short stories, but I have trouble keeping them short. I think I want to write a novel, but I just don't have the time. Maybe when the business really gets going ... I don't know."

"Have any ideas for a novel?"

Again the shoulders shrugged. "Not really."

Kate stared at the plants on the shelf above Jessie's head. Well, that subject had been exhausted pretty quickly. She groped for another one with which to replace it.

Agnes, Kate's old grey cat, wandered into the room and walked over to Jessie, cautiously sniffing her pant leg. Jessie, relieved to find any diversion, leaned over to pet her. Agnes immediately sat down, delighted to have such unexpected attention lavished on her by a total stranger.

Kate seized the moment to stare openly at Jessie. Jessie sat with one knee drawn up, her chin resting on it, her muscular body seeming tense and somewhat out of place in the crowded room. Kate felt the urge to run her hands over Jessie's wide, solid shoulders.

Minutes passed in silence as Jessie rubbed Agnes, her hands touching the soft fur, rubbing deeply into the muscles. Agnes arched her back and purred, pressing up against Jessie's fingers. Kate watched. Not particularly beautiful hands, but strong hands that seemed very knowledgeable about touching. Sensual as they stroked the small cat. Kate set her wine glass on the floor and reached out to catch Jessie's arm, pulling it to her so she could hold her hand. She ran a finger over the back, tracking the veins which shone pale blue under the skin.

"You know, Jessie, I asked you over because I really wanted a chance to get to know you better. I wanted time to talk more with you. But also because I am very attracted to you." Kate's tone was matter-of-fact.

"I wasn't sure," Jessie answered, staring at Kate. She did not withdraw her hand.

Kate quietly considered Jessie's response as she continued to rub the hand she held, fully aware of the faint flush that arose on the other woman's face. She waited.

Jessie cleared her throat carefully. "Kate . . . I'm feeling very self-conscious right now."

Kate glanced up, a puzzled expression on her face. "Why do you feel that way?"

Jessie refused to meet her gaze. "I . . . well, I've never met a woman I was so attracted to before, and I don't know exactly what to do. I mean . . ." Jessie fell silent, still staring at the cat who stood up indignantly now that she found herself so suddenly ignored.

Kate didn't understand. "I don't get it, Jessie. You talked about being a lesbian . . ."

"I really feel that I am a lesbian. It's just that I've never . . ."

"Oh, baby," Kate whispered. She reached out and put her arm around Jessie's shoulders. "So that's it. It's okay. I'm even more delighted and flattered that you're here with me."

"I'm glad you are," Jessie said a trifle bitterly. "I just feel silly."

"I don't think you're silly." Kate kissed her lightly on the cheek. She could feel the tension in Jessie's body. She wanted to laugh, but she was afraid she might offend the other woman.

"Maybe I should just go home."

Kate leaned around so she could see Jessie's face. "I really don't want you to leave."

"I don't know what else to do," she burst out in frustration. Jessie ran her fingers through her short, dark hair. "I can't even carry on a decent conversation with you."

"We don't have to talk. I don't mind sitting quietly with you. But I want you to stay tonight. We don't have to make love. We can just sleep together. I want to be close to you."

Indecision was in Jessie's eyes. She hesitated for several long moments. "All right," she said finally.

"Good," Kate answered, smiling. "We can talk in the morning." She stood up and offered her hand.

JESSIE LAY WITHOUT MOVING, without opening her eyes. Something was not right. The morning sun never fell on her face . . . And the smells were all wrong, the sheets odd against her naked skin. The feeling of disorientation nearly overtook her until she remembered—Kate.

She could feel the heat from Kate's body and sensed that the other woman was also awake though still and quiet, perhaps waiting for Jessie to open her eyes. Jessie remembered drifting off to sleep the night before, her back pressed firmly against Kate's breasts and belly, Kate's thighs curving under her buttocks, pubic hair tickling lightly whenever Kate inhaled. It had been very wonderful, soft and peaceful, and Jessie had relaxed into the quiet rhythm of Kate's breathing, finding sleep almost too quick and close. But now it was morning, and Jessie lay on her back, feeling the weight of Kate's arm across her stomach, feeling warm breath against her ear.

Jessie slowly moved her hand up to rest on Kate's arm. Then lightly, holding her breath, she stroked the soft skin, feeling the downy hair rise slightly under her fingers. She was acutely aware of the pleasant fluid heaviness in her thighs and stomach. Her breathing quickened suddenly when she felt Kate's mouth move against her ear, soft tongue flickering lightly. Then a quiet laugh made her finally open her eyes.

"I didn't think you were really sleeping," Kate whispered.

"No," Jessie admitted.

"Still feeling awkward?"

"Yeah, a little."

"I . . . want . . . you," Kate said slowly. She paused over each word, her mouth against Jessie's ear, the sounds seeming to slide into Jessie, leaving a warm trail through breasts, belly, and finally falling into a moist heap between her thighs. "You don't have to do a thing."

Jessie felt completely immobile for several moments. Then her stomach rippled involuntarily, and her hand moved up, almost without her knowledge, along Kate's arm, over her shoulder and down her side, coming to rest on her hip, tugging slightly as Jessie coaxed Kate closer.

Kate moved until she was over Jessie, their thighs pressed together, light and dark pubic hair mingling, stomachs touching at the slightest stirring or intake of breath. She held herself up on straightened arms, watching Jessie's face, watching as Jessie's hazel eyes darkened when Kate's long hair brushed over her ribs and breasts. Kate held back, wanting to be quick, feeling her own impatient rhythms rising, but she restrained herself. She teased gently, moving her body in concentric circles as she leaned down to give light, tantalizing kisses, only to pull back once more, listening to Jessie's breathing as it quickened and deepened, rubbing until the younger woman groaned softly and arched up to meet her. Jessie grabbed her with strong, certain hands, pulling Kate down to the full length of their bodies.

First time, Kate thought, as she felt herself tremble. She forced herself to move slow, slow, easing down a trail of kisses, light, insistent, coaxing. She paused as Jessie's hands found her breasts, touching tentatively, and she pressed forward against Jessie's fingertips.

Jessie almost reached to stop her as she felt Kate begin to move down her body. Men had done that, and Jessie had hated it. Then she heard Kate groan softly as she slid her face between Jessie's thighs and pressed her mouth to the wetness there.

"You feel so good," Kate murmured softly, "so good."

For some reason that Jessie didn't understand, the words released her tension. She felt herself relax, drawn into the dance of Kate's mouth and tongue. She held the back of Kate's head, her fingers curling tightly in the long, tousled hair, suddenly pulling Kate closer, wanting to take her inside and hold her there. Her body felt lighter, lighter, and then she came, suddenly, with a burst of color behind her eyelids and a soft, damp spring against Kate's face. Not thinking about gentleness, she pulled Kate hard against her until the last shudder broke and ebbed away. Jessie caught Kate's head between her hands and pulled her up.

"I need you to hold me."

Kate moved her body to fit around Jessie and wrapped her arms around her, feeling Jessie vibrate and then slowly begin to relax.

Jessie opened her eyes to find Kate watching her. She turned on her side and lifted her hand to touch Kate's still damp face. She was hesitant, careful, suddenly realizing that she had never touched anyone's face before and understanding why. It was an intimate gesture, a gesture she had never felt inclined to make. She let her hand drift down, cupping Kate's breast, marveling at the shape and weight, feeling the nipple harden against her fingertip. Then down the smoothness of Kate's belly, the springy, thick pubic hair. She heard Kate's breath catch as she slid her fingers into her, rubbing lightly, attentive to the motion of Kate's body, letting Kate show her what and where and how. She watched the expressions on the older woman's face as she touched, wondering if she, too, had had those same expressions, wondering if she would even know when Kate came. But the certain knowledge was there, and she followed the rhythm, feeling the pulsing under her fingers, following it down as Kate closed around her fingers, hard, trembling. Then she leaned down and rested her face against Kate's breast and listened to her breathing slow and quiet, like the calm after a storm.

2

JESSIE HAD MADE A HUGE, unthinking mistake.

She knew that now as she sat on the porch step, a can of beer clasped between her hands. She stared out at the pasture, oblivious to the grazing cows who passed slowly by the barbed wire fence ignoring her as they searched out tender grass.

Laura had been furious. At first, Jessie could not comprehend the reason for Laura's anger. The more she failed to understand, the madder Laura got. Finally Jessie had stopped talking. Laura had shoved the newspaper article across the table at Jessie, headline glaring: KLANSMEN SAY ORGANIZING WILL CONTINUE.

"Don't tell me they shouldn't be taken seriously," Laura had said through clenched teeth, her body rigid as she leaned towards Jessie. "Don't tell me they're clowns and the way to control them is to ignore them. They exist because people want them to exist. White people! And only white people can stop them. Did you even read this article? I can't believe you did."

"Of course I read it," Jessie had replied. "Why else . . ."

"Why is a damned good question! Is it because I'm black and we're friends? Is it because I'm the only black woman you know and you're doing a trip on me?"

Laura took a deep breath and leaned back in her chair. Jessie stared at her in stunned silence. Laura continued, her voice quieter.

"I want to tell you something. I know your intentions are good. But there are lots of folks out there with good intentions. And good intentions are absolutely worthless. Let me give you a little piece of reality to think about. In the early 1900s, my grandfather and grandmother bought fifteen acres of land in northern Georgia. They were farmers. The Klan paid them a visit. They burned my grandfather's house to the ground and rode through all the crops. Two years later, because my grandparents wouldn't leave, they came back. They burned the place again. They tore up the crops. But this time, they beat my grandfather and left him a cripple for life. He was a young man with a wife and five kids. They had to move into town and my grandmother had to do maid's work to support the family. Some local white men visited my grandfather and told him that they had heard there was some mischief brewing, but they hadn't taken it seriously. Mischief! Then those good-intentioned white men offered to buy grand-daddy's land from him. They bought it for twenty-five cents on the dollar.

"So you think about that. They are not a bunch of clowns. Have you ever seen that film, *Birth of a Nation*? Check it out. It still plays around from time to time. Just go to the graduate library and read all about the hearings that were held about the Klan. Read the testimonies of black women and men. Get some goddamned information before you start making conclusions. As far as I'm concerned, Jessie, you don't take them seriously, then you're as bad as they are!"

With that, Laura had left.

You don't take them seriously, then you're as bad as they are. Jessie lit a cigarette. Sick, she felt sick. She had gone to the library, but she hadn't been able to read very much. The accounts were horrible, endless testimony in volume after volume: stories of beatings and rapes, torture, men killed outright, women beaten bloody and left to die, people terrorized, crops and homes destroyed, black people fleeing for their lives.

Then she had checked through the newspaper files for more current information. It was there, some of it obscure, but it was there. She had spent the entire day reading the accounts, some on yellowing pages, some on microfilm.

She had come home intending to call Laura and apologize, but she found she could not pick up the telephone.

Jessie threw away the cigarette butt with a disgusted flick of her wrist.

"It was a stupid, ignorant thing to say," she blurted out suddenly. Kelly looked at her mildly. "Stupid. Stupid!" She glared at the dog. "Sometimes I don't believe I should ever open my mouth! Stupid!" Jessie turned and stormed off towards the garden. After a moment of uncertainty, Kelly stood up and loped after her.

JESSIE LEANED OVER to pick up another armful of wood. She stacked it on the porch, loosely, so the air could circulate through it. It would be dark soon, and the breeze was cool. She wiped the sweat from her face with the bottom of her T-shirt. Jessie sat down on the step and picked up the file to sharpen the dull maul. Tomorrow she would can beans, and maybe some peas, too. Tomatoes were coming in so quickly she could not keep up with them. She shuddered at the thought of another tomato sandwich. Next year, she would know better than to set out ten tomato plants at the same time. Next year, she would know a whole lot more about everything.

There were chickens to do soon. She watched them as they pecked around the yard oblivious to her. One of the roosters strutted around the hens territorially as he jerked his head from side to side, his comb flipping wildly. Jessie kept a cautious eye on him. He had taken to attacking without warning or provocation. Many of the hens were laying now, giving her up to ten eggs a day. Mentally, she scheduled killing three of the roosters. She didn't need five roosters.

She needed to borrow Hollis' truck so she could pick up the old freezer she had bought from Mrs. Anna Washington. A lot of her vegetables could be frozen. And there was that new farmers' market with all of that fresh fruit. She wanted to make applesauce and jam. Jessie sighed. There was just not enough time.

She stood up and stretched. Kate would be coming soon. Jessie gathered the tools and headed to the woodshed with them, conscious of the sudden burst of energy that had come when she thought about Kate. She laughed. Time enough for some things.

Jessie ran warm water into the bathtub and stood silently watching the whirlpool current that formed as the water deepened. She had seen Kate several times but still felt shy with her, especially when they made love. Kate took the lead there, and Jessie wasn't entirely satisfied with that. She understood why Kate felt like she should take the lead, why Kate would feel a certain amount of responsibility, but she didn't like her own passiveness.

Jessie peeled off sweat-soaked clothes and lowered her body into the water until it lapped at her chin. The last time she and Kate had made love Jessie could feel a tension in Kate's body, as though something was being held back, restrained.

Kate probably thought she would frighten Jessie if she let the passion go, if she showed how she felt. Jessie splashed water on her face, wishing she knew how to let Kate know that not only was it okay, but that she wanted it. She wanted it.

This would be the first time Kate had ever come to Jessie's house. Briefly, Jessie wondered what Kate would think of the ramshackle old place, the dog, the cats, the chickens, the garden. Last night, Jessie had heard a bobcat scream from the woods down near the marsh. Maybe Kate wouldn't want to know that, at least not during her first visit.

Jessie eyed her body through the water. Kate said she was beautiful. Jessie closed her eyes. Her body was many things, but she never thought of it as beautiful. After all, she had been told often enough that it was not even acceptable—stocky, wide shouldered, a slight bulge at the waistline, ample hips and thighs.

She never thought of herself as fat. No, fat did not fit. But definitely chunky, in a nice solid sort of way. Of course, she didn't mind Kate thinking she was beautiful. She just didn't fully believe her.

But Kate, Kate was beautiful, in every conventional sense of the word—willow thin, long blonde hair, blue eyes. Men stared at her whenever she and Jessie went out together. They would wink at her and try to engage her in conversation. Jessie had never seen a woman more capable of cutting a man cold than Kate, however. She had a real technique, acidic and very effective.

Jessie sat up suddenly and reached for the washcloth. What are you doing, she thought to herself, sitting here daydreaming about her when she'll be here in half an hour? And what did it matter that Kate was beautiful? Would it be any different if men found her ugly? Or just unappealing, as they seemed to find Jessie? Jessie soaped her body slowly. It disturbed her that she was so attracted to such a conventional-looking woman and had not been attracted to other women who very much looked like dykes. What did that mean? What the hell, she thought tiredly. You don't have to have a reason for everything.

KATE STOOD ON THE PORCH, sipping wine from the glass Jessie had handed her. The moon was almost full, and the pasture behind the house was clearly visible. Jessie leaned against the door frame, one hand holding her wine glass, the other shoved into her pocket. She, too, stared out at the pasture, seemingly lost in some faraway thought. Kate watched her quietly.

Jessie was something of an enigma to Kate: intense, quiet, almost impenetrable at times, but given to wild flights of fancy, soft whimsical humor, with a gentleness that sometimes belied her exterior toughness. But Jessie was tough, and hard. Kate felt that as clearly as she felt the tenderness in the younger woman. Balancing the two notions of the woman who was now her lover was very difficult. She had never before met anyone quite like Jessie.

Kate knew she was a dominating sort of person, used to having her way and the upper hand in her relationships. She tended to barnstorm through life, through ideas, and through lovers. She had never considered her lovers to be her equals, although she had often wished they were. Now she was quite aware that she was involved with someone who she instinctively knew was her equal in every way, and it made her very nervous.

Kate did not yield to the slow, soft motion in her body, the quiet rising of want. She continued to stand near the steps, outwardly still, wanting Jessie to make the first move this time. The thought surprised her. She never waited for anything, and she certainly never waited for sexual overtures. For all her brashness, Kate knew Jessie was shy. Still, she waited, wanting that new balance, wanting Jessie to come to her.

Jessie had yet to really let go with Kate, to drop the guards and fall completely into the lovemaking. Kate wondered if she ever would.

Jessie's want was not so easily stilled. She finished the wine much faster than she had intended and then automatically reached for a cigarette. As she started to light it, a sudden breeze flicked out the match. Kate glanced at her, her attention caught by the flare of flame in the dark. All you have to do, Jessie thought, is go over to her. Just go over.

Kate was caught off-guard when Jessie's arms closed around her and pulled her close. There was still a bit of tentativeness in the gesture, and Kate held herself still in the circle of Jessie's arms. She could feel the hard muscles of Jessie's body, ridges of stone under the soft clothes and skin, the body of a woman used to physical work. Jessie's hands were calloused and scarred. She was strong; Kate knew that, too. For a moment, Kate felt a breath of fear. Jessie held her gently but more firmly than before, her face resting against Kate's neck. Yet, for a brief second, Kate was afraid of the strength. Only in a man's body had she ever felt that power.

Jessie was surprised by the sudden rise of wanting. The sensation was completely new and disconcerting—almost like a roughness, a need for immediate contact, a need to be able to feel Kate against her, to press her body into Kate's until skin merged. She wanted to take her, fiercely. The thought surprised her. Uncertain, she turned Kate to face her and pulled her close, closer, until her arms ached from tautness and her breathing deepened, rasped in her throat. She could go no further until she had some sort of sign from Kate that it was all right.

"You're very strong," Kate said quietly. "Yes."

The silence was long. Jessie almost backed away. She felt a rejection, but she couldn't understand exactly what it was or where it came from. Then suddenly, she felt Kate exhale a long, pent-up breath. Kate tightened her grasp on Jessie and kissed her firmly.

"Hey, Jess?"

"Yeah?"

"I have a sort of strange request."

"What?"

"If we went into the pasture, do you think the cows would step all over us?"

Jessie leaned her head back so she could see Kate's face. "The pasture?" she asked in a puzzled voice. "Why on earth do you want to go ..." She paused, then began to grin. "Are you sure you want to go out there?"

Kate eyed the meadow. "Is it safe?"

Jessie followed her gaze. "Probably. The cows are most likely in the woods for the night. I could get a blanket and a flashlight."

"Why don't you?" Kate grinned.

"Okay. But the bugs are going to eat us alive."

"I'll take my chances."

"Then I'll get a blanket."

When Jessie returned to the porch, she was no longer nervous. She was in her territory now—the pasture, the grass and sky, even the cows. She threw the blanket over her shoulder, switched on the flashlight, and reached for Kate's hand.

"C'mon. There's a stand of trees on the far side where the grass isn't so tall. Even if the cows come out, the trees should keep them away. They're pretty skittish, and if you so much as look at them hard ..."

Jessie's voice ambled on as she hurried Kate through the gate and through the tall, wiry grass. She could hear Kate breathlessly trying to keep up, but she did not slow her pace. She felt light, and she could have walked all night. A sudden low noise drifted to them on the wind. Jessie could feel Kate start in fright.

"It's okay. That's a barred owl. Probably hunting down in the marsh. There are lots of owls around here."

"I've never heard one before."

"I love the way they sound," Jessie said softly as she stopped walking and began to spread the blanket. Kate watched her, some of her earlier bravado vanishing. She felt the meadow stretching out around her.

"I thought you were going to spread the blanket under the trees. Aren't we going to be trampled out here?"

"We're close enough to them. Anyway, at this time of year the meteor showers start. You can lay on your back and watch them, all different colors." Jessie stepped back and inspected the blanket. Then she turned to Kate who was watching her intently.

"I have to admit that I'm a little nervous," Kate said.

"About what?" Jessie asked as she put her arms around Kate.

"About being out here in this openness."

"Nothing will bother us. The only thing we might see would be a rabbit, or an owl flying overhead."

Jessie's mouth was insistent. Kate's nervousness disappeared as Jessie unbuttoned her shirt and pushed it aside impatiently. She pressed her mouth against Kate's, then moved down to her breast. As they lay down on the blanket, Kate could feel the grass against her ankles, cool and vaguely damp. Then she forgot the grass and the meadow as she sank into wild, impatient rhythms that matched Jessie's fierceness, pressing into Jessie's hands and mouth, urging, coaxing her, and finally tangling her fingers in Jessie's short, dark hair and moving her down, holding her there, there.

"THERE'S ANOTHER ONE," Kate exclaimed delightedly.

Jessie lit a cigarette and stared up. "I missed that one. They sure are beautiful."

"So are you," Kate said.

"Yeah, well," Jessie replied, embarrassed. "I won't be so beautiful with all these chiggers."

"What in the world are chiggers?"

"You've never heard of them? Well, they are also known as redbugs, and they are these tiny, tiny little creatures who bite and burrow into your skin. The bites itch worse than anything."

"Sounds awful."

"I have a feeling you'll know for yourself by morning. It takes a while for the itch to start."

"I hope not. I hate to spoil this moment, but I'm getting very cold."

"We could go in."

"I think I need to."

"Okay."

They dressed in silence. Jessie suddenly felt self-conscious as she pulled on her jeans and slipped into her shirt. Had she been too rough, too . . . uncontrolled? She felt a surge of embarrassment. What did Kate think?

JESSIE GROANED AND TRIED to open her eyes, still locked at the edge of a dream. The sound didn't fit. Somewhere there was a pounding noise, almost like a hammer on a block of wood. She stretched out her hand but could feel nothing. The noise was not pleasant.

Jessie finally woke to Kate shaking her. "Jessie, someone's at the door. Do you want me to get it?"

Jessie sat up quickly, reaching automatically for her jeans. They were not in their usual place on the foot of the bed. Stumbling hastily to her feet, she finally located them in a heap of clothing on the floor. She tugged them loose and pulled them on, swaying and tripping. Nausea rose; she had gotten up much too quickly.

"I'll get it," she muttered. "It might be Ben Carpenter, and I would never be able to explain you if you weren't fully dressed." She shrugged into her shirt, paying no attention to the detail of getting the correct buttons into the appropriate holes. Shirt askew, hair standing on end, and barefoot, she left the room.

"All right," Jessie said as she fumbled with the dead-bolt lock on the door. Her hands would not cooperate, and it took three attempts to slide the bolt free from the tumblers. When she opened the door, Denny and Val stood on the porch.

"I was asleep," she explained.

Denny glanced at her. "That's pretty obvious. What are you doing still in bed? It's almost eleven."

"I got to sleep kinda late," Jessie mumbled as she tried to smooth down her hair with the palm of her hand. "This is really sort of a bad time. I mean, I'm not awake and . . ." Her voice trailed off as Jessie noticed her shirt and set to matching buttons and buttonholes. Denny looked at Val who was trying very hard to hide her smile.

"Well, it's high time you were up. Got any coffee?"

Jessie followed Denny into the kitchen, still fumbling with her shirt. Denny took down the coffee pot and calmly began measuring coffee into the drip basket.

"Look, it's great that you two came all the way out here to visit but I . . ."

"We're not here just for a visit," Denny explained patiently. "We're supposed to have breakfast and plan the benefit dance, remember? You moved the sugar again, Jess."

Jessie grabbed the sugar bowl and thrust it at Denny. "Damn. I forgot. Look, uh . . . I'll make breakfast. I think I have enough of everything." Jessie jerked the door to the refrigerator open and peered inside. When she emerged, she was clasping milk, eggs, cheese, and butter to her chest. She kicked the door closed with a bare foot and set things on the table. "I can make omelettes." Jessie reached for a frying pan.

Kate stepped into the kitchen, hair tousled, sleepy-eyed, heading for the bathroom. She was wearing Jessie's robe.

"Hello," Denny said, a note of delight in her voice. Jessie flushed furiously as Denny glanced at her, her gaze teasing wickedly.

"Oh, Kate. This is Denny Stevens and Val Berns. Kate Robbins." Jessie gestured vaguely between the three women and turned back to the frying pan, her face a deep shade of red. Somehow, her privacy felt very invaded. She wasn't ready for this.

"I knew the face but not the name. Hi, Kate," Val said as she offered her hand.

Denny nodded, still grinning. "Good to see you again, Kate. We were just starting breakfast before we settle into a meeting. Want to join us?"

Kate nodded and smiled. "Sure. Let me get some clothes on and I'll help."

She disappeared in the direction of Jessie's bathroom. Denny made no attempt to hide the giggle as she turned back to the coffee pot.

Jessie dropped a heavy hand on Denny's shoulder. "One word out of you and I'll toss you out of here on your ear, Denny. I mean it."

"Me? I thought I was being perfectly polite," she protested.

"Not one word," Jessie repeated grimly as she left the room.

Val touched Denny's arm, and they both burst into muffled laughter.

JESSIE FINALLY RELAXED when Val and Denny drove away some two hours later. She poured another cup of coffee and dropped into a chair on the porch, propping her feet on the ledge. She lit her first cigarette of the day and inhaled deeply.

Kate came up behind her and slid her arms around Jessie's neck, slipping her hands inside the partially open shirt to cup Jessie's breasts. "Your friends are very nice."

"Yeah, they are. But Denny does give me a hard time."

"Bad kind of hard?"

"No. Just teasing the hell out of me."

Kate sat down in a chair opposite Jessie. "Will she give you a hard time about me?"

"Probably."

"Well, I guess it would be hard to resist the temptation to tease, especially after my fatal entrance wearing your bathrobe.

I thought you were just making breakfast. If I had known they were here, I would've been a lot more respectable looking when I came in."

"You looked fine. It's just that I've never had a lover before, and Denny knows that. I was feeling a little self-conscious."

"Well, she can only get so much mileage out of it."

Jessie glanced at her, grinning. "You don't know Denny. She gets light years out of every story. And each time she tells it, it gets more stupendous."

"Does it bother you?"

Jessie laughed as she shook her head. "Not really. I'm just mentally bracing myself. Denny knew I was interested in you, and I haven't seen her since I started seeing you."

Kate's eyebrows went up slightly as she helped herself to a cigarette from Jessie's pack and lit it, her gaze never leaving Jessie's face. "Really? You haven't told me about that."

Jessie ran her fingers through her hair. "No, I guess I haven't."

"Are you going to? If you'd like."

"C'mon, Jessie. I love these kinds of stories."

"Well, it's just that I was attracted to you and was trying to find out about you, what you were like. You know." Her smile was self-conscious as she continued. "So I asked Denny because it seems like she knows everybody in these parts. She zeroed right in on it and told me I should by all means have dinner with you and then come back and tell her everything."

"Did you? Go back and tell her everything, I mean."

"No. I haven't seen her. I'm sure she's been wondering."

"Looks like she got her confirmation this morning."

"But the next time I see her, she really will want all of the details."

"And what will you tell her?"

Jessie glanced at Kate, her expression teasing. "I don't know. Maybe I'll tell her it's none of her business."

"Or?" Kate asked, also smiling.

"Or maybe I'll tell her you are an incredible lover."

"What? No lurid details?"

"I'm sure Denny's imagination can supply more than I ever could. I'm equally sure she will put it to good use."

"You don't take them seriously, then you're as bad as they are."

LAURA'S FACE LOOMED OVER JESSIE, her voice angry, her eyes narrowed. "Why do you want to be friends with me, white girl? Who do you think you are anyway?"

Jessie couldn't speak. When she opened her mouth, only whispers emerged, whispers no one else could hear. Laura turned and began to walk away. When Jessie tried to follow, her body would not move.

Laura kept walking, and Jessie felt herself sinking down into some kind of thick wetness. It slicked her body, and when she raised her arm, it dripped in gelatinous drops down her chest.

She woke with a strangled cry, coming up from the bed as though she would leave it. Kelly sat beside her, tail thumping the floor, a low whine in her voice.

Jessie reached over and rubbed Kelly's head. It did little to quiet the large dog's nervousness. Jessie could hear the distant rumble of thunder. Abruptly, she swung her legs over the side of the bed, grabbing her jeans and shirt as she stood up. She started to pull on the shirt. The night was hot, heavy with humidity. Jessie glanced at the clock. Three o'clock. She threw the shirt onto the bed. She could be safely naked in her own house in the middle of the night.

Barefoot, Jessie went into the kitchen, took a beer from the refrigerator, and found her cigarettes. Kelly padded closely behind her. She pulled the door open and curled her body into the battered armchair on the porch, the light breeze cool on her skin. She popped the top on the can, lit a cigarette, and pulled Kelly's head into her lap. Far away, there were small jags of lightning, thin shards of yellow-white. Usually Jessie loved storms; Kelly always hated and feared them.

But Jessie paid little attention to either the storm or the dog, causing Kelly to push even closer for attention and reassurance. There was little Jessie could do to help Kelly's fear, but her inattention added to it. She rubbed the dog's head absently, her thoughts far away.

Laura. Jessie had known her for about two years. The beginnings had not been easy. Jessie had come into the lesbian community thinking of herself as a lesbian, looking for a group of women with whom she could share ideas and work, women whose political notions paralleled her own. She was adamant about not wanting to work with men. So she approached the lesbian community where, for a while, she was viewed as something of an oddity, a woman who kept to herself and volunteered little or no personal information. Jessie had been afraid she would not be accepted if the women in the community knew her lesbian identity was strictly political, and her personal reality did not, at that time, include sexual relationships. Women speculated about her to one another; she heard some of the gossip. A few asked her about lovers. Jessie never lied, but she rarely volunteered much information. The few women who did know were very close friends and quite accepting of her, even if they didn't completely understand her reticence about sex.

Laura had come onto the scene quietly at first. She had been very clear that her reasons for working with white women had everything to do with the lack of a black lesbian community in the area. White women seemed a bit unnerved by her presence, by her extensive political experience as well as by her color. Their response to her was awkward.

If Jessie was considered odd because of her intense personal silence, and Laura was odd because she was black, they were both considered a little weird and hard to deal with because of their head-on approach to organizing. Individually, each was quick-tempered, assertive, stubborn, and impatient. Jessie could remember more than one occasion where they turned meetings upside down when one or the other got angry over the prolonged process of nitpicking politics.

Because they usually agreed with one another, Jessie and Laura often found themselves working together. With almost no outside help from the community, they had organized a march to protest the rape of a local college student, a march that had drawn much publicity and media coverage. By the end of the event, Jessie and Laura were friends. It had happened slowly.

One night, after a particularly long and involved meeting with a local anti-nuke group, Jessie and Laura decided to go to the bar together, having discovered they both enjoyed playing pool. The tension of the meeting was still between them, and their conversations were testy.

Finally, exasperated by Laura's ongoing string of derisive, anti-white remarks, Jessie had slammed the cue ball across the table without aiming and glared at Laura. "Dammit! Will you please stop talking about those 'damned white girls'? I am a white girl, and I feel like you're taking all this out on me. If you have a problem with me, then say so. Stop all the 'white girl' crap."

Laura leaned across the table and glared back. "Fine. Just as soon as you stop talking about 'women of color.' What color? I am a black woman. Every other woman there tonight was a white woman. Talk some reality, thank you very much."

"All right!" Jessie shouted.

"Good!" Laura snapped as she made her next shot. Abruptly she straightened and eyed her companion. "You know what I think we both are?"

"No. What?"

She smiled. "Mean bitches." Laura's voice was calm and content. "Mean damned bitches. And you know, I love it."

JESSIE WATCHED THE LIGHTNING, her beer almost gone. The thunder had ended, and Kelly had fallen asleep, her head still on Jessie's lap. Tiredly, she rubbed her eyes. She would call Laura tomorrow. They had to talk soon.

3

THE KNOCK ON THE DOOR startled Jessie. Immersed in a book, she had not heard anyone coming. She paused before opening the door.

"Who is it?" she called. The .22 rifle was loaded and leaning against the wall. She glanced at it, hating the fact that she found the presence of the old gun comforting. Kelly pressed against her leg, tail wagging but an alert expression on her face.

"Val and Denny."

Jessie opened the door, relief flooding through her. She didn't care for the fact that she was nervous about living alone for the first time in the year she had spent in the house.

Denny stepped inside and almost tripped over the gun. Replacing it against the wall, she looked at Jessie. "What's this for?"

Jessie motioned them towards the living room and locked the door behind them. "You know that button Val gave me that has STOP THE KKK on it?" Denny nodded. "Well, I wore it into Pete Davis' store the other day, you know, the store up on the highway? There were a bunch of local guys hanging out as usual. Pete read the button out loud, and you could've heard a pin drop in there. All the men stared at me, and one guy came over and sort of leaned against the counter beside me, looking at me hard. When I went out, I noticed that they all had rifles in the gun racks in their pickup trucks. Just as I was leaving, Davis asked didn't I rent that old farmhouse down at Ben Carpenter's place. Everyone in the place heard him. It's got me a little scared. I keep watching for men in white sheets."

Val sat down on the sofa, her expression thoughtful. "I've been in that store a couple of times. I think you have a good reason to be scared. Place gave me the creeps. It reminded me too much of the Klan hangouts in Mississippi and Georgia when I was down there several years ago. They weren't your usual good old boys. Something different about them."

Jessie sat by the desk. She could hear thunder in the distance, and Kelly was pressed tightly to her thigh, trembling at the sounds. She stroked the nervous dog absently with one hand while she closed the book she had been reading with the other.

"So what brings you out here tonight?"

"Just a visit. We wanted to pass along what we had heard about the march planning. We tried to call, but you didn't answer."

Jessie's interest rose sharply. "What's going on with that?" Val tucked her long legs beneath her and accepted the beer Denny handed her. "It is definitely going to happen. The newspaper today reported a Klan spokesman as saying they would not tolerate any interference with their rally and warned us that it's happening on private property. They have a point there. They have the law on their side if we go on to posted private property without the owner's permission, which he isn't likely to give because he would have to be a Klan supporter himself."

"So what was decided?"

"I can't believe Val and I sat through another one of those meetings last night," Denny said, sipping her beer. "There were a lot of rash statements being thrown around, but I think most of the people are beginning to settle down. It's just that there were so many damned men. It's been a long time since I've done any political work with men. The gay guys were okay. But the het men are harder to work with, some of them anyway. A whole lot more men than women."

"But there are women involved?"

"Oh yeah," Val answered, "just not nearly enough to suit us."

"And the straight men were so resistant to input from dykes," Denny interjected. "I'll give credit where it's due to those who did listen, but there weren't many of them."

"The general layout for the demo is pretty simple. We're supposed to meet at the Cary town hall that night at seven o'clock. Then we'll carpool everyone to the edge of the farm where the Klan rally is happening. The idea is to prevent people from walking alone and exposing themselves to individual attacks. We're going to carpool back afterwards. The news media will be there. The Klan is hot stuff these days. We'll demonstrate at the edge of the farm, staying off private property. Then we go home."

"Sounds almost ridiculous when it's actually described like that," Jessie said.

"Yes, it does," Denny answered quietly, "but I'm pretty nervous about it. I think some of the men may show up with weapons."

Val looked at her. "There's no way to stop that unless there's a body search of each and every person before the march. People won't submit to that. If they are going to be armed, I just hope they have the good sense to keep the weapons out of sight."

"I don't know," Denny replied dubiously. "I don't think the Klan will just have their rally and ignore us. Those men talking guns were scared. If a Klansman threatens them very much, there's always the distinct possibility they might pull out those guns."

"But there's not a whole lot the Klan can do if we don't trespass," Jessie said in a firm voice. She hadn't considered the fact that people might be armed.

Denny glanced at her. "There's plenty they can do. They aren't known for obeying the law. That's why we felt it was very important that no one walked around alone."

"You said we, Jessie. Have you decided to come along?"

"Yeah. I think so. I feel like I need to do something. Every time I hear the news or pick up a paper, there's the Klan. And every time I see it, I think of Laura."

Val looked up, a frown furrowing her face. "Say, is everything okay between you two?"

Jessie sighed. "No. It's not okay. Not terrible but not okay."

"What's going on?" Denny asked curiously.

"Oh hell. It's all my fault. If I would ever learn to stop and think before I opened my mouth . . . Laura was over here for breakfast a few weeks ago, and I showed her a clipping from the campus newspaper. It was an expose on the Klan. So I blithely gave my ignorant opinion that they are clowns and the best way to deal with them is to ignore them." Jessie heard Denny's quiet moan. She continued, "I know, Denny. I know."

"So what do you think now?" Denny asked as she sat down beside Val, her hand resting on Val's arm.

"I think I'd better keep my mouth shut until I know what I'm talking about. Laura's been pissed at me before but never like this."

"She probably had her guard down, Jess. You and she have been friends long enough for her not to constantly expect you to say things that can hurt her."

Jessie rubbed her face with the back of her hand. "Well, after that run-in with Laura, I took her advice and went to the library to read some of the testimonies from past Klan investigations. It made me sick. It was actual transcripts, and what was being said was horrible. The fact is, I haven't wanted to see any of that so I didn't. What Laura said to me stopped me dead in my tracks. Those men at Davis' store made it a very personal point to me, too."

"What are you going to do?"

"We are talking. It's just that this is going to take some time to work through."

Val sipped her beer. "Take it to heart and go on, Jessie."

"I know," Jessie muttered, rising and heading towards the kitchen. "I know."

THE OLD WOMAN EYED HER as Jessie shifted her rear on the hard cane-bottomed chair. Dorothy Carpenter pushed her glasses up then clasped her hands around one bony, pale knee and leaned forward.

"Yes'm. I asked Papa why did he go through the men's ward. And do you know what he tole me?" She didn't wait for Jessie's answer but plunged ahead, intent on her story. "He tole me that he just wanted to see what they was doing there. He just wanted to look around for a spell, I reckon. They was crazy, ever' last one of 'em. I don't ever want to go back to one of them hospitals. But I guess if I need it and cain't help it, well, then I'll just have to go and be done with it. But I don't think I'll ever go crazy. Takes an educated person to go crazy, and I reckon I'm not smart enough for it." The old woman fell silent, watching the birds in the driveway in front of her house.

"Why did you and your father go to the mental hospital in the first place?" Jessie asked.

Dorothy Carpenter was a storyteller. Jessie had spent many hours on this porch listening to Dorothy weave her tales, some told straightforwardly, some highly embellished and recounted with a tiny, wicked smile on her face. But this was by far the strangest Jessie had heard.

"We was there to pay a visit to my aunt. She'd been there goin' on eight years, and I reckon she was crazy. Least that's what they said. I remember it like it was yesterday. Her lyin' there, not sayin' a word to nobody. Sometimes, she knew folks. Most of the time not. Or else, she didn't care to. I 'spect that myself. But she kept her hands clenched into fists with her thumbs inside like this," Dorothy demonstrated with her own hands, "and her fingers clenched down tight over her thumbs. Been like that the whole eight years. Nobody could open that woman's hands. It like to made me sick to look at her, sick to my heart and soul. She was a pretty woman 'fore she got put in there. But her skin was as white as pastry flour, and her eyes didn't seem to have no color to 'em.

"And her hands, Jessie, I wisht you coulda seen her hands. Her thumbnails had done growed clean through her hands and was stickin' out the other side. The nails of her other fingers had growed into the meat, too. Nurses said they had tried to open her hands and cut them nails but they couldn't do no good with 'em. Finally, they just gave up tryin'. I guess a woman clench her fists long enough, ain't nothin' nobody can do about it. Reckon it could happen to any of us."

"They grew through her hands?" Jessie asked incredulously, not wanting to believe the story. Mrs. Carpenter glanced at her, sensing the disbelief.

"That's what I'm tellin' you, ain't it? Woman, I seen it with my own eyes! And she let a man do it to her!" Dorothy leaned forward, her hands flashing in agitation as she spoke. "She was a young gal and she got with child and had to get married. After the child was born—pretty baby girl it was—that man of hers pointed her and the baby in one direction, and he took off in the other, and she never saw him no more. She let some no 'count man drive her plumb crazy. Her mama had to raise that baby girl. I don't aim to go crazy. But if I do, ain't gonna be on 'count of no man. This'n here," she pointed at Ben who was dozing in his chair, "he done tried for near forty years.

He tried long and hard. If forty years ain't enough to make me crazy, then I guess I won't ever be. Here I set. I just as soon shoot myself right square in the head as let a man do somethin' like that to me."

Jessie leaned back and lit a cigarette. Her landlady went on, switching to a new tale, one that was light and humorous. Jessie smiled automatically in the appropriate places, but she wasn't really listening. The image of the woman's clenched fists wouldn't leave long enough for her to appreciate the next story.

She thought of the clenched fist: rebellion, anger, power. She had used it herself in demonstrations and rallies. Anger. She thought of her mother, standing in the kitchen, angry with her father, her fists clenched as she cried silently by the sink. She thought of how her fists clenched automatically when threatened, when in pain. Abruptly, she shook the image from her mind and stood up. She had to go home. Jessie tried to ignore the look of disappointment on Dorothy's face.

"I have to go and cook dinner. I haven't eaten today." Mrs. Carpenter nodded, her face quickly cleared of any expression. "Maybe we'll see you tomorrow then."

"Probably." Jessie smiled and started down the driveway to her house. The light was fading rapidly with the approaching storm clouds, and she still had work to do. There was wood to be cut. The last of the vegetables from the day's picking had to be cleaned and stored for canning. Kelly leapt out of the shallow ditch and nipped playfully at Jessie's elbow. Breaking into a run, she raced the dog home. Kelly reached the porch yards ahead of Jessie and turned to bark triumphantly.

Jessie rubbed the dog's head as she cast an appraising glance up at the purple sky. She wondered what would have happened if that woman had ever had a chance to use her fists.

"WHO ARE ALL THESE MEN?" Jessie whispered to Val who sat next to her.

"A strange mixture, isn't it?" Val said. "Are they all planning to participate?"

"It's beginning to look like it."

Jessie leaned back in her chair and crossed her arms. The number of men in the room made her uncomfortable. When Val had called and asked if Jessie wanted to come to the meeting, it had seemed like a simple thing to do. Now she wasn't so sure. For every woman she could see, there were at least five men. The room was hot, and the open windows did little to relieve the stuffiness of too many bodies in a too small space. Jessie rubbed her eyes with the back of her hand. She was tired. She had stayed at the bar much too late the night before and had gotten up early to finish the canning she had postponed. Where she wanted to be most at that particular moment was in bed sleeping, not in the middle of a meeting.

Jessie searched through the crowd for familiar faces. There were a few—women she had seen at other meetings or at parties. Mostly the room was full of strangers. She watched the expressions on the faces of the women she could see from where she was sitting. They appeared to be listening, but they exchanged looks of distrust and disbelief.

" . . . All I'm saying is that we can't take it for granted. They will be armed. It's a Klan rally and they are always armed. They post guards and everything. I think it would be stupid for us just to walk up to the fringes without being armed, too. What if they start shooting at us?"

Jessie finally located the owner of the voice, a young man with short hair sitting near the door. She nudged Val and pointed him out. Val nodded, a frown on her face.

The man continued. "Look, it's impossible to predict what might happen. They might ignore us. But I don't think so. I think they might simply start shooting. And I, for one, do not intend to stand there and be a helpless target."

Another man jumped up from his chair, a look of incredulity on his face. He ran his hand through his long hair and then slapped his thigh. Anger or frustration? Jessie couldn't decide.

"I can't believe this! It sounds like the showdown at the OK Corral. This is not the 1800s, man. This is now. And the quickest way to get those people to shoot at us is to show a weapon of any kind. That's crazy. You would be putting other people's lives on the line with your gun!"

"The constitution gives me the right . . ." Short-Hair doggedly persisted.

"Fuck the constitution! It's only a piece of paper. It does not give you the right to screw around with the lives of other people!" There were murmurs of agreement from around the room. A woman rose and raised her voice so she could be heard over the noise. "I am not willing to participate in a demonstration where people are carrying weapons. I thought we were trying to prove a point here. If we go in carrying guns, then we aren't any better than they are. We will endanger ourselves and everyone who participates. We could easily provoke an attack."

Short-Hair leapt up, pointing a finger at her. "I think it's time you started living in the present! The pacifist sixties are over! People do not respond to the nonviolent theory anymore. This is a violent society, and we have to protect ourselves. Anybody, and I mean anybody, who takes to the streets unarmed is a damned fool!"

"Then I'm a damned fool!" she shouted in return, "But I do not intend to arm myself, and I do not intend to let men like you set me up to be shot at because you can't deal with your own fear and need for violence!"

Another woman rose, her face flushed angrily. "You won't get any women to participate if that's your plan."

"We don't need the women, darlin'," he sneered.

The long-haired man threw up his hands in disgust. "Oh shit, man. You are a damned fool. A stupid, damned fool. What do you mean, we don't need the women?"

"Just what I said! We would make a greater show of force if the men were there with ..."

Shouts of "sit down" were heard from others in the room. Short-Hair stared them down. "Those men at that rally will laugh at the women. They will not laugh at men. They are men, and they will have to respect a show of force by other men! As for the dykes in here ..."

"Do some research, prick!" roared one large woman as she pushed her way through the crowd towards him. Short-Hair backed away a step or two when he saw her size. She stared down at him, not lowering her voice in spite of the fact that she stood less than a foot from him. "There are women in the Ku Klux Klan, too. Women don't just sit back and sew the bedsheets together anymore, fool. They participate. Did you see the latest issue of *Southern Exposure*? Didn't you even notice that that person on the cover with the child was a woman? A woman in Klan drag with her grandson, for chrissakes? You just glanced at it and assumed it was a man, didn't you? Well, it wasn't a man. There are a lot of women in the Klan. And besides, a lot of Klan violence comes down on women in this society, especially black women and Jewish women. So you can take your bullshit and stuff it! You need us! And we aren't going to leave to pacify your male ego!"

The cheers came not only from the women. Men clapped, too, as she continued to loom over the very silent short-haired man. Jessie nudged Val with her elbow. "Who is that?"

Val laughed. "Her name is Moon. That's all she answers to." The long-haired man held up his hands to try to restore order in the room. Gradually the noise level dropped. When he was able to speak and be heard, he turned to face Short-Hair. "I think it would be best for all concerned if you left, man. Just pack it in and go."

Complete silence reigned as everyone stared at Short-Hair. "You can't throw me out," he sputtered in confusion.

"The hell we can't. You said we don't need the women. Who we don't need is you. We don't need your disruption or your violence. Just get out."

The crowd echoed him, loudly. Finally, the short-haired man grabbed his backpack and started towards the door. "You cannot stop me from participating in the demonstration!" he yelled as he left.

The long-haired man sighed. "I don't know about everyone else, but I could use a short break. What do you say?"

Standing in the yard, Jessie lit a cigarette. She stared at Val. "I can't believe this. Have you been sitting through meetings like this for the past two months?"

"They haven't been anywhere near this eventful. I don't know who that guy was making all the noise. I haven't seen him before."

The large woman who had shouted down Short-Hair suddenly loomed over them. "I think he's an agent."

"Moon!" Val's shout was one of undisguised delight. The two women wrapped into a crushing hug. Jessie watched, grinning. It wasn't often she saw another woman as tall as Val Berns.

"It's been a while since I've seen you," Moon said to Val.

"It sure has. How are you?"

"Okay, whatever that means," Moon answered, shrugging her massive shoulders. Val turned to Jessie.

"Jessie, this is an old friend of mine from at least fifteen years ago. Moon, this is Jessie Pyne."

Jessie held out her hand. "It's good to . . ."

"The hell with shaking hands." Moon laughed as she grabbed Jessie in a hug that almost enveloped Jessie's whole body. "Good to meet you, too, Jessie Pyne. Yeah, Val and I go back to Civil Rights days in southern Georgia. Say, Val, I hear Laura is living around these parts, too. Is that a fact?"

"Yep. In Durham."

"I have to look her up. I've missed my daily fights with her." Moon looked at Jessie. "We didn't really fight, but goddess, did we ever have some great arguments! Nobody's made me think like that since I left Mississippi."

"I can understand that."

"So you know Laura, too? Lucky you! So how do I get in touch with you, Val? I want to have dinner with you real soon."

"I'm in the book. Durham, Alabama Avenue."

"Alabama Avenue?" Moon laughed loudly. "Okay. I'll call this week. Take care of yourself. See ya, Jessie."

Moon pushed back into the building. Jessie crushed out her cigarette and shook her head. Quite an impressive woman.

Val looked at her. "I'll tell you about Moon on the way home.

You ready to go back inside?"

"I guess so."

VAL STIRRED HER COFFEE, then sipped. There were circles under her eyes and she looked tired, even though she smiled as she talked. "So Moon came to Jackson, Mississippi, from Georgia. She was all heat and ready to take on the world. There was a group of whites who were trying to find a way to work with the blacks in the area and having some difficulty. We all felt, blacks and whites, that a visible, strong all-black movement was essential. And yet many of us whites wanted to do whatever we could. So some of us started working as support groups, mostly staying in the background, except when we could serve some specific purpose with our whiteness and visibility. Things like gathering information, sometimes managing to get into meetings, things like that. We couldn't do much though because we were so obviously outsiders. Most of us weren't even from the South, and our accents gave us away pretty fast.

"Moon came down. She was very outspoken and pushy. She also overstepped the bounds frequently. She was an open lesbian, a fact which freaked almost everyone out. Moon was very big on security and thought what we called security was totally inadequate. She and Laura clashed hard several times, but the security thing united them. Laura was going crazy over the number of workers who were harassed or caught out alone and beaten up, some very badly. Finally, the group told them to work it out and shut up. They refused to do it until everyone agreed they would follow whatever guidelines and procedures were drawn up. The argument went on for days. In the end, the two of them literally talked everyone else into it. What Moon and Laura came up with was a fairly simple check-in and buddy-type system so that we got the most self-protection possible no matter where we were. They also tightened up security around conversations and meetings so that very little of our planning got out to the public. We were hassled less and got a lot more work done. We knew where everyone was almost every moment, and that made us feel a lot better. We also didn't have any more incidents of workers being caught and beaten up. I think we were just lucky that no one was killed.

"About a year after she arrived, Laura and Moon became lovers. No one understood it, and it caused a hell of a lot of problems for Laura. Moon was sort of ignored, and she didn't think who she slept with was anyone's business anyway. Laura, on the other hand, was challenged on the basis of the entire black liberationist politic."

"How did she stand up to that?" Jessie asked.

"It was rough on her. Moon wasn't black, and she wasn't a man, and Laura caught fairly constant hell for a while. But they stayed together for almost two years, until Moon wanted to move on and organize migrant workers and Laura felt very strongly that she needed to remain within the black Civil

Rights movement. They parted as close friends, but I don't know how much contact they've had since then."

"I'd sure like to get a chance to talk with her."

"You probably will. She doesn't usually breeze through a place. She tends to do what she calls 'squatting' for a while, so I expect she'll be around. I'm glad she seems to be fully recovered."

Jessie glanced at her. "Recovered from what?"

Val signaled for the check. "About twelve years ago when Moon was in Mississippi, she was shot by the Klan and left for dead. One of the workers found her and got her to the hospital. There was a lot of nerve damage to her left arm and hand, and the doctors weren't sure she would ever have full use of them again. But she seems to be okay."

"The Klan, huh?"

"Yep. The Klan." Val looked at Jessie. "They seem to come into almost every conversation these days, don't they? I'm beat. Let's go home. Want to stay in town tonight? It's awfully late."

"That would be great."

Jessie followed Val out of the coffee shop. The Klan. The Klan. Why had they arrived so hard in her life?

4

WHAT THE HELL WAS HAPPENING? Jessie ran.

Which direction? Where? She heard pounding footsteps behind her, and she tried to increase her speed. Hands gripped her shoulder and jerked her hard to the side. She felt herself slipping. Painfully, her shoulder struck the pavement and she rolled. Under something. A truck. She was under a pickup truck. She felt a body slam into her, and Denny shouted into her ear.

"Are you all right?"

Jessie nodded and slid further under the truck, seeking safety between the wheels. Denny shook her. "Do you know where Val is?"

"No," Jessie answered, trying to catch her breath. "I lost sight of her when everyone started running."

"Jesus," Denny muttered.

The shouts and screams were close now. Jessie suddenly panicked. She was under a truck. What if the driver . . . She started to wiggle away, but Denny grabbed her and pulled her back.

"Where the hell are you going?"

"We've got to get out from under here. We could get killed lying under a truck!"

"We're safer under here than out there." Denny clung to her.

Jessie tested her arm as best she could in her cramped position. It seemed okay. Bruised and sore, but okay.

Then she saw the woman fall just on the other side of the wheels. A black woman, young, on the ground. Suddenly, all Jessie could see were hands and feet, hands pounding, feet kicking. The woman was silent, and still.

Jessie struggled to pull away from Denny. "Let go!"

"Jessie . . ."

"Let go, goddamit!" Jessie broke free from Denny's grasp and rolled out from under the truck. The woman was sprawled on her back, unmoving, blood all over her face. One man still stood beside her, his leg drawn back. Just as Jessie jumped to her feet, he kicked out, into the side of the woman's head. Then he looked at Jessie, his gaze daring her to interfere.

She took a step forward, not knowing what to do. The man stepped over the black woman's inert body and grabbed Jessie by the shirt. He shoved her against the truck and laughed as he ground his knee into her pubic bone. When he let go, Jessie doubled up, gasping from the pain. Only supposed to hurt men, she thought fleetingly, as she saw him disappear into the edge of the woods. She dropped onto her knees and bent forward in an effort to minimize the pain.

The sudden silence was as frightening as the gunshots and screams had been. Jessie held herself very still, taking deep breaths and feeling the pain subside a bit. Then she realized that she was leaning over the woman. She felt Denny beside her, but she could not tear her gaze from the woman's face. Finally she reached out and felt for a pulse. There was the tiniest flicker beneath her fingertips.

Val dropped to her knees beside Jessie, appearing out of nowhere. Her breathing was labored. She touched the woman's face.

"Oh hell. Oh hell," she said, over and over, like a litany.

Denny touched Jessie's shoulder. "Are you all right? Did he . . ."

Jessie shook her head. "I'm okay. I got a knee in the cunt."

"Get an ambulance, Denny."

As Denny ran down the road, Val pulled a bandana from her pocket and gently tried to wipe the blood from the woman's face. "What happened, Val? What the hell happened?" Jessie asked.

Val shook her head. When she spoke, her voice trembled and cracked. "I don't know. I saw two men with guns. They fired them into the air. Then all those men burst out of the woods with heavy sticks in their hands. They started chasing people, clubbing them with the sticks. Some people tried to fight back, but most of us just ran. I think a lot of people are hurt. This was stupid. We should've been watching for something like this!"

Jessie instinctively jerked back when she saw the boots beside her. A tall, uniformed highway patrolman stood over her, glaring down from under the round brim of his hat. He touched the black woman's leg with the toe of his boot, a look of disgust on his face. "Stay with her," he ordered, as he moved away. Jessie bit off an angry retort. The pulse in the woman's neck was fainter now. Be here, she thought silently to the woman. Be here.

JESSIE SAT IN THE ARMCHAIR, staring out the window, watching the afternoon sun drop behind the trees. She ached with exhaustion. Her mouth was coated from too many cigarettes and beers, and she needed a bath. Still, she sat.

In spite of the afternoon heat, she was cold. She wrapped the light blanket more tightly around her. She could hear Val and Denny talking in the kitchen.

One man shot to death. Old Short-Hair himself. A white woman badly wounded with a knife. The black woman had died on the way to the hospital. Lots of other injuries. The black woman's name was Etta. Etta Thomas.

Jessie glanced at the clock. Time for the news. For the first time in hours, she stood up. She turned on the television set and stood in front of it. The newscaster looked alien to her, far removed from the reality of her world, too tidy in his dark jacket and carefully combed hair. He gave his report in a modulated, neutral tone of voice.

"Violence erupted last night during an anti–Ku Klux Klan demonstration at Jennings farm outside Cary. Two people are dead, one woman is listed in critical condition, and at least fourteen others are reported seriously injured from a battle between Klansmen and demonstrators. Police reports say…"

His voice droned on and Jessie listened. She heard Val and Denny come into the room, and she could feel them standing close behind her, also listening to the report. Jessie finished her beer and lit another cigarette, ignoring the rawness of her throat. There were few pictures. The news people had packed up their gear and were leaving when the whole thing started. The demonstration was over. Everyone had been heading back to the cars together, just as planned. The photographs being used by the television station were taken by a bystander.

As she listened, Jessie slowly became aware of her surroundings, the quiet breathing of her friends, the sound of the frogs starting to sing, Kelly's panting. She tossed the blanket onto the chair and went into the bedroom. As she reached for the rifle, she noticed that her fists were tightly clenched, the nails pressing half-moon indentations into the palms of her hands. Abruptly, she grabbed the gun and the box of shells and went outside.

Her hands were shaking, and her stomach was knotted with sickening tension. She picked up a beer can from the window sill and set it on the grass. When she had walked about fifty feet from the can, she lifted the rifle and took careful aim. Then she fired.

Reloading, she quickly sent fifteen shells into the can and the ground around it. Over and over. She stopped only long enough to shove the .22 caliber shells into the magazine, and then she fired in almost continuous bursts, taking three or four seconds to empty the chamber.

If she had had a gun, could she have used it? Would she have? If she had gotten out from under the truck sooner, could she have stopped those men? What could she have done? The sharp cracks from the rifle did not drown out the memory of the men's laughter. Jessie could still hear them as clearly as if she stood beside them.

She reached for more shells and found the box empty. A heavy tiredness settled into her body as she went to retrieve the can. It was ripped to shreds by the bullets.

Val was leaning against the dogwood tree watching Jessie. She wrapped her arms around her chest as if cold, and there were tears in her eyes as she waited.

Jessie passed her on her way back inside the house. Still hugging herself, Val fell into step with Jessie. "I didn't know you could shoot a gun like that."

Jessie glanced at her. "No reason why you should. All I killed was a can."

Val stood by the door. Denny was working on the car. "Come and stay in town with Denny and me for a few days, Jessie."

"Why?"

"It doesn't feel safe out here right now."

"I don't want to come into town."

Val ran her fingers through her thick hair, an agitated expression on her usually calm face. "It's not safe," she persisted.

"It's as safe as your house."

"Bullshit, Jessie. Look, I am scared. I don't know if I can stay out here with you."

"I didn't ask you to stay, Val. To be perfectly honest, I would rather be by myself right now."

"Use your head, Jessie. You are an eyewitness. It's not safe out here. You're too isolated."

"Dammit, Val. Stop mothering me! I don't need it!" Jessie's voice cracked with strain, and there were tears in her eyes. Val stepped forward and impulsively pulled Jessie close to her. They stood there for a long moment, silently locked hard against each other. Then Jessie straightened up and wiped her eyes.

"I think I'm a complete wreck, Val."

"So am I. So am I."

"I'll come and stay tonight. But I have to come home tomorrow. There's too much for me to do to be away from here for more than a day."

"I need to call Kate. She's probably pretty worried."

"Probably."

Jessie sighed. "Let me get some things together and feed the animals. Then I'll be ready."

"I'll take care of the chickens," Val volunteered. Jessie nodded and disappeared into the house.

JESSIE'S MOOD WAS FOUL. She cursed the press and slammed reams of paper. Nothing in her day was going right. She had messed up several plates, could not get the ink and water balance right on the press, and now she had dropped a rag into the rollers which had fouled the gears. She sat down on the stool and lit a cigarette, taking deep breaths, trying to calm herself. If she kept on like this, she might as well close the shop and just go home.

Laura came into the room and stood staring at the press. The rag protruded like a snake's tongue. Calmly she reached into Jessie's shirt pocket and removed a cigarette.

"You quit smoking," Jessie reminded her.

"One every week or two is not exactly heavy-duty smoking," Laura answered mildly. "I posted the closed sign on the door. We're going home."

"There's too much to do for us to . . ." Jessie began.

Laura silenced her with a gesture. "Ridiculous. You aren't getting anything done anyway, Jessie, and you know it. Besides, I can't stand hearing you yell anymore. I've been listening all day."

"It hasn't been a good day," Jessie said defensively.

"I know. You need to go home and relax a while. Go work in your garden. Get rid of some of this tension. Otherwise, I'm afraid you might really wreck the press."

Jessie threw a rag on the floor. "People are so damned full of advice these days!"

"What's eating you?" Laura demanded. "I'm a partner in this little venture here, and I have a right not to have to listen to your tantrums all day long!"

Jessie turned to face her. "What's eating me is a picture I can't get out of my mind! The picture of a woman dying flat on her back, in the middle of a road, with blood all over her face! That's what's eating me, Laura."

"So what are you going to do about that?"

"If I knew what to do about it, it wouldn't be bothering me so damned much!" Jessie did not lower her voice. "What really gets to me is whenever I think about Etta Thomas, I see your face. It could have been you!"

"Honey, I've known that every day of my life," Laura said softly.

"Well, I just figured it out!"

"I'm glad you finally did."

Jessie stared at her and felt the anger drain away. "Yeah, okay. I get your point. Can we be friends again?"

"We never stopped being friends. I just wanted you to think a little."

"Well, I'm thinking."

"So why don't you think at home? I could stand a little time off myself."

"All right," Jessie muttered. She reached for her pack and flipped off the light switch. Laura propelled her towards the door.

"I'll see you in the morning," she said with finality.

"Yeah." Jessie walked to her car. It was early yet. Maybe she should go home and work in the garden. Suddenly, she felt too restless to make the long drive back to her house. She threw her pack into the back seat and started down the street. She would have a beer, then maybe she would be ready to go home.

5

JESSIE STARED AT THE WALL, her hands shoved into the pockets of her jeans. The light outside was fading but she didn't notice.

Kate sat quietly on the sofa, her gaze firmly fixed on Jessie's broad shoulders. "Jessie . . ."

"Not now, Kate. Not right now."

It had been going on for a long time, this fight. In some ways, it had started nearly a month ago, right after the demonstration, right after Jessie had met with Val, Denny, Laura, Moon, and some other women to discuss what had happened. They had decided to start a group and to put out a newsletter, open and visible opposition to the Ku Klux Klan. Kate had not liked the idea from the start and had been very vocal about it.

But now the afternoon dragged on with an argument that seemed endless. Jessie felt they had gotten nowhere at all. Kate could not, or would not, understand anything Jessie was saying, anything Jessie was feeling. Jessie had seen it coming; she had simply tried to avoid it. She knew Kate opposed her every Klan-related thought and action. This afternoon was just the culmination of all the disputes and tensions.

Kate rose and approached Jessie slowly, tentatively placing her hands on Jessie's shoulders. The strength in her lover's body still scared Kate a little. She had seen Jessie throw large slabs of wood around as if they weighed nothing. She had felt the barely restrained force when they made love. She had seen Jessie angry and had watched her hit the side of the house with her fist, seeming not to notice the pain Kate knew she must feel, or even the split, bleeding skin on her knuckles. Kate felt inept and clumsy by comparison.

"Can't you understand that I'm afraid for you?" Kate asked softly. "I'm afraid something terrible might happen to you. What are you hoping to accomplish?" Kate turned Jessie around, holding onto her arms. "Jess, these people kill. They don't play games."

Jessie pulled away from Kate's light grip, a touch she felt was meant to restrict more than anything else. She didn't notice the hurt expression on Kate's face as she started pacing the length of the room.

'That's the whole point. I was there. I saw what they can do. It's my whole nightmare, seeing it played over and over. I can't let it be just a nightmare, and I feel that's what you're wanting me to do."

Jessie picked up her beer and downed the last of it with one large gulp. Her hands shook, from memories, from too many cigarettes, from exhaustion. The whole conversation was going in circles with no resolution or end in sight. Kate appeared to want her to just give in completely. Jessie unclenched her fists with great effort, but she did not look at Kate.

Kate sighed and lit one of Jessie's cigarettes. She was running out of words. But Jessie wasn't listening anyhow so what did it matter?

"I'm not asking you to forget anything. No one should forget what happened, including you. But I am asking you to use some common sense."

Jessie slammed the empty beer can down on the desk, her face flushed with anger. "And just what the hell do you call common sense, Kate? I don't understand. Everyone goes around thinking this sort of thing can't happen to them. I doubt any one of those three people who died would've thought it was possible either. But they are dead. Two women and one man are dead. I was there, too, but I wasn't a target."

"This time," Kate muttered.

"Kate, I swear, if you don't stop baiting me ..."

"I'm not baiting you! Dammit. You're trying to take on something that's so big no one even knows how many people are involved. And you're trying to do it with a tiny group of women and a newsletter. I admire your courage, but I question your tactics. What are you going to do other than call attention to yourself? I don't think even the Klan would pay much attention to you except that you are a witness to a murder and are expected to testify in court. So you put out an anti-Klan newsletter. What's it going to prove? They already know who you are, and this isn't going to make you any less of a threat to them. John O. Public does not care!" Kate's voice increased in volume as she spoke. In her mind, she had her own private nightmare; she could so easily see Jessie lying on the ground, beaten bloody or dead. She tried to clear the picture from her mind. She couldn't function when she thought of it. All she could feel was a deep, incapacitating fear for Jessie, and for herself.

" ... that in this little town, there is a junior KKK club in the local high school? And that's a fact. We have got to make some kind of start, Kate. More people will join in."

"Why don't you recruit those people first then? The old adage about safety in numbers is true, you know."

"There are three dead people who very much disprove that old adage."

Kate recoiled from the sarcasm in Jessie's voice. This was going absolutely nowhere, and she was afraid they would only end up hating each other for the seemingly insurmountable differences between them, rather than being able to see what was really going on. Kate dropped onto the sofa and rubbed her tired eyes.

Jessie turned on the lamp, holding back tears of frustration by sheer willpower, wishing for another beer, wishing Kate would simply go home and leave her alone. Everything had seemed clear and resolved until Kate had arrived that afternoon, a copy of the newsletter in her hand.

Kelly, who had been watching anxiously from the corner, crossed to Jessie and shoved her cold, damp nose into Jessie's hand, wagging her tail slightly, seeking reassurance. Jessie rubbed the dog's head in an agitated manner, then tried to send her back to the corner with a gesture and an abrupt command to "lie down." Kelly moved a few feet away and sat, watching Jessie intently, her tail thumping on the floor from time to time as she grew more nervous about the disagreement.

"I don't want to live in a world of constant fear, Kate. I reject that. I think it can be changed. Something has to be done. That's what I want. I want to try."

"But it's not realistic," Kate answered, her patience almost completely gone. "The world isn't fair. It's okay to have a vision of people righting all the wrongs. But you are an idealist, Jess. Sometimes I think your trouble is that you can't see around your own visions long enough to acknowledge the reality. Your anger comes from not being able to have the vision, all the peace and goodness. We all know the world is a lousy place . . ."

Jessie whirled around so suddenly that she knocked a stack of books off the corner of the desk. Kelly whimpered uneasily.

"For god's sake, Kate! What do you think I've been talking about for the last two months? This whole fucking society is supposedly set up on the premise of peace and goodness and freedom. And it doesn't work! Sure, I have ideals. Everyone has to have a few. But my sense of reality is damned clear. Killing people seems like a pretty big reality. And we give our permission to those people every time we keep our mouths shut. My own silence makes me a target for them."

"And that's not enough? You're trying to make it even easier than before!"

"No! They do it because no one tells them they can't. I am not giving my silent consent anymore. I'll go down screaming, thanks."

"So why don't you just wear a sign that says Shoot me, I'm willing? I think there's more to be gained by simply staying alive while we try to effect change. Confrontations in the streets will only get people hurt. Have you thought seriously about that? What if we all just walked right out there and became targets? What then?"

Jessie was surprised by Kate's biting anger, but she met the older woman's gaze evenly, fighting the impulse to grab her and throw her bodily from the house.

"They can't possibly get all of us."

"But they can get a lot. What then?" Kate demanded, her eyes narrowed and piercing.

"We get killed every day, Kate! You're working for the battered women's shelter. You should know that better than anyone. But what do you think black people faced when they took to the streets in the sixties? They faced guns and clubs, the Klan, law enforcement officials, firehoses, dogs, and death. But they stayed in the streets. They took the chance!"

"Yes, and some people, like Roy Wilkins, stayed behind the scenes and fought for change from within."

"Are you trying to tell me that Roy Wilkins could have accomplished all that if there weren't also people in the streets forcing confrontations, forcing people to take notice?"

"There's the key word, Jessie, also. All I'm trying to say is that there are also other ways of doing things, not just one way, not just your way."

"I don't want to take cowardly ways of dealing with this."

There was a long silence in the room as Jessie lit a cigarette and dropped into the armchair.

"Now are you saying that not wanting to march in the streets is cowardly?" Kate's voice was tight.

Jessie's hands were shaking, and she almost dropped the matches. She was stammering over words, anger clashing with speech, her feelings frayed, all acuity gone, destroyed by the long hours of beating her head against Kate's solid wall of resistance.

Kate wanted to grab her and shake some sense into her, make Jessie at least acknowledge the other sides to her own arguments.

"I think we have to take some chances if anything is ever really going to change."

"And no one can do anything any other way?"

"I didn't say that."

"Then tell me exactly what you are saying!"

"What the hell good would it do to try it any other way? We have tried almost everything. We have talked and begged and even threatened. What has changed? What is different? If anything, it's worse. What good would it do to hide . . ."

"Hide?" Kate sputtered.

"Yes, hide! Hide behind the powers that be and try to make something out of nothing. They aren't going to give it to us because we're good and we don't make trouble. We have to create something from the bottom up and then let them know we won't shut up and go home until things are different."

"Do you think I am being cowardly for not taking to the streets?"

Jessie stared at her, then turned to put out her cigarette. Rising from the chair and crossing the room, Kate was on her in a flash of a second, grabbing her by the shoulders and whirling Jessie around, her fingers digging deeply into Jessie's flesh. Jessie slammed her hands upward, breaking Kate's grip. She grabbed Kate by the shirt and pushed her back, afraid to be too close, knowing she might hit her if Kate touched her again.

"Don't you ever grab me like that again, Kate."

"You answer my question!" Kate shouted. She moved towards Jessie again but then noticed Jessie's clenched fists and rigid expression.

"Your problem is, Jessie, that you can't stand the fact that we don't think exactly alike, that I see things differently from you. Or that I might, just might, be able to see some things more clearly because I'm not in the middle of them. All you want from me is an across-the-board yes to everything you think, feel, or say. You will not get that from me! But don't you ever insinuate that I am a coward again. I won't take that from you."

Kate was crying, but Jessie just stared at her. Then she turned and walked into the kitchen. She jerked open the refrigerator door and peered inside, then slammed it with a muttered curse. Stomping into the living room, she picked up her car keys, wiping her own tears away with the back of her hand. Kate still stood in the middle of the room, looking drained and fearful.

"I'm going for more beer," Jessie said.

"I could go with you."

"I don't want you to," she flung over her shoulder as she left the room. She slammed the door and stepped outside. The chilly air stung. She could feel her damp cheeks draw tightly, and she wished she had another door to slam.

6

BETH PARRISH PULLED the old bathrobe tightly around her as she sat down at the kitchen table and opened the morning paper. She never really read the paper; instead she looked at headlines and pictures, at the display ads and grocery specials. The news was always too full of murders, disasters, crises, and Beth found it depressing.

She sipped her tea contentedly, the silence in the small house unbroken except for the occasional rustle of a page being turned. She loved this time of the morning, the only time she had for herself, to be alone, to be still and quiet. It was her ritual, although she never would have thought of it as such. After the boys went off to school and Hank left for work, Beth would put on her faded pink bathrobe, the terry cloth worn nearly through in places, make herself a cup of mint tea, and sit down at the Formica-topped kitchen table with the newspaper and the silence.

She didn't remember exactly when, or even why, she had started taking this time for herself. In her mind, she thought she had simply found herself doing it. Beth frequently didn't remember the beginnings of things, only that they were now and therefore must need to be. She had not made a conscious choice to continue her morning ritual; she just did it. She never told anyone about it, never shared the secret of the time stolen from her busy day and given to herself as a precious gift. And of course, she had to be careful about it. Hank had come back to the house unexpectedly one morning and had almost caught her sitting at the table, lost in a daydream. Since that day, she had been much more discreet, never relaxing so completely that she might not hear his key in the lock or the sounds of Karen next door coming over to borrow something.

Beth unconsciously stroked the worn pattern of the soft robe. Her best friend in high school had given it to her as a birthday present the year they graduated. She had never understood why Hank hated it so much. Well, it was getting pretty ratty and old now, but he had hated it even when it was new. Maybe Hank just didn't like anything that was given to her by anyone other than himself. He always found fault with the clothes Beth's mother gave her from time to time, on her birthday or at Christmas. Sometimes, he even forbade her to wear things he especially didn't like. So she kept the robe hidden away from him, afraid he would demand that she throw it away or that he would do it himself. She didn't want him to get mad over the robe. She hated for him to get mad.

She lifted the cup to her mouth. Hank also hated for her to drink hot tea. He said it was a snobby habit and that Beth was acting uppity. Beth never pointed out to him that he drank iced tea by the pitcher so why shouldn't she drink hot tea once in a while? You couldn't argue with him. When Hank was at home, Beth drank iced tea or coffee. She kept the box of mint tea hidden where she thought he wouldn't find it, behind the flour or shortening, being careful to move it from time to time because Hank would sometimes get these wild notions that he needed to check things out. He would methodically go through drawers, cabinets, and closets for no apparent reason other than to berate Beth about her housekeeping. Sometimes he actually seemed to be looking for something, although Beth knew better than to ask what for. Hank hated for her to question him.

She eyed the paper sleepily as she turned the pages. They were wrinkled from Hank's rough handling at breakfast. Sighing, Beth wondered what it would be like to have a fresh paper, to be the very first one to open the crisp sheets and see the headlines. Startled by this unexpected thought, she glanced quickly around the tiny kitchen, almost expecting someone to have heard what she had not said out loud. She flipped guiltily to the comics. Being the second person to read the paper wasn't so bad. Besides, Hank was her husband, and he was supposed to have the best of everything.

Sometimes, though, it was difficult to always put Hank first. Beth knew that was the way it was suppose to be, but Hank was so hard to please and so much the Big Man. Sometimes, he just acted plain silly, like a big, spoiled kid. Or mean.

Sighing again, Beth started to gather the paper up. There was a lot to do—grocery shopping, laundry, and the house needed to be cleaned. As Beth carefully folded the paper to deposit it in the trashcan, her eye caught a picture on the front page of the local section. It was a picture of a black woman, lying on what looked like a street, with two white women kneeling beside her. One of the white women had her back to the camera, but Beth could see the other one quite clearly, a stocky, intense looking woman with dark hair, glaring at the camera as she held the black woman's hand. Beth looked at the headline, MURDER TRIAL SET FOR FIRST OF YEAR, and the column header, Klansmen Claim Self Defense. She abruptly folded the section into the middle of the paper and carefully placed it in the trashcan.

HANK MOTIONED TOM AND EDGAR into the room and towards chairs. The room was cloudy with cigarette smoke and stuffy from inadequate ventilation. In spite of the fact that someone had obviously been smoking heavily, all the ashtrays were clean.

"Glad you could come over. I want to get through this as fast as I can so we don't have to miss any of the ballgame. Hey, Beth! Bring a couple more beers out here."

The men were silent as she hurried into the room and handed them the cold cans of Miller. Her movements were quick and nervous. Hank ruffled her hair casually before taking his beer from her hand.

"Thanks, hon." There was little warmth in his voice.

Beth understood the dismissal and left the room as quickly as she had entered. She went down the hall, checking the sleeping children, pulling up blankets and turning off lights. Then she went into the bedroom she shared with Hank and started to close the door. A thoughtful expression settled over her face and she hesitated. Hank had been awfully agitated lately, and he had spent a lot of time on the telephone with his friends talking in a low voice, glaring at her every time she came into the room. She had overheard snatches of the conversations; they were always about some woman. Whatever it was, Hank was certainly upset.

Beth closed the door resolutely. Obviously, it was none of her business what they were talking about. If Hank wanted her to know, he would tell her. She sat on the edge of the bed and bent down to remove her shoes, glancing at the closed door. Unbidden, the picture from the newspaper flashed into her mind. *MURDER TRIAL SET FOR FIRST OF YEAR.* The woman staring at the camera, the black woman lying on the road. She stared at the doorknob and strained to hear any bits of conversation that might drift down the hall.

"THERE'S TROUBLE," HANK SAID, watching the faces of the two men sitting across from him. Tom looked bored; Edgar looked puzzled. Edgar almost always looked puzzled.

"It doesn't have to be big trouble. No one wants it to be. I have been asked to deal with it before it has the chance to get any bigger."

"Get to the point, Hank," Tom said in a low voice.

Hank bristled slightly. Tom had a longtime habit of challenging, directly and indirectly, what Hank considered to be his authority. Hank assumed that anyone who had the ear of the head of the state Klan organization also had authority. He had Baker's ear; he rarely let anyone forget or overlook that fact. He also had inside information, access to police records and documents, information that made him a valuable man.

"I take it you've heard of a broad named Jessie Pyne?"

"Sure. She's supposed to testify at John Layton's trial," Edgar answered.

"Well, Baker doesn't want her to testify. But he wants to keep a low profile, too. Doesn't want the organization involved in any way that could be traced. He doesn't want any fingers pointing his way, if you get my drift. Now, in addition to being the only eyewitness to that nigger's death, this Jessie Pyne has also started up an anti-KKK newsletter. She and a bunch of other broads are talking it up pretty big. Ordinarily, Baker wouldn't pay them any mind. But this is not a good time. They're already circulating this thing pretty widely, and they're giving speeches. One of those liberal churches has them slated for some kind of workshops. Folks are beginning to pay attention, which is exactly what Baker doesn't want to happen.

"I have been asked," Hank paused dramatically, "to explain to her that no one ever wants to see another copy of this rag she's putting out. I have been asked to explain to her how dark it was that night and how unlikely that makes her identification of whoever killed that nigger. I have been asked to explain to her that she just needs to shut her mouth and stop spreading all her stupid lies. I have been asked to see that this is done as quickly and quietly as possible. I assured Mr. Baker that I knew two men who could do the job and that everything would be fine."

BETH COULD HEAR the low hum of Hank's voice from the living room, but she could not make out any words. With a sigh, she slipped between the sheets and turned off the lamp. Maybe, for once, he would be quiet when he came to bed and not wake her up.

"I CAN'T DO THAT, Tom, and you know it." Hank felt a twist of panic as he felt his control over the situation slipping.

"Well, I guess you'll have to go back and tell Mr. Baker that you can't deliver. That ought to really excite him. Impress him, too." Tom's drawl grew more pronounced as he talked, his enjoyment obvious. "Of course, you probably won't have a job after he gets through."

"Look," Hank struggled to keep the rage out of his voice, "I told him I would arrange to plant a weapon that could be traced back to that Etta Thomas and make this a clear case of self-defense. And John Layton has four men who are willing to swear he was nowhere near Thomas when she was getting her head kicked in."

"Afraid of getting your nice blue uniform dirty, Parrish?" Tom grinned his delight at the turn of events. "Get this straight. We haven't said we would do it. But we have said we won't do it unless you come along."

"I serve a purpose when I stay behind the scenes. There's no one else in this town who can . . ." Hank's chest felt tight.

"Face it, Hank," Tom interrupted. "You're a real chicken-shit, and you hide behind that uniform. I always knew that. You think you're really something because you can leak a few things out from the department once in a while. Well, I got news for you. Time for the boy to become a man. And you aren't the only one who knows Bill Baker. I'm pretty sure your police captain would be very interested to know that one of his sergeants is a Klansman."

"You prick," Hank said softly, his voice dangerously low. "Time for you to stop beating your meat and your wife and do something a real man would do. Oh, you can still be the brains. You can even be the leader. But you're going to be there, old buddy. Right there. You're gonna prove yourself to me, man to man."

JESSIE PULLED HERSELF OUT of the battered Volkswagen and walked towards the house. She was tired. The press had broken down, and she had spent the entire day trying to figure out what was wrong with it. She pushed the door open and began the ritual of feeding the dog and the cats. They milled around her feet until Kelly chased Lystra and Sadie from the room, asserting her right to be fed first. Jessie set Kelly's bowl on the floor and then spooned cat food into a dish as the two cats sneaked cautiously past the dog.

The air was unexpectedly chilly, even for late September. Jessie went into the study, deciding she would build a small fire in the woodstove. Absently, her mind still on the problems with the press, she crumpled newspaper and placed it inside the stove, adding kindling and small logs. Then, lighting the paper, she closed the door to the stove and sat down in the armchair to wait for the warmth. She was hungry but was too tired to think about cooking. Maybe she would make a sandwich later.

She had started into the kitchen when she heard a car pull up the long driveway. Checking to make sure the rifle was handy, she pulled back the corner of the curtain and peered out. It was Kate, walking towards the house in much the same way someone might walk to their own execution—her steps slow and heavy, head down, hands shoved into the pockets of her peacoat. Jessie took a deep breath and went to open the door, aware that all of her defenses had risen.

Kate came into the house, her smile tentative and cautious. Jessie motioned her into the study, then went back into the kitchen. When she joined Kate by the stove, she held two large mugs of tea in her hands. She gave one to Kate who accepted it silently. They drank without speaking. Jessie was determined to wait Kate out on this one.

Kate stood close to the woodstove, absorbing the heat, wondering what to say first. "I didn't come here to apologize," she blurted out finally.

Jessie looked at her squarely. "I would hope not."

"Can we talk?" Kate asked after another long silence.

"If we could manage to do that it might be helpful," Jessie answered, her voice soft but tight.

Kate sighed audibly. It was not going to be an easy conversation; she could already see that. She unbuttoned her jacket but did not take it off. "Jessie, I meant what I said to you."

"So did I."

"I know. But I also want you to know that I am very frightened. Not just for you but for everyone involved in this."

"People have to make their own choices. Kate. I'm not forcing anyone to do anything. And we do discuss risks. No one is doing this without being aware that there are some very real potential dangers involved."

I'm glad to hear you're doing that." Kate sat down on the sofa, tucking her legs under her for warmth. "Jess, I care about you very much. I don't want to see you get hurt."

"We've been over this and over this. I take that risk by simply getting out of bed every morning."

Kate tried to head off the anger she heard in Jessie's voice. "I know. We all do. What I came here to say is that I know you're doing what you feel you have to do. I won't do anything else to try to make you change your mind. But I will raise objections, loudly, if I feel you're overlooking something. I won't maintain silence."

"All right." Jessie watched her carefully as she stroked the cat who had jumped into her lap.

"I will go right on doing what I've been doing which is working on the shelter. That's all I want to do. It's where I feel the most personal urgency. I don't want to fight the Ku Klux Klan right now. And I don't want to take to the streets."

"That's your choice, Kate. I'm not going to judge you for that."

"It felt like you were the other night."

Jessie was silent for a moment. "I didn't mean to do that, and I'm sorry if I sounded that way. I care about you, too, but you are only one part of my life. There are other things I need to do, and I won't if I'm always worrying about our relationship, worrying about what you think of my decisions. We don't have to agree. You have a right to your thoughts and feelings even when you totally disagree with me. I will try to listen to what you think and feel, but I won't always take your advice, or even welcome it. And I won't change for you. You need to know that now. I also won't defend myself to you. I would like to think you're basically on my side whether or not we agree, that you're my friend in spite of the differences."

"But if we're lovers . . ." Kate began.

"I want us to also be friends," Jessie said quietly. "Aren't we?"

"I hope so. It's what I want."

"And lovers, too?"

"Both. Greedy woman, aren't I?"

"Yes. But so am I."

"Good. I was hoping you were."

Kate stared into her cup then looked up. "Much as I hate to admit it, the newsletter is really well done."

"Thanks. Everyone is working very hard on it."

Silence lingered in the room as Jessie and Kate studied the floor. Jessie didn't know what to say. She wasn't used to fighting and did not know exactly what one did when it was time to become friends again.

"I shouldn't have grabbed you like I did the other night."

It was an evening of confessions. Jessie looked at Kate. "No, you shouldn't have. And I shouldn't have reacted the way I did either. I don't want it to happen again. We were both scared and angry. It's too easy to take it out on each other."

"I'm sorry."

Jessie smiled quietly. "Don't be sorry. I learned something about myself the other night. I have a lot of anger, and there's violence right along with it. That's unnerving because I've always thought of myself as a nonviolent person. But that's not true. It's there. Since the demonstration, I've found myself drifting into some very violent fantasies. When you and I were fighting and you grabbed me, I was very close to hitting you. Too close."

"I'm still a little scared. I don't know where all of this will take us or how we will be able to be together. I've never had a relationship like this one."

"Neither have I. But it could be exciting."

Kate crossed the room and sat down on the arm of the chair. Jessie reached up and touched her face gently. "Actually, Kate, I think we're doing pretty well."

Kate's voice was light. "Does that mean we go on seeing each other?"

"I guess so. What do you think?"

"I think I'd like that."

Jessie raised an eyebrow, imitating one of Kate's mannerisms. "You *think*? Would you like to stay here tonight and make sure?"

"Are you going to help me make up my mind?"

"I am certainly going to do my best to be helpful."

Kate laughed softly and slid onto Jessie's lap. "Maybe we can just sit like this for a little while."

Jessie wrapped her arms around Kate and breathed in the scent of her. "For a while."

7

BETH HURRIED from the bathroom to the bedroom clutch-ing her robe around her, her hair wrapped in a towel wound turban-style on her head. She could hear the two boys in their rooms in bed according to Hank's orders, but making just enough noise to communicate their dissatisfaction over the decision. It was Friday night and usually they would be allowed to stay up until nine-thirty. But it was only a little after eight, and they had been in bed for almost half an hour.

Beth toweled her hair briskly, staring at her reflection in the mirror. There were dark circles under her eyes, probably from lack of sleep. Hank had been in a horrible mood ever since that meeting on Monday, yelling at every little thing, slapping the children, not eating well, grinding his teeth in his sleep. This last created a sound that grated so heavily on Beth's nerves that she was unable to sleep through the noise. But she didn't dare get up, knowing how angry Hank would be if she got out of bed for anything other than to check on the children or make a quick trip to the bathroom. So she had not slept except for a few hours all week. Then tonight, Hank had abruptly ordered her to put the kids to bed and to make herself scarce. Tom and Edgar were coming over, and the three of them had business to discuss. Beth didn't mind being excluded. She didn't like Edgar. He was always dirty, smelled of beer, and had a whining voice which drove Beth crazy. But she especially did not like Tom. In fact, she was desperately afraid of Tom. He was always very nice to her, but there was something about him—Beth didn't know exactly what it was—that made her think he was ... evil. That was the only word she thought fit him. Mean all the way through, and evil. She stayed as far from him as she could.

HANK CHUGGED HIS BEER and chain-smoked as he sat at the kitchen table and waited. Tom and Edgar would be there soon. But it would be just like Tom to be late deliberately just to irritate Hank. The man had no respect for anything or anyone. And he was dangerous; Hank knew that. He hated the man. Hank grinned. One of these days, Tom Riley would step out of line somewhere, and Hank would have the pleasure of blowing the sonofabitch clear to kingdom come. One of these days.

Hank had heard Tom's stories of what he did in Viet Nam. The boy was proud of himself. Hank scratched his chin thoughtfully. He had not gone to Nam, even though he had volunteered. Damn the Army anyway. Tom liked to rub Hank's face in the fact that the Army wouldn't let him go, that Hank had had a cushy supply job in the states while the real men were out killing Congs. Tom claimed to have kept count of how many men he had killed, most of whom he claimed to have shot up close. Hank didn't totally believe him. On the other hand, Tom seemed to be exactly the kind of man to do the things he claimed to have done, to men and to women.

Hank glanced at the clock. They were twenty minutes late. He lit another cigarette. Tom had put him in a very bad position. Much as he wanted to be an active member of the organization, his job meant too much to him. He had a rep around town—a very tough, mean cop, the kind folks didn't argue with. Punks stayed out of his way, and judges usually ruled in his favor when cases came to trial. Mostly, Hank liked the power the uniform gave· him. He liked the fact that almost everyone got a little bit nervous when they saw him. And he loved the feel of the equipment against his hips—the gun, the cuffs, the nightstick. He had a chance at another promotion in the spring, if nothing went wrong. He was going to make damned sure nothing went wrong in spite of that bastard Riley. He would break him, too, one of these days. Tom was a mean, temperamental shit, but Hank knew he was meaner. Nobody crossed him and got away with it. Not people on the streets, not men on the force, not even his own wife.

His thoughts shifted briefly to Beth. He was going to have to get tougher with her. He had been so busy lately, he hadn't had much time to think about her. Things were getting slack around here. He had had to wait almost twenty minutes for dinner tonight. But then, she was a woman, and you had to stay on top of women. These liberal, pantywaist men might not think so, but Hank knew better. He knew women were sneaky, conniving little bitches, and he just wasn't willing to put up with much from them. You had to watch them every second. He had broken Beth in right, from the beginning. She had never doubted he was the boss.

Opening another beer, Hank wondered what it would be like to be a bachelor, to have no ties or responsibilities. He sighed. If Beth hadn't gone and gotten herself knocked up when they were dating, he wouldn't have all these worries. She had probably done it on purpose. All women wanted to be married, to have a chokehold on some poor guy, wrap him around their fingers, and try to control his life. Well, he might've had to marry her, but he sure hadn't let her bother him very much. That was never going to change either. She was his, and he was in control. She might've trapped him, but she would never own or control him. He'd see to that.

The doorbell rang and Hank rose. About time they arrived.

BETH HEARD THE DOORBELL and then heard the sound of voices. Hank was leading the men into the kitchen; she caught a glimpse of them as they crossed the hall. She pushed the door shut quickly, not wanting Tom to see her.

When she started to take off her bathrobe, Beth realized that the door had not latched. Crossing to it, she listened for sounds from the boys' rooms. They were both quiet. She started to push the door closed when words drifted down the hallway.

Beth frowned. They had been talking about some girl last time, too. She wondered what was going on. Suddenly Hank's voice was louder, and Beth quickly, silently, closed the door. Better mind her own business and stay out of trouble.

HANK GLANCED DOWN THE HALL to make sure Beth was not around. The door to the bedroom was closed. Stepping back into the kitchen, he lit a cigarette and studied the two men who sat at the table. "It's got to be done. There's no way she can be allowed to testify in court. Even if I rig the evidence, Baker doesn't want her to testify."

"You know the deal, Hank."

Hank knew the deal. When he had called Baker earlier to try to back out as carefully as he could, Baker had been very clear about what would happen if Hank failed. Hank nodded towards Tom. "I've been thinking about that. I've decided it probably would be better if I did go along. That way, I can keep an eye on things and make sure they go like they're supposed to."

"Yeah?"

"Yeah. I can make sure you don't fuck things up."

"You'd better watch your mouth, Parrish," came Tom's tight response.

"And you can go fuck yourself, Riley. You'll do exactly as I say." Hank leaned over the table as he spoke.

Tom sprang to his feet, fists clenched as he twisted to free himself from the chair. Edgar jumped up and slammed a restraining hand against Tom's chest.

"Ease off, Tom. You too, Hank."

"I don't want to ease off," Tom said through clenched teeth. "I want a piece of that mother."

"That'll be the day."

The two men glared at each other for a long, tense moment. Edgar maintained his position between them, knowing that if either of them struck the first blow, he was running for cover. Finally, Tom grinned tightly and sat down, his body taut. "I'll give you this one, Hank. We got work to do. But one of these days, I'll catch you, man. I'll catch you."

"Would you quit your bickering and let's get to it? I'm tired of sitting around talking. I want something to happen!" Edgar slapped an open palm on the table. Tom nodded in agreement, his gaze never leaving Hank's face.

'I agree. But first we have to figure out what we're going to do." Hank opened the refrigerator door and took out three beers which he handed around. Opening his, he sipped and waited for suggestions.

"You're supposed to be our fearless leader," Tom drawled. "I thought you would have it all figured out."

"Well, I don't. I do know that no matter how we come down on her, we have to be damned careful. This is going to take some planning." Hank resisted the urge to light yet another cigarette. He didn't want Tom to see his nervousness.

Hank kept his free hand in his pocket, his fingers curled tightly around his pocket knife. If anything should go wrong, anything, he could be in deep trouble. He'd be off the police force. No way he'd ever get a job as a cop anywhere.

"Baker wants us to scare the piss out of her," Hank said, his voice carefully controlled.

"So, how do we do that? All this shit over some girl is stupid. She ain't nobody worth worrying about. Let's just beat the hell out of her and be done with it," Tom said angrily.

"That's one option," Hank answered, "but don't you think we can find some other way to start? Save that for just in case she doesn't take a potent hint?" More than anything,

Hank wanted to avoid a face-to-face confrontation with Jessie Pyne. No matter how badly they frightened her, she still might go straight to the police. They had to be careful, dammit. Very careful.

"Personally, I don't want to spend a whole lot of time messing with this broad. Let's just do it right the first time and get it over with." Tom drummed his fingers on the table top.

Edgar spoke up. "Well, if Baker wants to keep a low profile, I think we should do something pretty hard and straight but keep our faces outta that girl's line of sight."

Hank's knees went weak with relief. "You got an idea?"

Edgar nodded thoughtfully. "I think we ought to find out where she lives and pay a visit while she's at work. You can get her address, Hank. And we can redecorate the place for her, leave a note. She should be able to understand what we're telling her from that."

"And if it doesn't work?" Tom asked. "Then we beat the hell out of her."

"I'll get the address tomorrow," Hank said.

Tom and Edgar nodded. Then Hank handed out another round of beer. This would work. And this would be the end of it.

LAURA POKED HER HEAD into the back room and shouted over the noise of the press. "Hey, Jessie! You have a phone call!"

"Do me a favor, Laura, and take a message?"

Laura shook her head. "It's Denny, and she sounds real upset. You'd better talk to her yourself."

Jessie muttered as she turned off the press. Work was still backed up from last week when the press had broken down for two days, and she didn't want to waste precious time on telephone calls. The small shop had suddenly been flooded with jobs, all rush. She crossed the room to the extension phone and jerked the receiver off the hook. "What is it, Denny? I'm really..."

"Jess, I'm at your house, and I think you need to come home right now." Denny's voice was tight.

"Denny, I'm backed up to my ears with work," Jessie said impatiently. "I won't be able to leave here before midnight. It'll have to wait."

"Somebody broke into your place, and they completely wrecked it. You need to come home!"

Jessie held the phone in stunned silence. Finally, she found her voice. "I'll come home."

"Good. Kate's here, too."

"Why . . ."

"We came to start painting the kitchen." Denny cut her off impatiently.

"I'll be there in half an hour," Jessie said, and then hung up slowly. Who would break into her house? Almost two years there and she had never had any trouble before. Laura came around the corner and peered at Jessie.

"What's going on?"

"Denny says somebody broke in and wrecked my house."

Laura stared at her. "Burglars?"

Jessie shook her head. "I don't know. I have to go home. Can you handle things here?"

"Go on. I'll be fine."

Jessie nodded her thanks and headed for the door.

SHE CLIMBED SLOWLY OUT OF THE CAR, uncertain as to what to expect. Denny was waiting for her in the yard, and Jessie could see Kate standing on the porch.

"Jess," Denny said hurriedly, "I didn't want to get into all of it over the phone, but there's something you need to know before you go in there."

Jessie looked at her, alerted by the nervousness in Denny's voice. "Is it that bad?"

Denny nodded. "It's really a mess. They've torn up furniture, scattered trash all over the place. They even wrote stuff on the walls. And . . ." Denny hesitated, not looking at Jessie.

"Go on," Jessie prompted, feeling a sudden surge of alarm. "It's Kelly, Jessie."

Jessie stared at her. "Oh, shit!" She ran towards the house ignoring Kate as she burst inside.

Nothing Denny had said prepared Jessie for the chaos in front of her. Nothing seemed to be standing, or even in one piece. Tables and chairs were smashed, dishes broken. Trash was everywhere, the smell sickening. She could see the overturned woodstove in the other room, the room she had so recently changed into a "study," a place in which to write. Now ashes were scattered all over the floor. Then Jessie looked up. Written across the faded blue walls in large, red spray-painted letters were the words *nigger lover*, *queer*. Jessie could only stare. She felt nothing.

Finally, she started into the study, but Denny pulled her back. "Don't go in there."

"What happened to Kelly? Did they hurt her?" Jessie's voice was hushed. Denny nodded. Jessie brushed past her and walked into the other room. It was as bad as the rest of the house. The sofa and chair had been slashed and cotton stuffing was strewn around the room. Her desk had been overturned, and her papers had been scattered and trampled on. Jessie glanced at Denny as she gestured towards the closed bedroom door.

"Did they wreck that room, too? Or is Kelly in there?" Denny didn't answer. Jessie opened the door and stepped in.

For some reason, they had not touched this room. Everything was exactly as Jessie had left it, the bed neatly made, clothes in their proper places, a book still open on the bedside table, the lamp upright.

Kelly lay in the middle of the floor. Jessie knelt down beside her. No blood, she thought to herself as she touched the cold stiff body. The dog's eyes were open and fixed. Jessie wished she could read the final expression. She rocked back and forth on her knees, not understanding. Pain was beginning to replace the numbness and she fought it; there was too much to do to give into it now. Too much to do. Denny touched her on the shoulder.

"What happened, Denny? What did they do to her?"

There was a long pause before Denny answered her voice a pinched whisper. "They hung her."

Jessie turned to stare at her, a stunned expression of disbelief in her eyes. "They hung her? Hung her? Where?"

"From the tree by the porch."

"Oh, for . . . hung her. Goddamn, Denny, who would do that?" Jessie's voice cracked. She grabbed a shoe and threw it as hard as she could. It hit the wall with a loud thump and crashed to the floor. She leaned back on her heels and stared at the dead setter.

"I'll bury her for you, Jessie."

Jessie stood up abruptly. "I need to do it. Just go home, Denny, and take Kate with you. I need to be alone for a while."

Denny shook her head. "We'll stay out of your way, but we're not leaving. We can start cleaning up. Call if you need us." Denny touched her sleeve and then left the room. Jessie didn't move.

SHE PUT THE SHOVEL in the shed and stood at the edge of the pasture smoking a cigarette, watching the sunset. Digging had been hard. Kelly was a large dog. Had been. Had been a large dog. She wiped the sweat from her face and shivered as the chilly night air penetrated her damp clothes. Her hands shook and her stomach was in knots. She felt as though she might throw up. Where were the cats? Were they all right?

Jessie threw the cigarette on the ground and crushed it under her heel. She walked to the other side of the house, not wanting to go in to the mess and the people. Jessie paced around the huge, sweet gum tree studying the branches, trying to find a sign of what had happened to Kelly, of why. The circle tightened as she walked, faster and faster, her hands clenched into tight fists deep in her pockets. There was no sign, not a broken branch, not . . . An indentation in the ground caught her eye. Jessie knelt and studied the footprint. Anger was immediate, surging. Jessie stood up, hands dangling at her sides, stifling the urge to scream the rage. As she started towards the house, she tripped over a log. Dogwood. The thought registered unsummoned. Dogwood. A killer to split. A killer . . . to split. She placed the log against the old stump she used as a block and picked up the heavy maul. She tapped a wedge into place then stepped back and brought the maul down with a loud crash of metal on metal. The log cracked. She worked in another wedge, rolling the log onto its side. Three strokes and the log split. She tossed it aside and reached for another. Over and over again she brought the maul down, faster, as she swung her grief into each blow. Down. Metal against metal. Sparks flew when her aim was off. Down, metal retorts like shots in the dark.

"I could," she muttered, "I could. I could kill them. I . . . could . . . kill . . . them." Her voice grew louder as she chanted.

She worked for almost an hour, until the muscles in her shoulders and arms felt torn from place, until she was hoarse from the words she had forced from her throat. Blisters rose on her hands. The pile of split wood grew. Jessie didn't notice the darkness, the blisters, the tears, the fierce ache in her body. She swung the maul, driving her anger into the wood, harder and harder, hearing only the shell-like retorts. She didn't feel the skin shredding on her hands. She didn't hear Denny's car leave or Kate coming onto the porch.

She turned to grab another log, but there were none left. She dropped the maul on the ground and stared at the woodpile. Kate came down the steps, took Jessie's arm, and led her inside without saying a word.

There was a fire in the woodstove. Denny and Kate had managed to get it upright and had replaced the vent pipe. Pillows from Jessie's bed were on the floor in front of the stove. Kate motioned for Jessie to sit down so she could hand her a cup of coffee. Jessie dropped onto a pillow and accepted the hot cup, then almost dropped it. She turned her hands over. They were raw and bleeding. Kate's face tightened, but she said nothing. She left the room and returned with a pan. Setting it on the floor, she rolled back Jessie's sleeves and immersed her hands in the water.

"Denny and I got most of the mess up. Some things can be fixed. Most of the dishes will have to be replaced. The cats came home a little while ago. They seem fine. I fed them." Kate's tone was quiet and conversational. She sat close to Jessie but did not touch her.

"Who would do this, Kate? Who would tear my house up and . . . kill my dog?"

Kate hesitated for a moment then reached into her pocket, bringing out a slip of paper. "This was hanging on the door when Denny and I arrived here this afternoon." She held it out so Jessie could read the words. "You didn't see anybody. You can't identify anybody. But we know who you are, and we can come back again. Tell the D.A. you have nothing to say in court."

"Oh, god." Jessie's tone was even and low. "I guess that answers my question."

"Yeah."

Kate carefully dried and bandaged Jessie's hands. Then she slipped her arm around her lover's shoulders and pulled her close.

Kate pushed her own terror down. If they would do this, wreck a house and hang a dog, what would they do to Jessie?

Jessie's voice was shaking. "They're trying to scare me off. They're trying to get me to say I lied, trying to scare me into not testifying in January. Kate . . . they killed my dog. They hung her."

"I know, Jess. I know, baby." Kate lit a cigarette and tried to steady her hands. She had to be calm right now. "Are you going to stay here?"

"What?" Jessie seemed confused.

"Jessie, have you thought what might have happened if you had been home when those men came?"

"No."

"I'm not asking you to make any kind of decision right now. I know you can't. But please, honey, think about that. Those men obviously thought they had nothing to fear. They came in broad daylight. It could have been you instead of Kelly. I really believe that."

Jessie picked up her cup awkwardly and sipped the cooling coffee. "I love this old place. I don't want to give it up."

"I know," Kate whispered, "but I'm so afraid for you. I'm so scared they'll do something to you. I know how horrible men can be. Please don't stay here. Come to my house tonight and just think about it. Please, Jessie."

Kate's hands were shaking visibly. She was scared to leave Jessie alone, and terrified at the thought of staying there with her. What if they came back? She watched Jessie's pale face silently, willing herself to be quiet, forcing herself not to bodily carry Jessie out to the car and drive her away, drive them both away from the danger Kate felt throughout the house. She could feel Jessie's anger, pain, confusion, not spoken out loud but filling the room, surrounding them both.

Kate felt a wild urge to run, to leave and not come back. She couldn't take this. She couldn't just stand by and watch Jessie get hurt. And she couldn't put herself into the position to get hurt either. She had been hurt enough, too much. She knew about men. She knew what they could do. They had shown her over and over. And there was nothing she could do to protect Jessie. Nothing.

Jessie was numb. All she wanted was to sleep. She looked at Kate quietly. "I'll get some clothes, and we can go to your house."

Kate sighed with relief as Jessie rose and went into the bedroom. Once she got her into town, once Jessie got some sleep, then maybe she would understand. Jessie had to leave this house. She had to.

"YOU'VE GOT TO MOVE INTO TOWN, Jessie. It's very dangerous for you to be way out there alone. It's too damned far from everybody and everything."

"I don't want to be forced out of my home, Val."

"You've got to protect yourself."

"It's like admitting defeat."

"It's like being alive!"

Val, Laura, Denny, Kate, and Jessie were all crowded into the small back room of the print shop. Jessie was exhausted. She had not slept much the night before, and the bandages on her hands made it nearly impossible for her to work. She was tired and irritable, sick of this line of argument, having heard it already from Kate.

"So I run away. The next thing they'll be trying to tell me is that I can't do the newsletter anymore. And what about the trial?"

"Ignoring what happened is just plain stupid." It was Val again. Jessie glanced at Laura who leaned against the wall, arms folded over her chest, a silent, watchful expression on her face.

Finally she straightened, stretched, and spoke for the first time. "You remember that story I told you about my grandparents, Jessie?" Jessie nodded. "Well, it was every bit true." Laura turned and left the room, quietly closing the door to the shop behind her.

"Next time," Denny said, "they might wreck more than just your house, Jessie."

Jessie jumped to her feet. "And just where would I go? They can find me if they want to, no matter where I am."

Val's answer was quick. "You can live with Denny and me. God knows, we've got enough room in that old house. The idea is to discourage them. Knowing you're not alone in some house way out in the country just might do that."

Jessie turned her back and picked up her knapsack. "I have to think about it."

Val kicked at a case of paper. "I hope you live long enough to make up your mind. Are you going back out there tonight?"

"Yes!" Jessie shouted, tears filling her eyes. "Now if you will be so kind as to get out of here, I'll lock up and go home!"

The women left silently, not looking at Jessie. She locked the door tiredly. Maybe they were right. She tried to brush the tears away, but it was futile. She felt a surge of pain and moaned quietly. She couldn't stop thinking about Kelly, hanging from that tree. She was glad she hadn't found her there. Jessie looked at the lights and the buildings and felt the surroundings close in on her. She hated the city. Hated it. The need to break down and cry nearly choked her as she climbed into the car and drove away.

JESSIE ROLLED OVER and looked at the clock with a sleepswelled eye. Four-thirty in the morning. She stretched, pulling the covers up under her chin. She could have sworn she heard voices. Maybe she had been dreaming.

The crash of glass breaking brought her straight to her feet. She jerked on jeans and a shirt and went carefully into the front room, staying away from the windows and trying to avoid the broken glass she knew must be all over the floor.

A brick lay in the middle of the room. She heard the sound of a car engine starting up and then the car drove away. She stood in front of the broken window, her gaze fixed on a burning cross in the front yard.

VAL, DENNY, AND KATE arrived in less than twenty minutes. They piled out of the car and stood in the yard. They could see Jessie standing by the porch, her face lighted eerily by the flames that were slowly burning down.

Finally, Jessie crossed the yard to join them, wrapping her arms around Kate and burying her face in Kate's shoulder. Kate held her, feeling rigid muscles, feeling her tremble.

"I can't even put it out," she muttered. "There's no hose to use to put it out."

No one answered her. The women stayed close together, watching the flames die out.

All of them jumped when Ben Carpenter's voice sounded from the corner of the yard. "I wanta talk to you, Jessie."

"What do you want, Ben?" she asked tiredly.

Carpenter grew closer, glancing from the cross to Jessie to the women holding onto her. A frown creased his face. "I cain't have this, I cain't."

"What do you mean?"

"I got to have you gone. Today. I want you to pack up and move outta here. Cain't be having the Klan burnin' crosses on my property. You be gone from here, I mean it. You hear me now?"

There was no friendliness in Carpenter's voice. He peered at her nearsightedly.

"Ben, look . . ."

"Don't argue with me, girl! I been thinkin' there was something' strange about you for a long time. I let you stay because my wife liked you. But I cain't have this. I ain't gonna tell you but just this once. You ain't outta here by this evenin', I'll get the sheriff to throw you out. You understand me?"

"A day isn't enough time to . . ."

"By evenin'. That's my final word. Get your friends here to help you." He gestured towards the group.

The blue light caught Jessie's attention as the sheriff's car pulled into the driveway followed by the highway patrol.

"What the hell are the cops doing here?" Jessie asked angrily.

"I called 'em, that's why. I gotta protect my property." Ben's voice was hostile as he walked across the yard to meet the men getting out of their cars. The women looked at each other.

"I guess we'd better get busy," Kate said briskly. "We can start packing and get a truck later today."

"Guess we'd better," Val agreed.

Jessie stood for a moment longer watching the flames dying on the cross and listening to the laughter from the men at the corner of the yard. Then she slowly followed the others inside.

JESSIE SAT ON THE SOFA and read the brief article in the county newspaper. She tossed it aside in disgust. The paper said that the Klan denied all knowledge of the incident, and that the police were convinced it was a prank played by locals. They had written it off as a hostile joke. Even the District Attorney's office had told her not to worry, that she had to expect some hostility. Jessie grabbed her jacket and headed for the door. She was going to be late for work.

JESSIE TOOK THE MAIL from the box and looked through it. A small envelope addressed to her, the handwriting unfamiliar, caught her attention. Opening the door, she dropped the rest of the mail on the table and opened the letter. As she read, she sat down abruptly.

Nigger-lover. Queer. We don't need your kind around here. There won't be any more warnings. To you or your friends.

8

"SO WHAT IF SHE MOVED into town? What does that prove? She hasn't contacted the District Attorney's office. The trial is still going to happen. So let's just stop bullshitting around and really let her know we mean business."

Beth stood just inside the bedroom door and listened to Tom's voice as it drifted down the silent hall. It was beginning to make some sense to her. They were doing something bad to somebody, a woman called Jessie. She crossed her arms over her chest and hugged herself tightly. Hank was going to hurt somebody: he was going to hurt this woman.

Hank glared at Tom. "I suppose you still want to beat the hell out of her, don't you?"

"Damn right. Nothing else is going to work. Sometimes, you have to make your point in person, face to face."

Edgar looked at Tom thoughtfully. "Risky. She could identify us if she sees us."

"She won't be talking to anybody when we get through with her," Tom answered with a slow smile.

"I guess you'd be happy just to kill her?" Hank's voice dripped sarcasm.

"I wouldn't mind. But we don't have to kill her. We can put some righteous fear into her, so much she won't open her mouth to a soul. She'll agree to anything just to make us leave her alone. I guarantee it." Tom's last sentence was spoken so softly Hank almost could not hear it. For the first time, he felt a slight jolt of fear when he looked at Tom. The man is crazy, he thought to himself.

"I'd like to get my hands on her for just a few minutes," Edgar said, a tight grin on his face. "I know exactly what she needs."

"I'll bet you would show her a thing or two," Tom said, also grinning. His face was flushed from the beer, from anticipation.

"Damn queer cunt," Edgar muttered. "I know what she needs."

"I still don't like it," Hank persisted. "If we go after her, people are going to know exactly where to start looking—it's too risky. I'd say yes if she weren't a witness and if the D.A.s office didn't already have a handle on her."

"You know what I think, Hank?" Tom's voice was taunting. "I think you're scared of this broad."

"Shut up, Tom."

"I didn't hear him deny it. Did you, Edgar?"

Edgar studied Hank for a moment. "Nope. That true, Hank? You scared of this girl?"

"You're fucking bananas, both of you. Why should I be scared of some little homo like this?"

Tom leaned forward, resting his elbows on the table. "Then prove it, man."

Beth closed her eyes and leaned her head back against the wall. Oh lord, she thought to herself, let him say no. Just let him say no.

Hank rose and took a beer from the refrigerator. He opened it and drank half in one long gulp.

"You two are crazy," he said, wiping his mouth with the back of his hand.

"And you," Tom said softly, "are a chickenshit."

He ducked as the beer can sailed by his head, missing him by mere inches. Edgar jumped up, putting himself between the two men.

"Now just hold it! We ain't gonna get anywhere with you two fighting like a couple of bitching old women. Hank, what we tried didn't work. Now unless you got a better plan, I say we go with Tom's idea. I don't want to keep messing around with this girl forever."

"I don't have anything better."

Tom laughed. "Now you're talking! We'll scare the pure bejesus out of her." He winked at Hank. "Ever had a genuine lesbian before, Hank, my man?"

Hank shook his head. "No."

"Well, this will be the first. Don't expect a whole lot. After all, a cunt's a cunt. C'mon Edgar, let's get out of here so Hank can get back to his little woman." Tom stopped in front of Hank. "Edgar and I will check it out, and we'll be back in touch in a couple of days. Don't go getting cold feet on me now." He laughed and left the room, Edgar close behind him.

Beth bit her lip as she slumped against the wall. She strained to hear what was said next, but there were no other sounds from the kitchen. She leaned closer to the door. Suddenly, Hank was there filling the doorway, his face livid with rage when he saw her. He grabbed her by the arm and jerked her up against him.

"What the hell are you doing?" he roared into her face. "You were spying on me! Just what did you hear?"

Beth hung in his grip, trying not to cry out. "Hank . . . the kids."

"The hell with the kids!" He threw her onto the bed and stood over her, his face drawn into an ugly mask of hatred, his fists clenched at his sides. "What did you hear?"

"Nothing . . . I didn't hear anything, Hank. Honestly."

"You're lying! You heard it all, didn't you? You fucking bitch! How many times do I have to tell you to keep your nose out of my business?" He drew back his hand and slapped her across the face, knocking her back on the bed.

"I'll teach you to go listening at doors!" He glanced wildly around the room, then seized a belt from the chair. He wrapped the leather around his fist. Beth covered her face with her arms as she saw the wide, flat buckle flash through the air and towards her.

THE GREY LIGHT IN THE ROOM let her know it was dawn. Hank had not moved all night, sleeping on his side, his back to her, one arm thrown over his head. As she turned over, Beth had to bite her lip to keep from crying out. Her body screamed protest with every movement. Last night had been the worst yet. He had hit her before but never like that. She finally got into a sitting position and thought she might faint. Through her thin nightgown, she could see the livid bruises and smears of blood where the belt buckle had struck her. Slowly, she pulled herself to her feet. Beth made it into the bathroom and swallowed some aspirin. She gagged repeatedly as she tried to force them down, and she ended up hanging over the toilet bowl retching until she felt her insides would shred. Then she slowly slid to the floor and burst into tears, her hand clamped over her mouth, her other arm wrapped around her shrieking body.

JESSIE DRIED HER HANDS and tossed the grimy rag into the cannister. She was finally caught up. She didn't know if it was good or bad, but she felt a huge sense of relief. It meant she could have the whole weekend to herself. Maybe she and Kate could go to a movie. Or a picnic on the Eno River. The weather was supposed to be nice. She wiped a smear of ink from the side of the press. This would be her first full weekend off in nearly two months.

Laura came into the back room and sat down on the stool. "Are we really caught up?"

Jessie nodded. "Amazing as that seems. What are you going to do with your weekend?"

"Sleep." Laura's answer was quick and definite.

"Doesn't sound half bad," Jessie answered with a grin.

"I thought I might write up that story about my grandparents for the newsletter. What do you think?"

"I think it sounds like a great idea."

"Well, I'll see what comes out on paper. Have a good weekend, Jessie. I'll see you Monday morning."

VAL PULLED THE CORD to signal her stop. She had almost an hour to kill before she met Jessie for dinner and their weekly newsletter meeting. She sighed softly, thinking how much better she felt since Jessie had moved into her house. So far, there had been no more trouble. Maybe that was the end of it. Standing up, she made her way down the aisle of the bus.

THE THREE MEN WAITED at the back corner of the small parking lot. They had been there since six and had seen Laura leave. Tom leaned casually against the streetlight pole, smoking a cigarette. Edgar paced in small, endless circles.

"Calm down, Edgar. You're as nervous as a cat."

"I ain't nervous! I'm just tired of waiting." Edgar's voice was snappish. Tom smiled at him.

"You won't have to wait much longer. She should be coming out to empty the trash any minute now. She and that nigger broad are as regular as clockwork."

Hank shoved his hands into his pockets. The temperature was dropping rapidly as the sun set. He didn't want to be there. What if she remembered their faces? He would rather these two idiots handled this, leave him out of it. At least he had thought to bring sunglasses. That was better than nothing.

Tom seemed to read his thoughts. "Want to back out, Hank?

Just say the word."

"Go to hell," Hank muttered.

"There she is!" Edgar's voice was a harsh whisper. Tom dropped his cigarette on the ground.

"Let's do it."

Jessie strained to lift the heavy can over the edge of the dumpster. She should have gotten Laura to help before Laura had dashed out for her much-awaited dinner with Moon. The last time Jessie had attempted to empty the trash barrel alone the entire can had gone over the edge, and she had had to climb inside the dumpster to retrieve it. Getting in had been relatively easy; getting out had been a little more difficult.

She set the empty can on the ground and bent down to pick up the loose paper that had scattered on the sparse grass. Stretching muscles stiff from standing all day, she watched the thin cirrus clouds whip across the sky. Val would be there soon. Jessie stifled a yawn; she would just as soon go home to bed. It had already been an exhausting day. She also needed to go to the grocery store. She was out of cat food, and she didn't dare appear at home empty-handed.

"I want to have a word with you, girl." His voice was soft. Jessie jumped back instinctively and slammed into yet another man who grabbed her arm. She jerked free from his grasp but there was nowhere to go. The dumpster was directly behind her.

"What do you want?" Her voice was strained to a whisper. "Just to have a little talk with you. For now. So you just keep your mouth shut and listen, and maybe that's all we'll want." Jessie heard the threat clearly. She watched their faces, searching her memory for some clue, some recognition of them. Nothing came.

"It must be real lonely for you with your dog dead," Tom said softly, smiling at her. We know how much you loved that old dog of yours."

Jessie stared at him. The fear that surged through her was immediate, bitter. Her stomach knotted, and for a moment she was afraid she might vomit.

"Now, we tried to make a point when we visited your house. We thought you would understand what we were trying to tell you. But you're awful stubborn. You know that? Moving into town didn't solve a thing, girl. This ain't no game we're playing here." Tom's voice became harsh. "This is the real thing, Jessie Pyne. And you'd better back down right now or your friends will be finding pieces of you a week from next Christmas."

"Or maybe you'll be finding pieces of them," Edgar added with a low giggle.

Jessie would have been less afraid if Tom had shown some outward sign of anger. But his face held an oddly blank expression that chilled her. Edgar stepped forward suddenly and grabbed the front of her shirt. Several buttons popped loose, and Jessie was acutely aware that her breasts were visible.

"Ain't you got nothing to say? You been talking big up 'til now. I seen those interviews with you in the newspaper, and I even seen you on TV. You speak when you're spoken to, girl!" Edgar shook her.

"I heard you." Jessie spoke through clenched teeth.

"Good. I heard once that there ain't no cure for stupidity, and I'm hoping that's wrong. Now it's simple, so you listen up. One, you shut up tight as a clam. Two, you stop putting out that fucking newsletter of yours. It's a pack of lies. Three, you tell the D.A. that you made a mistake, that it was dark, and that you really can't identify nobody. You didn't see nobody kick no nigger woman. You hear me?" Edgar was staring at her breasts.

Jessie said nothing, too afraid to speak, too proud to give in.

Tom glanced skyward and sighed. "Maybe that saying was right after all, man. Look, we're trying to give you a second chance here. There won't be a third."

Edgar ran his hand down her chest. There were no choices left. Jessie kicked out as hard as she could, catching Edgar squarely on the shin.

"Goddam!" he yelled. He released her abruptly and clutched his leg. "Goddam, you bitch!"

Jessie feinted to the left, seeing one slim chance to make it past them to the door of the shop.

But Tom had seen it, too. Suddenly he was in front of her, blocking her way. His arms hung loosely at this sides. Jessie knew the danger in the way he held his body, in the calm stare, the beginnings of a smile on his lips. She lowered her head and catapulted her body forward, anger mixing with the intense fear. She *had* to get to that door.

She didn't see the fist coming. She felt it instead, body and unyielding against the side of her face. The blow slammed her back and shoulders into the dumpster. Her head cracked against the cold metal. There was blood in her mouth, a ringing in her ears. Her face felt numb; there was no pain in her jaw, only blinding jolts in the back of her head. Tom jerked her to him, his breath warm on her cheek.

"You're not talking so big now, are you? Go on. Fight back. I like that."

All clarity vanished as he hit her again. Dazed, Jessie tried to kick him, to break his grip with her hands.

Tom laughed. "You can fight harder than that. Better yet, why don't you ask me to stop? C'mon, beg me to stop. Say it real nice."

Jessie clamped her mouth shut. She would not say a word.

He beat her methodically, forehand, backhand, holding her upright by the front of her shirt. Vaguely, Jessie was aware of her shirt tearing, of the laughter of one of the other men. She hung in Tom's grip, feeling the pain as it raced through her, sharp, shooting pain that increased with each blow and brought sickening nausea rolling to the back of her throat. Blackness swam through her head, and she yearned for it, grasped for it with all the strength she had left. Tom shoved her back against the dumpster and aimed his blows at her body, using his fists on her breasts, ribs, and belly. He would not let her faint.

"What the hell are you doing, Tom . . ."

The blows stopped abruptly, and Jessie slid to the ground, her back still against the dumpster, her legs unable to support any of her weight.

"I don't want you to kill her," Edgar said as he pushed Tom away. "I want a crack at her."

"We'll all get a crack at her, old buddy. Don't you worry about that."

"Now's the time then. Why don't you go first, Tom? After all, you been doing all the work. What about you, Hank? You gonna get in on the fun?"

Jessie heard the voices dimly but the words made no real sense to her. Names. She heard names.

There was laughter, then hands grabbed her and pulled her onto her knees. Someone locked rough fingers into her hair and pulled her head up. She felt cloth brush her face and heard the sound of a zipper sliding down its short track. She tried to raise her arms to ward off what she suddenly knew was about to happen, but she couldn't move. Keeping her eyes closed, she fixed her spinning thoughts on some blank space she found in her mind. Hold on. Hold on. Choking her, Tom came with the same violence that was in his fist when he hit her. She tried to spit when he withdrew, but she was too weak for even that.

She tried to concentrate on the cold, damp grass against her buttocks as they pushed her down onto the ground and pulled her jeans to her ankles. Pain shifted, changed, lessened, increased, as one man finished and another took his place. She didn't know how long it lasted or how many times. At one point, she was aware of the heavy pressure of a body on top of her but felt nothing between her legs. Her wonder was brief; she could find no answers. She felt them shift in turn. Time seemed to stop, isolating each thrust into an eternity of fear and agony.

Then a voice spoke close to her ear. "You just got a second chance. You remember what we told you."

Jessie could hear them laughing, talking, as they walked away. She lay on the wet grass, her pants still around her ankles, shivering from the cold. She managed to roll onto her side, and she threw up weakly, coughing and choking, her hands groping uselessly for her jeans. Val. Val was coming . . . she would help. Jessie tried to pull up her pants. She didn't want Val to see her like this.

She had heard names. Numbly, she tried to fix them in her mind. Tom . . . Tom and Edgar. Tom and Edgar and. . . .

VAL PUSHED OPEN THE DOOR to the shop and stepped inside. It was really getting cold outside. Maybe an early winter. She stuck her head through the doorway to the back room and called out, "Jessie? Jess, you back here?"

There was no answer. That was odd. They had a definite date for dinner. Jessie would never just not show up. Then Val noticed the back door ajar. Jessie was probably at the dumpster. Val wandered around the room. She didn't know the first thing about presses, and she was intimidated by them. She walked around the machine, peering at it carefully, trying to figure out exactly how it worked.

She glanced at her watch. Jessie was certainly taking her time out there. She walked to the door and stepped outside. "Jessie?"

She wasn't sure it was Jessie at first. Then she looked more closely and gasped. Kneeling beside her friend, Val put her hand on Jessie's shoulder. There was blood all over Jessie's face, and she was not moving. Val touched her chest and felt an immediate surge of relief when the slow motion assured her that Jessie was alive. She jerked off her coat and covered Jessie with it, then ran inside to the telephone.

9

KATE DID NOT RUSH into the hospital. She closed the door
to her car and walked slowly across the parking lot, starting
whenever a light cast her shadow on the ground near her.

Val had not given her any details over the telephone, saying only that Jessie was hurt very badly, and she thought Kate
should come to the hospital right away. Val had hung up before Kate could ask any questions. Kate forced her mind to
blankness as she walked towards the brightly lit emergency
entrance; she could not give in to her imagination.

Kate stopped short of the doors. Puffs of hazy smoke rose
in front of her face as her breath quickened, condensed, and
whitened in the cool night air. She hesitated so long that the
security guard approached to ask if anything was wrong. She
shook her head and pushed through the door.

It took all of Kate's will power to keep her from turning
around and running from the building. Sheer terror filled her
as she watched the activity around her—patients being trans-
ported on gurneys, portable X-ray machines being wheeled
down the corridor, carts loaded with mysteriously covered
trays pushed by her. There was little curiosity, only tiredness,

in the eyes that met hers as she walked down the hall, willing herself to move forward.

The smell always made her feel sick. Disease, blood, and antiseptic—a revolting combination, even if some of the smells were manufactured by Kate's imagination. But they brought back memories of being a child. No matter how much she steeled herself not to think, it came back.

Seven years old, lying on a stretcher in a cubicle, green curtains drawn around her, screaming from the pain in her broken shoulder and ribs. Her mother squeezing her arm, desperately explaining to the suspicious doctors and nurses that Kate had fallen from a tree. Kate's terror when her father had walked in, his eyes bloodshot from drinking, his hand almost crushing her thigh as he leaned close and told her what would happen if she said a word to anyone. Her mother trying to make him leave, saying Kate wouldn't tell them; she wouldn't want those awful strangers to take her away from her family and put her into an orphanage.

Kate tried to shake the memory away. Three times they had brought her to emergency rooms. Three times her mother had managed to convince hospital staffs and case-workers that Kate had had accidents. Kate remembered lying on a narrow bed in the pediatric ward, the rails surrounding her like prison bars, her mother close by watching as Kate lay stone-faced and staring at the ceiling; her mother swearing that *this* time, when Kate was well, they were going to pack their bags and go away, just the two of them, far away from her father and her older brother. Just mama and her. She never believed her. And it never happened.

An arm dropped over her shoulders, breaking her free from the painful thoughts. Val. There was a bitter taste in Kate's mouth, and she was trembling. She thought she could smell blood.

Val led her to an uncomfortable plastic chair and handed her a paper cup filled with lukewarm coffee. Kate looked at her, noting the deep, hard lines in Val's face. *Exhaustion? Fear?* Kate groped in her pocket for a cigarette.

"Let me tell you what I know," Val said quietly.

"Is she okay?" Kate's voice was surprisingly steady.

"No. But she is alive, and she will be all right in time. I don't know all the details. I haven't seen a doctor in over two hours. Kate, Jessie was beaten up very badly. Her nose and several ribs are broken. She lost a couple of teeth. They said she would need stitches in her eyebrow and mouth. Her spleen is ruptured. They have her in surgery now. It's going to take time for those things alone to heal."

Kate stared at her. "What do you mean, *those* things alone? Is there more?"

Val nodded slowly. "Jessie was raped, maybe several times and maybe by more than one man. So far there's no way of knowing details of what happened to her. She was unconscious when I found her, and even if she came to while they had her in the E.R., I doubt she could've said much that would be coherent."

"When did all this happen?" Kate felt her stomach start to churn sickeningly, and she spilled coffee on her pants as she tried to set the cup on the table beside her.

"I found her around seven. I don't know how long she had been lying there before I came."

Kate glanced at her watch. Ten o'clock. At six she had been working on a painting. At six-thirty she had taken a break for dinner. Maybe if she had . . . Kate stood up abruptly, staring out the dark window. Val began pacing the length of the long, narrow waiting room.

HER FEET WERE MIRED. *She moved, forcing her body against hands she could not see, trying to run towards the open door, but she moved only a few slow, thick inches. Her shout for help was deep and drawn, a low rumbling whisper that fell from her mouth to the ground, words shattering at her feet. Men surrounded her, their enormous heads cracked with silent smiles. She could see the fist as it came slowly through the air, hours to reach her face, hours until she tumbled back against the coldness of something metallic and unyielding, and then felt the ground beneath her. Her mouth made no sound this time when she opened it, spilling warm blood instead of words.*

Jessie fought against the dream, her hands flailing the air, jerking at the IV tubing. Kate leaned over the bed, careful not to touch her but getting close to Jessie's ear.

"Jessie, wake up. It's a dream, baby. Wake up." Kate continued to call her softly until Jessie lurched into wakefulness, her eyes bright with terror and pain.

Kate was quietly insistent. "It's okay, Jessie. It's over. It was a dream, baby, a dream. You're in the hospital. There's no one else in this room except me and you. Nobody else." She repeated the words over and over, like an incantation, until Jessie's body relaxed somewhat and her breathing slowed. Finally, Kate touched her, placing a gentle hand on Jessie's shoulders. "I'm right here with you, Jess. I'm going to stay here. Nobody's going to hurt you anymore."

Kate's voice droned on. She wasn't aware of what she was saying. She was watching the expression in Jessie's eyes. And she knew the moment Jessie remembered. She felt it like a hot, piercing pain in her chest as Jessie's eyes filled with tears, and she turned her head away.

The shock of memory jarred Jessie, sending cold shards of fear through her as she clamped her eyes shut against the vision. But it was behind her eyelids, too, and for a moment she thought she might scream.

She felt Kate's hand close around her fingers, and she gripped it tightly. Breathing was agony, and she panicked at the tight constriction of something wound around her chest. Kate was talking to her, stroking her shoulder. Blackness swirled on the edge of her consciousness and she welcomed it, invited it. From a great distance, she heard Kate's voice.

"Sleep if you want to, Jess. If the dreams come back, I'll be right here."

TOM WHOOPED LOUDLY and dropped into the armchair, propping his feet on the scarred coffee table. He cracked his knuckles and stretched his arms over his head. Edgar sat on a kitchen chair, the back against his chest, whistling softly, tunelessly, and grinning from time to time.

Hank leaned against the wall near the door, an unsmoked cigarette between his fingers. He had said nothing since they left Jessie Pyne lying in the grass. He looked at his two companions as he fished around in his pocket for a match. There was no way they could know. No way to tell.

"Do you think we killed her?" Hank asked flatly.

Tom rolled his eyes towards the ceiling and fingered his moustache. "No. But I guarantee we shut her up."

"I don't think she'll have anything to say," Edgar added with his leering grin.

His face was still flushed, and his hands moved constantly, drumming his knee, rubbing his crotch, jingling the change in his pockets. He could still feel the adrenalin surge, soaring along on the power he felt in his body. Strong. He could go out and do it all over again. Edgar wished Tom had not hit her so much. He liked for women to know, to know clearly, what was happening to them. Yeah, he'd done that. Slapped a broad silly when he was through with her. Make sure she'd never forget Edgar Davis. But Tom did have the right idea; if they weren't scared of you, make them scared. Make them piss-in-their-pants scared. So scared they'd do anything you say. Edgar didn't want Jessie Pyne to die. Nope. He wanted her to live, and to remember.

He rubbed his shin gingerly. Hard to walk without limping. Hell, she probably cracked the bone, hard as she kicked him. He chuckled softly to himself. The way she kept trying to pull her pants up when they were leaving. He hoped she was awake when people found her, awake so she'd know how stupid she looked, lying there with her bare ass hanging out for everybody to see. Edgar laughed out loud.

"You're awful quiet over there, Hank. You got nothing to say?" Tom asked, his voice tinged with sarcasm.

Hank glanced at him. "I think we've said it all."

"Hell, you haven't said a word. I want to hear what you think. What's the matter? Didn't you have a good time? You sure dropped your pants fast enough. What did you think of your first queer?"

"It was okay," Hank answered with an uneasy smile. They didn't know.

"Yeah, well, like I said before, a cunt's a cunt."

BETH WAS FRIGHTENED. Where was he? He had worn old clothes when he left, faded jeans and a torn shirt, that old, ragged windbreaker he refused to throw away. Hank was always so careful about how he looked when he went out. Where would he have gone, looking like that?

Beth sat at the kitchen table working a crossword puzzle. Hank always laughed at her. He said she was too stupid to work those things. But she always finished them, and they were always right. She had made straight A's in high school. Hank didn't. He couldn't work the puzzles, so Beth never let him see her finish any of them.

She studied the list of clues, her dark head bent over the folded newspaper. Three across, belonging to or occurring each day, seven letters, starts with D. Beth picked up her pencil, D-I-U-R-N-A-L. Where was Hank? Beth wondered if it had anything to do with the woman he had been discussing with the other men. She wondered if he was with Edgar and that Tom. She rubbed her face carefully. It was still very bruised and swollen from the beating he had given her, and she carefully remained at home, hidden away. She didn't want anyone to see her like this. It made her ashamed.

HANK SLAMMED THE CAR DOOR with a violent gesture. What had happened? Tom and Edgar thought they had won. Stupid idiots. She never backed down an inch. Hank didn't believe she would remain silent. She would run straight to the D.A. and tell him everything. Stupid idea! He should know better than to listen to Tom.

He started up the short sidewalk to the front door. More importantly, what had happened to him? Was he getting soft? He had faked it pretty good back there, lying on that girl and humping away like he was really enjoying himself. Watching Tom beat her up had turned him on. But something had happened as soon as he unzipped his pants and climbed on top of her. He went limp and soft. Never did get it up again. What did that mean? His mood was vicious as he jammed his key into the lock and let himself into the house.

BETH KNEW THE MOMENT she saw Hank's face that she had made a serious mistake by waiting up for him. She took a tentative step in his direction but stopped when she saw his expression. There was blood on his jacket.

"Are you all right, Hank? I was worried . . ."

Hank grabbed her with a choked cry and slammed her against the refrigerator. Beth screamed, her body too tender and battered to withstand any more abuse. With one quick motion, Hank slapped her across the mouth. Beth could smell the liquor on his breath, but he wasn't drunk. She knew that.

"You just can't stop shoving your nose in, can you? I'm not a boy, and I don't need a mama to wait up for me. You're supposed to be in bed! Where I go, what I do, and when I come home is my business! One of these days you're going to make me so mad, I'm gonna kill you!" He shoved her towards the door. "Get in the bedroom! Get in there where you belong! Get out of my sight!"

Beth ran down the hall and into the bathroom. She locked the door behind her. She wouldn't come out, not this time. He would have to beat the door down to get her out. She sat down on the edge of the bathtub and leaned her folded arms on her knees.

HANK FINISHED THE BEER with a last long swallow. He was beginning to feel the effects of the alcohol. He was a man, by god, and it was high time she learned that. This was his house and she was his wife and she would do whatever he told her to do. Waiting up for him. Hank snorted. He dropped the beer can into the trash and turned out the kitchen light. She should've been in bed, minding her own business, either sleeping or waiting for him. Hank's eyes narrowed. Yeah, waiting for him, in bed.

He opened the bedroom door. Beth was not there. His fury surged as he tried the bathroom door and found it locked.

"Open this door, Beth!"

"I'm scared of you, Hank! Leave me alone. Please!"

"I'll give you a reason to be scared," he muttered as he· slammed his shoulder into the door. He heard wood crack. "Teach you to be a decent wife. I should've done this a long time ago."

The door gave, and the lock broke when he hit it for the third time. Beth huddled in the corner, her eyes wide with terror. Hank grabbed her by the arm and dragged her into the bedroom, throwing her onto the bed. He ripped buttons off his shirt as he wrenched it free from his body.

"Teach you to talk back to me. Teach you to be minding my business. I'm the man of this house, and you're about to learn how much of a man I am. Take that gown off!"

"Hank . . . no . . ."

Hank pulled his underwear off and dropped it on the floor. He loomed over Beth, swollen, hard, and angry. With one quick gesture, he ripped her gown open and dropped on top of her. Beth's screams were muffled by his shoulder, and after a few moments, she stopped fighting.

All she ever wanted was her own newspaper, she thought fleetingly. Then she closed her eyes against the pain and tried not to think at all.

10

VAL LET HERSELF into the house quietly. She closed the door behind her and turned on the lamp by the sofa. Dropping her coat onto the chair, she headed into the kitchen and to the refrigerator. She poured a glass of wine and stood by the table, sipping it rapidly. For the first time in years, she felt like getting quickly and quietly drunk.

She glanced at the clock. It was almost three. She would have to wake Denny and tell her what had happened. Maybe she should wait until morning. Val refilled her glass. Denny would be furious if she didn't wake her up. Val knew she wasn't going to sleep anyway, so she might as well have company. Kate was supposed to call if Jessie came to. Val had made her promise that.

She hadn't wanted to leave the hospital, but Kate had convinced her it would be better for Jessie if not too many people were around her when she finally woke up. It had been hard to look at Jessie. Her face was swollen almost beyond recognition—bandaged, bruised horribly. Still, Val had not wanted to go, especially after she had seen how shaky Kate was once she reached the hospital.

Val carried the glass of wine into the living room. The sound of a key in the lock startled her. She turned to see Denny come through the doorway.

"I didn't expect to find you up. It's late." Denny kissed her lightly on the cheek as she passed Val on her way to the closet. She hung up her coat and closed the closet door. "I had a great time tonight. I'll tell you, Laura and Moon are quite a combination. Say, were they ever lovers?"

"Yes," Val answered absently.

"That figures. They look like they might be again." Denny stopped suddenly and stared at Val. "Val, are you okay?"

Val shook her head. "No."

"Hey, what's wrong?" Denny's voice was soft as she put her arms around Val and hugged her gently. "What is it?"

"Jessie was beaten up and raped last night, Denny. She's in the hospital."

"Jessie?" Denny's voice was confused. Her arms dropped away, and she stepped back from Val, a look of disbelief on her face. "Jessie?"

"Yeah, Jessie."

"But . . . what happened? How did you find out?"

"I found her when I went by the shop to meet her for dinner. She's really hurt, Denny."

"Is she going to be all right?"

Val nodded. "Yes. They had to do surgery on her. Whoever did this knew what they were doing. She's going to be a while recovering from it."

"She was raped, too?" Denny's voice was toneless.

"Maybe several times. They don't know for sure. They had brought her back to the room after surgery, and Kate is with her. I came home because Kate thought it would be better if only one person was with Jessie when she woke up. Maybe she's right. I don't know."

"Is there any more wine?"

"A little."

"I think I'll get some."

Denny came back into the living room a few minutes later with a small glass in her hand. She sat down beside Val on the sofa and put her hand on Val's knee, squeezing lightly. "We need to tell Laura," she said.

"I know. But it's so late, and there's nothing anyone can do right now."

"How badly hurt is she?"

"Oh hell, Denny. Broken nose, broken teeth, concussion, stitches in her mouth and face, bruised, ruptured spleen, broken ribs. And raped."

"And you say Kate is with her?"

Val nodded. "She's supposed to call as soon as Jessie wakes up and let me know what's going on."

"Gonna be a long night."

"Yeah. I think so."

JESSIE DRIFTED IN AND OUT of reality. Now, instead of welcoming sleep, she fought to stay awake. When she slept, the dreams came, nightmares that terrified her. But when she was awake, very little around her made any clear sense. She had trouble focusing her eyes. One of the nurses said that was because she had hit her head. She didn't remember.

The police came. She told them to go away. Jessie didn't want to talk; she didn't want to remember for them. She said she didn't know who the men were. The police didn't believe her but they left. Val had stayed with her, quietly furious, until Jessie had drifted off to sleep in spite of herself, exhaustion outweighing fear.

KATE THREW HERSELF INTO WORK for the shelter. They had a building now, donated rent free for the first year, and they were moving furniture in, each woman feeling the need to get it open as soon as possible. Kate moved in an ever-present circle of fear. What if they knew who all of Jessie's friends were? What if they came looking for everyone else, too? From the trunk in the spare room, Kate took out the gun she had stolen from her father's drawer when she ran away from home. She knew how to use it. Her hands shook as she loaded the shells into the heavy revolver. But she kept it with her, wherever she went.

IT DIDN'T HURT QUITE so badly to walk. A few days had made a difference. But Beth's body was still sore and stiff, the bruises blue and purple. She moved around the small kitchen in silence, gritting her teeth against the pain whenever she had to reach or bend. Walking and sitting were different agonies, and she still felt torn inside. She was afraid Hank had really hurt her ... there ... but she was too afraid and ashamed to go to the doctor. He would want to know what happened and she couldn't tell him.

She now avoided Hank's angry, brooding gaze. She did not speak to him any more than she had to. She did what was required of her around the house, but she did it mechanically, woodenly, her mind often a blank. Hank had not touched her again but she was watchful of him, starting violently if he came up behind her unexpectedly.

They were all at the table. Even the boys seemed subdued in Hank's presence. Beth carried bowls of food to them, helping the younger boy serve his plate, cutting his meat for him. When she stroked his hair as she straightened up, he pushed her hand away, glancing fearfully at his father as though expecting Hank to disapprove of Beth's gesture.

Hank was watching his youngest son quietly. "Whose boy are you?"

"I'm your boy, Daddy," Mark answered nervously.

Timmy chimed in from the other side of the table. "I'm not anybody's boy. I'm a man. You said so, Dad. Said I acted like a man."

Hank frowned at him. "Don't get too big for your britches, Timmy. Eat your dinner."

Timmy turned a crestfallen face back to his food. Mark looked from his brother to his father, his expression puzzled. Beth sat down and sipped her iced tea, her face a carefully composed blank, her stomach a knot of tension.

Hank chewed and swallowed a mouthful of food before speaking again. "You haven't had any more trouble at school, have you, Timmy?"

"No, sir. You really musta told that principal a thing or two."

"I don't want them giving you a hard time for doing exactly what I tell you to do. I'm the boss, not them. I don't ever want to hear tell of you sitting next to any nigger kid, or playing with one, or eating at the same table with one. It's bad enough they're even in the same school. Decent white kids shouldn't have to be thrown in with trash. And I want you to watch out for Mark here. You're the oldest, so you're responsible for him. Nigger gives you trouble, you go right ahead and punch him out. Never mind the principal. I'll take care of him."

"Okay, Dad. Does that mean Mark has to do what I tell him?" Timmy was eyeing his brother with obvious glee. Mark looked at his father in alarm.

"He's not my boss, Daddy! He can't tell me what to do. It's not fair! He pushes me around enough!"

Hank leaned forward, frowning. "I'll tell you what's fair, young man. Timmy is the oldest, and he knows more than you do. And I trust him. Hell, I've seen you talking to kids I told you to stay away from. I can't trust you. I do trust Timmy. I want him to watch out for you and make sure you do what I tell you. And if those niggers start picking on you, you'll be glad to have your big brother around to help out. Won't just one jump you. They always jump in packs, just like dogs."

"But they don't mess around with me, Daddy," said Mark, stirring his potatoes with his fork. "I don't want Timmy telling me what to do."

Hank's hand flashed with amazing speed as he slapped the younger boy across the face. Mark dropped his fork and grabbed his cheek, but he didn't make a sound. He blinked rapidly as his eyes filled with tears.

"Watch your mouth," Hank snapped. "I'll tell you what you can want and not want. You'll do as I say and that's that. Now if you'd like to argue with me, we can go into the bedroom with my belt and see who wins the fight. You want to do that?"

"No, Daddy," Mark whispered.

There was a long silence at the table. Beth saw the quick, smug look that passed across Timmy's face. He's just like his father, she thought to herself. She rose and poured herself a cup of coffee. There was an excruciating pain in her stomach—hot, burning stabs of agony. Her hands trembled, and she spilled coffee as she poured. Hank snickered. Mark pushed his plate back abruptly and stood up.

"May I please be excused?" he asked.

"You haven't finished your dinner. Sit down, Mark," Hank commanded. "And you sit down, too, Beth! I get sick and tired of watching you jump up every few minutes. No wonder the kids don't eat. You're probably driving them nuts."

"I'm not the one doing the yelling, Hank," Beth answered softly as she sat down, both hands holding the cup tightly.

"I suppose you think I should coddle them the way you do?"

"Kids need kindness, once in a while."

Hank looked at the children. "Both of you are playing in your food. Get out of here! Go to your rooms!" The boys jumped up and left the room without a word of protest. Hank turned his gaze back to his wife. "Don't talk back to me in front of the kids, Beth."

Beth flinched. She started to stand up but changed her mind. She couldn't help either of the boys. If she left it alone, Hank would probably forget it much quicker than if she interfered. She stared into her coffee cup.

"I'm taking Timmy bow hunting next week," Hank said in a conversational tone.

"He's just a little boy, Hank. Don't teach him to kill things."

"If I say he's old enough, then he's old enough. I won't have you ruining him, too, Beth. You've already made a sissy out of Mark, but you aren't going to do it to Timmy. He's going to be a man. I'll see to it, even if I have to break his neck in the process. If I want to take him hunting I'll take him. One of these days he'll thank me for it. What will he ever thank you for? You don't know the first thing about being a mother just like you don't know the first thing about being a wife."

Unfamiliar anger flared in Beth, and she spoke before she thought. "Then why did you marry me?"

"I'll be damned if I know," Hank said as he rose from the chair. "You sure ain't no prize."

Beth sat very still, gingerly probing her anger like one would probe a sore tooth. She heard Hank turn on the television in the living room. Her whole body began to shake, harder and harder, until she felt she might crack from the vibrations inside, until she felt she might choke on the words that rose in her mouth, pushing at her lips. Her hands clenched the cup, sliding it around in small circles that grew wider and wider as her anger surged. Then, unexpectedly, she threw the cup on the floor, throwing as hard as she could. All anger left abruptly as she watched with horror. Hopelessly, she grabbed for it, but she was too late. The cup smashed against the tile floor shattering completely, shattering loudly. Beth jumped up from her chair, horrified by what she had done, fear replacing anger in great waves through her body. She crossed her arms protectively over her chest.

Hank stepped into the kitchen and looked at the broken cup. Then he looked carefully at Beth, his voice tautly controlled. "You did drop that cup, didn't you, Beth?"

"Yes. I dropped it," Beth whispered, her hand covering her mouth.

"Good. I didn't think you would ever throw anything, would you?"

"No, Hank."

He studied her for a long, tense moment then left the room. Beth took a deep breath and leaned against the counter. She shouldn't have thrown that cup. It wasn't right to break things. It wasn't right to be angry. Bad things happened when people got angry. A good wife didn't get angry. She wasn't angry. No, she wasn't. Beth grabbed the broom and started sweeping up the slivers of glass. As she knelt to pick up the larger pieces, a razor sharp edge sliced deeply into her finger. Beth stared as the blood welled up and began to drip onto the floor. Red blood on the green tile floor. She wiped at it hastily with her other hand, smearing it, afraid Hank would come back into the room and see what she had done. Bad to be angry, she thought silently as she reached frantically for the sponge. Bad, bad, bad....

JESSIE WAS UNCOMFORTABLE. The plastic bottom of the chair stuck to her skin, pulling and chafing at her thighs. She silently cursed the backless hospital gown and tried to shift her position enough to pull some of the flimsy material beneath her. The effort made her lightheaded and dizzy. Finally, she gave up, resigning herself to the torture of the plastic against her legs until the nurses came back to help her into bed.

It was her first time up in the five days she had been in the hospital. She had been eager to get up, to change locations, even if it was only a few feet from the bed to the chair. Jessie hadn't realized how weak she really was while she was confined to the bed. The five steps to the chair had been made with her leaning heavily on the arm of a sympathetic nurse, and when Jessie finally sat down, she was out of breath. It had felt like miles to the chair.

It scared her to know that she could not move herself around the small room without a great deal of help. She stared out the low window. It would pass as she healed; the weakness would pass. But she felt very vulnerable. Anyone could walk into a hospital. Anyone.

Val popped her head through the partially opened door and grinned in surprise. "Look at you, hotshot. When did they let you out of bed?"

Jessie smiled as best she could, relieved to have company. "About fifteen minutes ago. They practically had to carry me." It was still extremely difficult for her to talk. The swelling in her face and mouth had gone down some but not enough for her to speak very clearly. And she had to talk quite slowly in order to form the words. It was so frustrating that Jessie did not talk very much at all.

"NO." THE ANSWER WAS QUICK and terse. "Jessie . . ."

"It hurts."

Val put the small bag of food she was carrying on the bureau and kissed Jessie on the forehead. "It'll get better as you do."

"I hate it. I hate not being able to do things for myself."

"I know. You're so independent, it's probably driving you crazy." Val sat on the edge of the bed, swinging her long legs back and forth as she watched Jessie trying to shift her body in the chair. "How long are you supposed to be up?"

"As long as I feel okay."

"Do you feel okay?"

"Except for this chair I do."

"What's wrong?"

"Plastic. Nothing between my ass and the plastic."

Val glanced around the room and saw a towel on the chair near the bathroom door. She brought it to Jessie. "See if you can lift your rear up far enough for me to slide this towel under you."

Jessie leaned her weight against the arm of the chair, straining to raise up from the seat. Val slid the white towel into the minute space Jessie was able to clear for her, and Jessie sank down, the strain evident on her face. It took a minute for her breathing to return to normal.

"Better?" Val asked. "Thanks."

"Sure." Val sat on the bed again, resuming her leg swinging. "So, how are you doing?"

"Okay. I don't like people doing everything for me." Jessie's words were slurred, and Val leaned forward slightly, a frown of concentration on her face as she tried to make out what Jessie was saying.

"Relax and take it as it comes. You've been through a lot. Maybe you deserve to take it easy for a little while."

Jessie didn't answer. She looked out the window. She had not talked about what had happened to her, had not said a word to anyone. She worked very hard not to even think about it, trying to keep her mind carefully blank. She felt the blankness slip in now, with Val watching her so intently as if waiting for her to say something.

"Talk to me, Jess."

"No." The answer was quick and terse.

"Jessie..."

"It hurts."

"I know." Val's voice was gentle. She found herself wanting to wrap her arms around Jessie and rock her like a baby, have her feel okay again, without pain, without fear. Just like she had been before.

"You've got to talk sometime."

"I don't even think about it." Jessie's expression was defiant. "I think about going home, going back to work. Laura must be going crazy by now."

"Laura is fine. She told me to tell you things at work are under control, and that she'll be in to see you tomorrow. She said not to worry."

"I have to worry. I don't have insurance. This is costing me ... I can't afford it ... I can't pay."

"Jessie," Val interrupted softly.

Jessie looked at her, a tortured expression in her eyes. "I'm afraid that if I start, I won't stop. Ever."

"I know. You will stop when it's time to stop, though. But if you don't start, it will never go away."

Jessie struggled to push away the sudden flash of memory, the sounds of male laughter, the fist in front of her face, the cold ground beneath her. The pain. Always the pain.

"I can't cry," she gasped, her eyes full of tears. "I can't breathe when I cry. My ribs . . ."

Val knelt beside her and slid her arms carefully around Jessie, holding her as closely as she could without hurting her further. "It's okay. You don't have to say it all, feel it all. Not at once. Just don't deny it."

"Playing therapist, Val?" There was bitterness in Jessie's voice. She felt captive; she couldn't even leave the room to escape the conversation.

Val shook her head. "You know better than that."

"Kate said you found me," Jessie said suddenly.

Val nodded. "I did. I called for an ambulance. At first, wasn't sure you were alive." Her voice was matter of fact.

"How did you find me?"

Val frowned, puzzled by the words, uncertain that she had understood Jessie's question. "I came by to have dinner with you before the meeting. I found you by the dumpster."

Jessie shook her head. "I know that. How did you find me?"

Suddenly, Val understood. "You were lying on the ground, on your side. There was a lot of blood. Your shirt was ripped open. Your pants were down. I thought you were dead," Val answered evenly.

"I tried to pull my pants up," Jessie said softly. "I didn't want anybody to see me . . . like that."

"I don't think anyone would want that. You were very cold. I covered you with my coat and went inside to call an ambulance. Then I came back and sat with you."

Val could see Jessie's distress as she stared at her hands, clenching and unclenching in her lap. Jessie's lips were white as she pressed them together, a gesture Val knew must hurt her. For the first time since she had known Jessie, Val found herself hating the young woman's self-control.

Jessie closed her eyes and leaned her head back. "They were the same men who trashed my house."

"How do you know that?"

"They practically told me. They said they had tried to make a point but that I wouldn't listen."

"And so they came in person," Val finished for her.

"They said all I had to do was . . . to not testify at the trial and to stop the newsletter. They said if I promised them that, they would go away and leave me alone."

"Would they have?"

Jessie shook her head. "I doubt it."

"Did you promise anything?"

"No."

Val waited, wanting to say something reassuring but there was nothing but lies to offer. She didn't really believe everything would be all right, that it was really over, whether or not Jessie testified at the trial.

"There were three men."

"The doctors figured there was more than one."

"Three. Tom, Edgar, and . . . I can't remember the name of the other one."

Val stared at her in amazement. "Do you know them?"

"No. They called each other by name." Jessie's voice became a monotone as she spoke.

Softly, Val said, "Tell me what you remember."

"I don't know how much I remember. A lot of it is hazy, like a dream. They hurt me . . . one of them beat me. Tom. The guy called Tom. The other two stayed out of the way for a while . . . At one point, before he . . . hit me the first time, I thought I had a chance to make it to the door of the shop. I didn't get very far ... He used his fists, Val, and he liked it. If you could've seen the expression on his face ... He liked beating the hell out of me."

"I'm sure he did," Val said, the low anger carrying through her words to Jessie.

"I was almost unconscious when ... Edgar, I think, stopped him. Said he didn't want Tom to kill me. I knew if he hit me one more time, I would pass out. I wanted to. I really wanted to. Then they got me on my knees. Tom made me ... They all raped me, several times. I don't know how many, maybe only once each. Maybe more. I couldn't do anything to stop them. I tried, Val." Jessie looked at her. "I really tried. But my arms wouldn't move. I wanted to faint but I was there, for all of it."

In Val's mind, she filled in what Jessie could not say. Tom made me ... Val had a good idea what Tom had made her do.

"I'm scared, Val." Jessie was whispering, her eyes wide and dark in the dimly lighted room. "I'm scared they'll come here. What if they do? I can't do anything alone."

Val kept her close, patting her lightly on the shoulder. "I don't think they will. They may believe they've scared you enough to keep you quiet. And we can stay with you—me, Kate, Denny, Laura. We can stay with you all the time."

Jessie leaned into the circle of Val's arms, rocking back and forth. "They left it all with me. They beat off all their hate and left it with me."

"Hang onto that anger, baby. That's what will pull you through this. You need it. Pour it right back at them. They deserve all you can give and then some. Don't lock it away. Throw it right back."

"I'm scared. Scared to go home. The thought of being outside ..."

"We'll be with you. Count on that. We'll be with you for as long as you need us to be there. We'll help. Denny and I will do all we can. And you know Kate will help. She loves you."

"Then why won't she talk to me?" Jessie's words were pouring out now, streams of bitterness and uncertainty. "And why won't she come to see me when I'm awake? It's like she can't take it, like she can't deal with me now."

"Jess, when a woman is raped, it doesn't just happen to her alone. It puts every woman who knows her through some pretty big changes. It scares the hell out of us all."

"But right before the demonstration, we had this big fight. What happened to me was exactly what Kate was afraid would happen, what she warned me about. I feel like she's pulling away from me."

"Are you afraid she'll leave you?" There was a long silence.

"I'm just as afraid she'll stay."

11

KATE HAD BEGUN SLIPPING into Jessie's hospital room very late at night and spending the dark hours there, curled up in the armchair, only half-sleeping as she smoked endless cigarettes and kept a self-appointed vigil. They talked very little. When Jessie woke during the night, Kate would sit on the side of the bed and give her news about the print shop, word of the battered women's shelter, anything she could think to say that would not bring up the subject of what had happened to Jessie. Jessie spoke of herself in terms of pain level and mobility. Kate seemed content with only that information.

After ten days in the hospital, Jessie was able to move around a little on her own, although she still required help from time to time. Her strength was returning slowly. Kate watched her progress silently, wanting her out of the hospital, wanting her home in some familiar environment that did not hold such terrifying memories for Kate. She hated being there, even for Jessie's sake. But Jessie never asked her to come or to stay. As far as Kate knew, Jessie never asked that of anyone.

The hard chair made it nearly impossible for Kate to sleep deeply or soundly, and she welcomed the wakefulness even though she was slowly drifting towards complete exhaustion. Jessie's beating and rape had brought back Kate's dreams, nightmares she had thought long forgotten, dreams she had not had in years: her father, her brother, her mother's swollen, terrified face, the sounds of men laughing, the sound of a fist striking flesh, the green antiseptic of emergency rooms, lights in her eyes.

Kate had worked with battered women for nearly two years. Those women had not set loose the memories Kate so carefully locked away. Jessie had. And she not only brought back the memories themselves but all of the feelings that came with them—the fear, the pain, and the helplessness. Kate wanted to tell her. She wanted to tell Jessie that she knew, really knew, what Jessie was going through, but she could not find the words.

During the days while Jessie was in the hospital, a pattern quickly developed for Kate. She would drink coffee all during the daylight hours, cup after cup, until every nerve in her body screamed in protest. Then she would go home, take a shower, have one or two drinks, and go to the hospital. She did not sleep for more than a couple of hours each night.

Kate twisted her body in the chair, trying to find a comfortable position. She pulled the lightweight blanket higher under her chin. Jessie was dreaming; Kate could always tell. Jessie's hands were clenching and relaxing, her breathing labored as if in a race. Her legs beneath the covers twitched spasmodically. Kate watched, giving Jessie time to wake herself up. When she didn't, Kate stood up and went to her, calling her by name before she touched her shoulder.

Jessie's eyes flew open, containing the terror Kate had come to expect. She found herself remembering how Jessie used to wake up, her eyes soft and sleepy, friendly. Now she looked at her as though Kate were a complete stranger. And when she recognized her, the softness was still not there, only a memory of fear. Kate sat on the bed, holding Jessie's hand, waiting for her to calm down from the dream, to stop trembling.

"Are you okay now? Are you out of it?"

"Yes," Jessie nodded. "How long have you been here?"

"Since eleven. It's around two now, I think."

"Why don't you ever come when I'm awake, Kate?"

Kate looked at her. "This way, I'm here during the night. I'm here when you have the dreams."

"And when we don't have to talk to each other." There was bitterness in Jessie's voice.

"I didn't say that, Jessie."

"You didn't have to." Jessie looked away. "When I was still living in the farmhouse, Mrs. Carpenter told me a story about one of her aunts who died in a mental hospital. The woman had clenched her fists so tightly and for so many years that the nails had grown through her flesh so that they came through the backs of her hands."

"Was that story true?"

"I think so. It's become part of my dream. Sometimes lately I catch myself clenching my fists so tightly that I cut the skin on my hands. I dream about being like that woman, my fists always tight and useless, and my not being able to open them anymore."

"That's a terrible dream." Kate did not look at her.

"Yeah. It changes. It changes then to a man hitting me, and I want to hit him back but I can't because my hands are so twisted that they aren't really fists anymore. I try to call for help, but I have no voice. I keep thinking that if I could just open my hands, I could push him away and my voice would come . . ." Jessie trailed off and Kate started to stand up. But Jessie suddenly, harshly, gripped Kate's arm. "I don't know how to talk to you about any of this."

"Jess, we don't have to talk yet. You need to heal your body first and then we can talk. One step at a time, baby. It doesn't have to all be done at once."

"What is wrong, Kate?" Jessie demanded in a quiet tone.

Kate pushed her hair back with a quick gesture and reached for a cigarette. "Being here, in a hospital . . . it's hard for me. Not just being with you, knowing you are hurt and in pain. Just being in a hospital, period.

"Why?"

Kate exhaled a white cloud into the air and studied the book of matches she was holding. She offered a cigarette to Jessie who shook her head. Kate slipped the matches into her shirt pocket. "There's a whole lot about me that you don't know. I've never told you because there didn't seem to be any reason for me to say anything. I don't think now is a good time to get into it . . ."

"Tell me." Jessie was staring at her intently.

"It's just that I was in the hospital several times when I was a kid, and there are a lot of bad associations for me, a lot of painful memories. I don't usually think about them very much."

"But you are now." Jessie was grateful for a chance to think about someone other than herself. And she thought Kate was withholding something important, something Jessie very much needed to know.

"Yes, I am now."

"What happened to you?"

She looked at Jessie, her eyes narrowed and angry. "My father beat the hell out of me. He put me in the hospital three times, and those were only the absolute worst times when there was no way to keep me at home and take care of me there. So I know how it feels to have someone do that to you. I don't know how different it is being a child and being an adult. Or how different it is when it's done to you by someone you love or by someone you don't know. It's just that being with you has brought it all back."

The silence in the room lingered for a long time. Jessie watched while Kate smoked and forced herself not to pace.

She didn't want to talk about this, did not want to think about it right now. Jessie did not need to hear about her past; she had her own problems to deal with. She needed time to heal herself. Talking would come later when the time was right. Much later. Kate put out her cigarette.

"Were you ever raped, Kate?" The question hit Kate like a physical blow. She set the ashtray down, carefully keeping her back to Jessie, her eyes closed.

"Jessie, probably fifty percent of the women you know have been raped. Maybe even more than that. It happens constantly. But I don't think this is the time or the place ..."

"Dammit, Kate, I'm not discussing the subject of rape. I don't want statistics. I'm asking about you. And I'm trying to tell you about me. It happened to me, not to someone else out there you don't know." Jessie gestured outward from her body. The words were there rushing to come out, the need to say them to Kate, pushing them forward, tumbling them into Jessie's mouth.

Kate turned to face her. "It's almost three in the morning, Jess. Let it be for now. I know what you're going through. But you have time, baby. You do have time. Just get better and then we can talk, then we can work this through."

Jessie turned onto her side, her back to Kate. The words silenced Jessie as effectively as a gag. She closed her eyes, pretending to go to sleep. When she felt Kate return to the chair, Jessie rolled onto her back again, her gaze locked on the far wall of the room. Kate did not want to hear about it. Maybe no one wanted to hear about it. She felt completely alone, and an icy fear spread through her. People wanted to forget; they didn't want to be reminded. They wanted her to get well and get back to her life, not to talk about pain and fear, not to remind them about death. She felt a sickening rush of apprehension. They would try to make it seem like it had never happened.

Maybe Kate was right. She should worry about healing her body. Maybe it would start to go away when she was able to do things for herself, when she didn't feel so helpless and vulnerable. There was lots to be done. No time for dwelling on something she couldn't change.

For the first time, Jessie considered not testifying at the trial, wondering if that would make them leave her alone. Everyone would understand. No one would blame her.

Jessie choked back sudden tears. She would not let anyone see her cry anymore over this, most especially Kate Robbins. Then she felt a stab of pain in her hands. Abruptly, she straightened her fingers. Small half-moons on her palms. The nails had cut through to blood.

KATE SET CUPS OF COFFEE in front of Val and Denny, then pulled out a chair for herself. The morning sun cut bright yellow patterns across the old, polished wood table, and Denny traced them with her fingertip. They could hear Laura in the next apartment humming to herself.

Kate glanced at Val. "Have you been able to talk to Jessie?"

"Some. She told me part of what happened."

"How is she?" Denny asked, her eyes lowered.

"Physically, I think she's doing remarkably well. Emotionally, I'm not sure." Val shrugged. "She did talk, and that was good. I think she needs to talk."

"Not everybody talks," Kate said quietly, "and she needs to heal her body before she tries to work through anything else. She can't do it all at once."

"No, she can't," Val agreed, "but her body is pretty much healing itself. Only Jessie can heal the rest of it. She won't do that by not talking."

"What did she say happened?" Denny asked as she picked up her coffee cup and rose to stand by the window, her back to the other two women.

Val watched her. "I think they were Klansmen. At least, it sounds like it. Three men. Jessie said they called each other by name. She can only remember two of the names so far. I think the other will come to her eventually."

"That was pretty careless," Kate said in surprise.

"Maybe they thought she couldn't hear or understand them. Anyway, from what she told me things sounded planned out, like the whole incident had been well set up. And they were the same men who broke into her house. They told her that. She said only one of the men did the actual beating, but that all of them raped her. She doesn't remember how many times. She never lost consciousness, not until after it was over."

"Oh, hell," Denny breathed softly.

"I think she's lying there feeling helpless, feeling very vulnerable to another attack, worried that they might come back. Even though she can get around by herself now, she still couldn't do anything to defend herself. But I haven't asked too many questions. I didn't want to push her. She does need some time."

"She has that," Kate said, a bit too firmly. "She has all the time she needs."

"I know that. But I wanted her to know that her friends are willing to listen if she needs to talk. I don't think it's safe to assume that she will know we are here and willing. Especially as many times as she may need to go through it."

"I wish you wouldn't say anything else to her, Val."

Val looked at Kate, a shocked expression on her face. "What are you talking about?"

"I just think she needs to be left alone." Kate's hands were trembling as she lifted her coffee cup.

"Well, I'm sorry, Kate, but I can't honor that request. I was raped a few years ago. What I remember most was the feeling that I had to go looking for women I could talk to, that no one else would bring up the subject. They all talked about how willing they were to listen whenever I needed to talk. The whole responsibility was on me. And they weren't even very good listeners for the most part. They wanted me to say it so they could nod and be sympathetic and then get on with whatever they were doing.

Sometimes when I brought it up, women would pat me on the shoulder and change the subject, like they were protecting me from something by not talking about it. Most women stopped touching me. They wouldn't even look me in the eye. They wanted me to just get over it. I felt almost completely alone and isolated. Only a couple of my friends really stuck by me and worked with me. My lover left me. She couldn't deal with it."

The sudden crash startled them as Denny slammed her coffee cup onto the counter, spilling the hot liquid all over the floor. She turned to face them, gripping the edge of the counter behind her, her eyes narrowed.

"So what are we going to do?" she demanded.

"Whatever we can, Denny. As much as we can," Val answered.

"We can't just sit back like this."

"I don't follow you," Kate said, watching Denny carefully. "I'm not dealing very well with any of this. I never have.

Almost every woman I've ever been close to has been raped. It makes me so angry I want to hurt somebody. Now it's happened to Jessie. Only they almost beat her to death, too. I can't just sit and listen. Every time I hear about it, all those women go through my head. She's got her whole life to put back together now, and she shouldn't have to!" Denny's voice became increasingly loud as she spoke, and her hands sliced the air with quick gestures.

"She's got to live with those men for the rest of her life, in one way or another. Even when she's worked through it all to the point where she's not in immediate pain or fear, they will still be there. Things will happen to bring them back. I can't sit here knowing that and talk calmly. I want to take a crowbar and beat their fucking brains in! I want it to have never happened!"

"We all want it to have never happened," Val said softly, "but it did. Now we have to figure out how to be there for her."

"And they will be there, too!" Denny shouted. "How do we replace them with ourselves? How do we offer her more security, enough to offset what they've done to her? Will sitting around a kitchen table make her feel safe? What about the next time she has to walk down the street or go out to the dumpster? Are you going to be there, Val? What about you, Kate? You're so into being cool, saying she can take all the time she needs. What are you doing for her? I've listened to you, and you always sound like you're talking about a complete stranger!"

"Denny . . ."

"Don't take that tone of voice with me, Val!" Denny answered, glaring at her.

"I'm sorry. But I don't think jumping on Kate will get us anywhere at all."

"Where are we supposed to get us?" Denny snapped, smashing her fist on the table. "That woman is the closest thing to a sister I've ever had. I won't act like I feel calm and rational about this because I don't. I want to hurt them as bad as they hurt her." Denny's face was drawn, and her body trembled as she leaned over the table. There were tears in her eyes. Val couldn't separate the different expressions she saw there.

"So what do we do now? There's no way we could ever hurt them the way they hurt Jessie. We can never hurt them that bad." Denny grabbed her jacket from the chair and pulled it on, her gestures abrupt and jerky. "I have to go for a walk," she said as she left the room, slamming the door to the apartment behind her.

A heavy silence filled the room as both Kate and Val stared at their coffee cups, each filled with her own thoughts.

Val sighed quietly. "I'm glad she finally lost her temper. It's been building all week, but she wouldn't say anything."

"Maybe it's better to just get mad like she does," Kate said. "Maybe it would be better if we all just got mad."

"Maybe."

"I have to go over to the shelter." Kate rose to her feet.

"I think I'll go to the hospital. Just check in and make sure Jessie is okay."

Kate studied Val for a long moment, her expression guarded. She felt a surge of resentment but quickly pushed it down. If Val was willing to go through the listening, willing to go through the pain, then more power to her. Kate wiped up the spilled coffee and put the cups in the sink. She couldn't do it; she couldn't listen to what Jessie had to say. Maybe it would be better to have someone else, someone not so intimately involved. When Kate looked up, Val was staring at her curiously. Kate shook her head and left the room in silence.

DENNY STEPPED INTO JESSIE'S ROOM, somewhat calmer, and tired. She kept her hands shoved into the pockets of her jacket as she leaned over and kissed Jessie on the cheek.

"You sure look better in your own pajamas. That little gown they gave you did nothing for your image."

Jessie smiled lopsidedly. "I know."

"I checked at the desk on my way in, and they said you can take a ride to the coffee shop with me. What do you say?"

"Oh my god, yes! Anything to get out of this room."

Denny pushed a wheelchair into the room. "They insist you ride, but this isn't so bad. All I can buy you is coffee or a Coke, but I'll treat you to a beer as soon as you get out of here. I think they frown at the consumption of alcohol on hospital premises."

"Stuffy bunch," Jessie said, maneuvering herself into the chair. "You know how to drive one of these things?"

"Sure do. You're in the hands of an expert. I worked for one summer as a nurse's assistant while I was in college. Here we go."

Denny pushed the wheelchair down the hall and onto the elevator. The two women were silent as they watched the green numbers on the panel announce the passing floors.

Denny bought Cokes and brought the drinks back to the table. She sat down opposite Jessie and stirred her drink absently with a straw. "I hear they may let you come home in a couple of days."

"That's what they said this morning. I'll be very glad to get out of here."

"Would it be easier for you if Val and I moved your stuff into that downstairs bedroom? That way you wouldn't have to . . ."

"No, Denny. I want to be closer to you and Val than that."

"Sure. I just thought . . ."

Jessie touched her on the arm. "I know. And I appreciate it. But I don't think I could take being downstairs and have both of you upstairs. I think it would scare me to death every time I heard a noise."

"I see your point. Do you think you'll be able to handle the stairs okay?"

"I don't know. Probably, if I move slow."

"Well, I guess we'll have to wait and see. How are you feeling?"

"Much better. I can get around pretty well now. They've taken out all of my stitches, but I have to keep the rib binding on for a while yet. That's my main concern. I still can't take a deep breath."

"Well, the swelling on your face has nearly disappeared, and the bruises are almost gone. You look like you feel a lot better."

"Yeah. I think if it hadn't been for the head injury, I could have come home several days ago. But they wouldn't let me leave until I had had three or four days with no dizziness."

"Better safe, I suppose."

"I suppose."

"Jessie . . ." Denny began awkwardly. "I'm having a hard time with what happened to you. I want to be here for you but I get so mad every time I think about it . . . I walked out, well I should say I *stormed* out, of Kate's place earlier because I just couldn't stand talking about it. I want to listen and help, but I can't without losing my temper."

"I'm glad you told me."

"It's not you. It's them, the men. It's that it has happened to so many women I care about. It's hard for me. I love you, Jessie. You're my best friend, my sister. I can't stand to see you hurt. It makes me want to jump on every guy I see."

"Yeah." Jessie's voice was soft. "I need you to be here, Denny. I'm scared to death. I'm afraid to go back to work, afraid they'll come back. I know they know where I'm living in town. I'm scared they'll hurt you or Val." She hesitated. "I've been thinking about not testifying."

Denny stared at her in surprise. "You're going to back down?"

"I don't know what to do. But I have been thinking about it."

"Well, everyone would probably understand it if you did. Except maybe for the D.A. You could go to jail, I think." Denny tried to disguise the disappointment she knew was in her voice. Now was not the time to argue with Jessie.

"I don't want to be hurt again. And I don't think I could take it if they hurt anyone else. One of the men threatened that."

Denny's answer was slow. "I think you have to worry only about yourself, Jess, and let the rest of us make our own decisions. You felt so strongly about what happened at the demonstration, I can't see you backing down. I won't judge you if you do. I'm just saying I can't see you doing that. I think you would hate yourself for it."

"That may be, but I'm scared."

Denny covered Jessie's hand with her own. "I know."

BETH DROPPED THE NEWSPAPER into the trashcan and put her cup in the sink. She would finish the dishes later. As she walked towards the door, her eye fell on the folded pages and the headline seemed to leap out at her, SHELTER FOR BATTERED WOMEN OPEN IN DURHAM. She paused, hesitating, her hands held stiffly at her sides as she read the opening paragraphs of the article.

Durham's first shelter for victims of physical abuse and rape opened its doors this week at an undisclosed location in town. The shelter, called Refuge, is designed to temporarily house battered women and children, as well as victims of rape, while sources of aid are explored and new housing can be found for those in need. Refuge features living quarters for those who go there, as well as a small, mostly volunteer staff to provide counseling and to act as contacts to other related agencies.

In a brief news conference earlier today, director Kate Robbins stated that the location of the shelter is not being revealed to the public at large in order to offer as much safety and security as possible for those women and children who utilize the shelter. Arrangements have been made with local hospitals and law enforcement officials to provide information about and transport to the shelter for any woman and/or child who needs a place to stay until satisfactory arrangements for their well-being can be made.

Consultants for Refuge include several local doctors, lawyers, and counselors. Ms. Robbins stated that the network which has been structured with other agencies in the area, such as Welfare, Rape Crisis, Traveler's Aid, and Legal Aid, will enable staff members to provide immediate and varying resources for many different needs.

Ms. Robbins was quoted as saying that with the increasing number of reported cases of marital abuse and rape in this area, the existence of such a shelter is vital to the welfare and safety of many women.

A fold hid the rest of the article. Beth reached out a tentative hand and picked up the paper. A shelter. She had never heard of such a thing before.

She tried so hard—so hard—to be a good wife. She pulled her robe more tightly around her as she stared at the paper. *SHELTER FOR BATTERED WOMEN OPEN IN DURHAM.*

Spreading the newspaper on the kitchen table, Beth slowly ripped the article free. After a moment's thought, she hid it in a cookbook and placed the book far back on the shelf. Just in case. Just in case.

12

KATE PUSHED THE CHAIR BACK and rubbed her tired eyes. She had been doing paperwork since early morning. It was now nearly nine at night. She made a face as she downed cold coffee and emptied the overflowing ashtray into the wastebasket.

She had spent the day trying to make the operating budget she had drawn up in the beginning fit the actual money she had received for the center. It wasn't being easy. When she originally designed a budget for Refuge, she had gone through and trimmed every possible corner, paring the budget to the bone. The money she had at the moment showed that she needed to trim some more, but she didn't know where or how.

Kate was the only full-time salaried employee. As the Director of Refuge, she was being paid $9,000 a year. But even that money didn't come out of the budget; it was being paid by a Junior League group in town, at least for the first year. Some of those women were also on the Board of Directors. Kate's fundraising tactics had been instrumental in getting the shelter open. She had literally pounded the streets, approaching civic groups, churches, public service organizations; she had brought money in from many of them. She had written grants, backed the United Way into a corner, organized bake sales, yard sales, and auctions. She had begged from individuals. And she had done well. But it was going to be a tight first year nonetheless.

She still had to hunt for money. Opening the doors provided the shelter, but it did not bring in money. Most of the women who came through would have little or no money to donate. Indeed, many of them would need money themselves.

Kate sighed tiredly.

The light touch on her shoulder startled her. Kate whirled around to find Denny standing behind her.

"What are you doing here?" Kate asked in surprise.

"Val has been trying to reach you all afternoon, but the line's been busy. The doctor released Jessie today. She's at home."

"How is she?"

Denny shrugged. "Getting around pretty well. She seems to be healing very fast."

"She's a strong woman," Kate said softly. "Yeah." Denny's reply was short and flat. "I guess she's probably asleep by now."

"I just don't get you, Kate," Denny said tersely. She leaned forward, resting her hands on the desk. "How can you be so laid back about all of this?"

Kate pushed her hair away from her face. "I don't feel very laid back, Denny, believe me."

"Then you've got a damned good act together. You sure had me fooled."

"Look, I don't need..."

"To be perfectly honest with you, I don't particularly care what you need. I care what Jessie needs."

"And just who appointed you her guardian angel?" Kate exploded. "I won't have you on my back, Denny. So get off!"

Denny stared at her for a long, tense moment, anger sparking in her eyes. "She's my friend."

"And she's my lover!" Kate blazed. She fumbled for a cigarette, lighting it with shaking hands. She threw the pack onto the desk and went to stand by the window.

Denny watched Kate's reflection in the glass. "So what is it? What's eating you?"

"I feel completely helpless! I can't even separate the realities, where I stop and Jessie starts. How can I deal with her when I can't even deal with myself?"

"I don't follow you."

"It's a long story."

Denny's face was set, her expression hard. "Look, Kate, Val talked to Jessie quite a lot while Jess was still in the hospital. Jessie is afraid you'll leave her. But she's also afraid you'll stay, that the two of you will just fight and never work it out. She doesn't know how to relate to you right now. And it doesn't sound like you've given her much reason to feel secure. Maybe you're scared, too. But withdrawing like this is going to have only one result. If you want to talk some before you see Jessie, I'll listen. I don't pretend to be the slightest bit objective but I'll listen."

Denny leaned against the desk and folded her arms across her chest. Kate stared at her for a moment, resentful and torn. It had been a long time since she talked to anyone about what had happened. She resented the need to talk, hated the whole series of events which brought it all up. She knew none of Jessie's friends understood why she was acting like she was. But maybe talking to them would help. Maybe it would calm her down, help her not feel so vulnerable herself. And god knows it would be better than dumping it on Jessie. She glanced at Denny again, wishing the expression on Denny's face was friendlier. She took a deep breath and forced the words out.

"One of the reasons I work so hard for this shelter is because I was a battered child. Every time I went to the hospital to see Jessie, it all came back. I realized that I had never dealt with any of that, had merely pushed it down. It's been so long now, I don't even know how to begin. The fear is still there. So I went to Jessie's room late at night so I wouldn't have to talk, so I wouldn't have to remember very much. Jessie is quite smart. She would've known something was going on, and she can draw it out of me. She already has pulled a lot out of me. She has enough to cope with, and all I can offer her is my own fear. I'm terrified for her, but I'm also terrified for me."

"Why don't you tell her that?" Denny demanded, not willing to back down.

"I have, in various ways. I don't want to get into it right now, with Jessie or with myself."

"But how can you work with these women and children if you haven't dealt with yourself? It seems to me it would eventually tear you apart."

Kate shook her head. "So far I've managed to keep a certain distance from them because they're strangers. That may be surprising, but it's true. I can't do that with Jessie. She's too close, too important. I told her some of it because she pushed me one night, and I didn't know what else to do. But she hasn't heard the half of it, and I don't think I can listen to her without going through everything that's happened to me. At least, in my own head. How's that going to help her? The last thing she needs to be dealing with is my garbage."

"Maybe what Jessie needs is for you to be completely honest with her, and a little vulnerable. She thinks you don't want her anymore. True, maybe she can't really deal with what you call your garbage, but you're playing some kind of halfway game with her, staying there at night and not being there when she's awake, scared and lonely. I know there's got to be some comfort in knowing you're there, watching her while she sleeps. But what about when she's awake and wants you to hold her? What about then, Kate?" Denny's voice was hard. Clearly, Kate's explanation was not adequate to her.

"Look, Jessie needs good things right now. I'm not sure I'm a good thing for her."

"Do you want her?"

Kate answered softly, "I'm not sure what I want."

Denny drew back abruptly. "Then maybe you'd better figure that out first. I thought you loved her."

"I do, Denny. It's just that . . ."

"It's just that nothing! Sometimes you have to let go of yourself a little and just be there for people who mean something to you. What do you think is going to happen? Probably Jessie would be so relieved to feel she could do something for someone else. She feels so totally helpless. To be a little selfishly honest here, Val and I could use some help, too. We're doing all we can, but we can't give her some of the things you can give her. And she needs them from you. If you can't, or won't, then just say so and get out of her life. But stop taking two steps forward and six steps back. Jessie is in no shape for that. She needs so much she doesn't even know how to ask."

"Stop lecturing me, Denny!" Kate snapped. "We're all trying to do the best we can."

"Well, I don't think some of us are trying enough." She stared Kate down after several long moments. "Look, Kate, I didn't come here to lecture or to be nasty. But right now, I don't care about anyone else's feelings except Jessie Pyne's. As far as I'm concerned, I'll do or say whatever I have to to make things as easy for her as possible. I'm sorry if I upset you. But I kinda figure whatever any of us feel, it can't be half as bad as what Jess is going through. That makes me pretty unsympathetic. You figure it out, but for Jessie's sake, I hope you don't hurt her. I don't think she can take it."

Denny turned and quietly left the room. Kate wanted to stop her but she made no move to call her back. She dropped into a chair, leaned her head back, and closed her eyes.

LAURA SAT DOWN on the edge of Jessie's bed and kicked off her shoes, a blissful expression settling over her face.

"That feels soooo good. Feet were not meant to be stood on for fourteen hours a day." She eyed Jessie. "You look pretty good, woman. How are you getting around?"

"The stairs are hard, but other than that I'm making it okay.

How are things at work?"

"Well," Laura answered with a chuckle, "I can't say I mind a bit bringing the paperwork over here for you to do. Business is good. A lot of orders coming in."

"That's good to hear. How are you holding out?"

"I'm doing all right. I don't know as much about the press as you, but this is one way to learn. I've figured a lot of stuff out for myself since you've been gone from the shop."

"Well, I'm glad it's not driving you completely crazy." Jessie paused for a moment, then said in a very low voice, "There hasn't been any trouble there?"

Laura looked puzzled. "Trouble? No. Should there be?"

"I was worried that those men might come back. They threatened my friends, too."

Laura put her hand on Jessie's knee. "Everything is fine. No one has come around or bothered me in any way. Don't worry about me."

"It's hard not to."

"I know. But I'm okay. You need to be putting all your energy into yourself, and the account books."

Jessie smiled. "I'm glad you brought them over. Gives me something to do. I'm already so sick of reading, I could scream."

"And just think. Not a month ago you were moaning about how you never got to read these days."

"I know."

"Just can't be pleased, huh?"

"Circumstances..."

Laura leaned forward. "Hey, Jessie, I know it's hard for you. I really know that. But I guess the reason I came over here was to just pass some time with you, see how you were doing, talk, give and get some moral support. I want you to get well. I need you. It's not the same being at work, at meetings, without you."

Jessie looked at her. "I miss being there."

"Don't you miss me?"

"Of course I do. What kind of question is that?"

Laura laughed. "Just thought I'd ask. I'm real glad you feel up to doing the paperwork. If you do that, then I can take a good deep breath again. I'm afraid it's in a bit of a mess. I haven't had time to do very much with it over the past couple of weeks. Things are a little slower now, so I can get caught up on the other stuff I'm behind on. Did that make any sense?"

"Yep. It sure did." Jessie stared at the pile of papers at Laura's feet. "Looks like I'll have enough to do there for a couple of days."

"Honey, I brought you the bills, the checkbook, the accounts, the invoices, the orders; I brought you everything. You just have yourself a ball."

"I never thought I would be happy to see the checkbook."

"Everything was up to date until two weeks ago. I haven't touched any of it since then. Feel free to call me fifty times a day if you have any questions."

"Okay. You just remember you said that."

"I will."

"Yeah?"

Jessie reached for a cigarette. Her stay in the hospital had almost stopped her smoking. Once she arrived at home, she found herself going back to cigarettes, fighting her tense nerves. But she was only smoking five or six a day, a drastic change from the pack and a half she had been smoking before . . . the accident. "I'm scared about coming back to work. The doctor says I can probably come back under limited conditions sometime next week. Half days, no lifting, twisting, or bending."

"You can be queen of the front office. Me and that old press are about to come to an understanding. Can't have you messing around with a budding relationship."

"Yeah, I know, but..."

Laura reached out and caught Jessie's hand. "Honey, *I* know. You'll be nervous and scared. I'll be there with you. Until you're ready, we're not going to let you be caught alone at home or at work. Not even on the streets. But this is your business, your work. If it's too much for you, if the associations are too bad, then let's look for another place for the shop. But we'll all be there for you in every way we can. Lots of women have been raped and beaten. We have to start watching out for each other."

"It makes me feel so damned helpless sometimes."

"I guess so. But look at it this way; we're not doing it just for you. We're also learning how to protect ourselves."

"I keep thinking I should be able to do it all."

"Wouldn't that be nice?" Laura smiled. "Sometimes we have to do it all, and alone. But it feels pretty good, from time to time, to know that there are women who can and will help. Jess, you're going to have to do a lot of this on your own, most of it. So let us be there for you when and as we can."

"Yeah."

Laura reached for her jacket. "Well, I have to get going. Oh, by the way, Moon told me to say hello to you from her."

Jessie smiled. "How is she?"

"Doing fine. Just as opinionated, ornery, and sweet as she ever was. I'm supposed to have dinner with her later tonight."

"I'd love to see her again sometime soon."

"I'll tell her. She's been wanting to stop by, but she wasn't sure you would welcome a visit from a stranger."

"It would tickle the hell out of me. She doesn't seem much like a stranger."

"I'll pass that along, too." Laura leaned down and gave Jessie a careful hug. "I sure will be glad when I can squeeze

144

you again without worrying if I'm going to pop one of your stitches. See ya."

Jessie watched Laura go out the door. The room felt strangely empty after she had left. Jessie finished the cigarette and ground it out in the ashtray. Suddenly, she wanted to be with Kate very badly.

13

"I CAN'T BELIEVE THIS!" Hank said as he waved the newsletter in front of Tom's nose. "That stupid broad! Does she think we're just blowing our horns?"

Tom scratched his head. "She does learn slow."

"So much for your bright ideas," Hank said, tossing the paper onto the table. "All that for nothing. And you were so sure it would work, so sure we would shut her up."

Tom spread his hands, palms up. "The girl is obviously crazy, man. Nobody would open their mouths after something like that."

"Yeah, well, what happens if she's crazy enough to start talking?"

"She hasn't said anything. And she won't either."

Hank sat down and opened the paper, reading parts of it aloud. "Listen to this. 'Unite Against Klan Activities.' They're talking about pulling a bunch of different groups together for a mass demonstration. They say they're going to come back to the farm and protest our next rally. Didn't they learn anything? And there's the usual bunch of history in here. And some garbage about Klan terrorism, personal recollections by some local niggers, civil rights shit. There's even some stuff in here about a Klan hit squad, a terrorist group. And a whole thing about the junior KKK club at one of the high schools. She's getting too close to some things now."

"She doesn't do this newsletter alone, Hank. There are several other women who do it with her. Have you talked . . ."

"Hands off, is the word I get. Leave her alone. Do not make any personal contact with her or with any of her friends. We can do whatever we need to to scare her, but we cannot personally do anything to her. No physical damage, low profile. Don't show our faces. It's getting too close to trial time. That's what Baker told me." Hank rose and went to the refrigerator. He tossed a can of Miller's to Tom, then opened one for himself.

Tom stretched, cracking his knuckles loudly. "Well, we already know she doesn't scare so easy. We've done everything short of killing her, and she's still at it."

"I know that. But I get so pissed every time I see a copy of this rag that I want to . . . Wait a minute!" Hank said, staring at the newsletter. "Jessie Pyne owns a printing business. I'm pretty sure this thing is printed there and put together by that bunch of broads who are with her in this group. Maybe, instead of worrying about the people involved, we should take care of the machinery."

Tom glanced at him, a puzzled expression on his face.

"What are you talking about?"

"It's not going to hurt Pyne to know that we know all about her. Okay, we did a number on her house. Then we did a number on her. She's out of the hospital, and she's pushing her luck by continuing to put out this newsletter. My guess is she's scared but getting a little nervy because she hasn't heard from us. So, a message to the house where she's living now and a torch to her business. We know all about her, and she is not safe, no matter what she thinks."

"You mean burn her printing business?"

"Exactly. Let her know we are all around her."

A slow grin spread across Tom's face as he took in what Hank was saying. "You know, that's not half bad, Hank. I worked in a printshop once. There are usually enough chemicals to make the whole place go up. It would be one hell of a bonfire."

"Will you see Edgar soon?"

"Tomorrow night," Tom answered.

"Bring him by and let's talk this out. We need to move soon. I don't want her to start getting too calm."

JESSIE STACKED THE LEDGERS and account books into a pile and set them on the floor by the desk. It was all beginning to blur, and she couldn't make sense of the figures anymore. She leaned back in the chair and rubbed her eyes tiredly. It was nearly eleven; she had been at it for almost four hours.

She could hear voices in the living room but paid no attention to them. Val and Denny seemed to have an almost constant stream of visitors, and Jessie had come to ignore the activity. It usually didn't relate to her in any way unless she chose to participate.

She would be going back to work at the first of the week. Three days. Jessie pushed down the sudden surge of fear she felt when she thought about leaving the house, being out on the streets, in the shop. She didn't know if they knew exactly where she lived, but they did know exactly where she worked. What if they came back? The newsletter was out again. Maybe they had seen a copy. Probably, she thought quietly. It was one of the things they told her she had to stop. Jessie lit a cigarette. She rubbed her belly gingerly, feeling the ridge of fresh scar tissue where she had surgery. The incision itched, and now it ached from tension, from sitting too long in the chair, leaning over the books.

Jessie moved from the chair to the bed, pressing back against the pillows. What was she trying to prove? She had fought the depression for days, rationalizing that it came only from being confined, inactive. But it crept into her constantly, every time she dropped her guard the slightest bit. What was she going to prove? Maybe they were all just spinning their wheels. Who could stop those men? Kate might have had a point. A few women against so many men? Men who would batter and even kill. What would they do next time? Jessie knew there were few options left to them. If the beating and the ... rape didn't stop her, then what would? She shuddered in spite of herself.

When Val had asked her about continuing the newsletter, Jessie had wanted to say no. Now, she wasn't sure if she was being brave or foolish. Since she had said to go on, put out another issue, she had had terrible dreams about the men coming for Val, for Denny, for Laura. She dreamed she was there, watching, but could do nothing to stop what was happening. All her movements were in slow motion as she tried to intercede. It was not an unlikely consequence; Jessie knew that now.

And what would she do if indeed that happened? Someone might get killed next time. Next time.

Jessie put out the cigarette in the ashtray and slowly swung her legs over the side of the bed as she sat upright. It was something they all needed to discuss. In fact, an attack on one of the other women felt very probable considering all that had happened already.

A brief knock on the door was quickly followed by Val's head as she peered around to see if Jessie was sleeping. "Is this racket bothering you at all? We can ask them to leave if it is."

Jessie shook her head. "No. It's fine."

"Thought I'd check. How're the books coming?"

"I'm almost finished. Feels good to be doing something instead of just sitting around."

"I'll bet it does. I forgot to bring up your mail before, so I thought I would run it up. Here you go." Val dropped a handful of envelopes on Jessie's lap. "I'm going back down. Yell if you need me for anything."

"Sure. Enjoy yourself."

Val glanced upward. "What I would most enjoy right now is some quiet time." With that, she left the room and closed the door behind her.

Jessie glanced through her mail, an assortment of advertisements, solicitations, announcements. One envelope caught her attention. It was hand-addressed to her in a block print that looked familiar. There was no return address on it. She ripped open the flap and pulled out a single folded sheet of paper.

We visited your house and tried to make you understand. We visited you and tried to make you understand. We are always here, even if you don't see us. The newsletter is out again, and you haven't spoken with the D.A. You've had your last warning.

There was no signature. It was the same print that had been on the other notes. Jessie stared at the paper for a long time, her hands shaking, her mouth dry. Then she balled up the sheet and threw it across the room. Rubbing her forehead anxiously, she suddenly clenched her fists and rose to her feet.

"I can't stand this!" she shouted. "I can't stand it anymore!"

She did not hear the knock on the door or hear Kate enter the room. When she turned, Kate stood there with one hand on the knob, a frown on her face. "Jess, are you all right?"

"No!" Jessie screamed at her. "I am not all right! I am not all right! I haven't been all right in a long time. My house was trashed. My dog was killed. I was beaten up. I was raped. I am scared shitless to go outside. There are men threatening to kill me and hurt my friends. I have a lover who won't even talk about what's happening. And I have to testify at a trial against a fucking murderer. I am not all right!"

"It'll be okay, Jess ..."

Jessie whirled around, her fists clenched and her face drawn in rage and fear. "Don't mouth platitudes at me, Kate Robbins! I'm not some damned Pollyanna. I have a very good sense of reality right now. I had it beaten into me three weeks ago. And if you came here to just sit and stare and not talk, then you can just get the hell out of my room. Get out of my house! If that's all we can do together, then we don't need to even try. I can't deal with your silence. I feel like you're holding me personally responsible for everything that's happened. You sit there, and it feels like you're passing some kind of judgment. I can't stand it!"

Kate pulled away from Jessie's anger as if Jessie had struck her. She leaned against the door and watched Jessie pace across the room, her arms folded tightly against her stomach. For a moment she wanted to leave, to run from the room and never come back. She didn't want to deal with this, with what had happened to this woman who was her lover. And Kate loved Jessie more than she had ever loved anyone else. She knew that if she left the room, Jessie would never allow her to come back.

Jessie had stopped pacing, and now she stood staring at Kate, aware that Kate was making some kind of decision. The pain Jessie was feeling had little to do with her injuries; it hurt to see that Kate had to think about what to do. Silently, stonily, Jessie steeled herself to watch Kate walk out the door.

"Goddamn them!" Kate hissed suddenly. "Goddamn them all! Every last fucking one of them! They're going to do it to us. They have done it. There's no sense in even trying to pretend we can have something they can't destroy." She turned and walked to the window, her movements abrupt and jerky.

Jessie listened. She heard what Kate said, but her own pain was too great to consider fully what she had just been told. "Are you saying that we have nothing left? That they've taken it all? I don't believe that, Kate, but I don't have the strength to argue with you about it. They can take nothing unless we give it to them! But if that's the way you feel, then you should just leave. I can fight them or I can fight you, but I can't do both." Jessie lit another cigarette, burning her finger in the process. "Do you know what it's like to lay here night after night and wonder about every sound? Every squeak? Always wondering if they're here, if they're coming after you? Do you have any idea..."

"Yes!" Kate shouted as she whirled around. "Yes, dammit, I do know! You don't have any monopoly, you know. I have a brother, Jessie. A brother who is five years older than me. When I was twelve years old, he came home from a date one night drunk and mad because the girl wouldn't sleep with him. He came into my room and he raped me. He pinned me down to my bed, held his hand over my mouth, and he raped me! And it wasn't just once. He raped me many times, over and over, until he left home three years later. I was terrified. He convinced me that I would be held responsible if I told anyone. He said no one would ever believe me, that it was his word against mine. So every night, for three years, I lay in my bed, and I listened to every sound. I jumped at every noise. I never knew when he would suddenly show up. He left home when I found out I was pregnant, and I threatened to tell my folks that he was the father. He left in the middle of the night. And when I did tell mama that I was going to have a baby, and when I tried to tell her Rick was the father, she slapped me so hard I saw stars. She told me if I ever said that again, she would ship me off to a home somewhere. So I had to keep quiet. I had the baby, and she was put up for adoption. So yes, I know damned well how you feel! And right now, I relive it every time you mention what happened to you.

"I survived being beaten by my father and raped by my brother. Val survived being gang-raped. Laura survived a severe beating. Moon was shot and left for dead. We all survived! You will survive what happened to you, too. But dammit it, Jessie, I don't know what to do for you or say to you because it hurts so much. It hurts to know it happened to you because I love you. But it also hurts because I cry for me, too."

The tension left Jessie's body so quickly that she nearly sagged. A strange silence filled her as she reached out and pulled Kate to her, burying her face in the softness of Kate's neck, breathing in the scent of her, feeling Kate's tension also ease as she held Jessie tightly.

Then it was all there, sitting on the edge of everything—the hurt, the fear, the total terror—bringing the memories she had pushed down, the feelings she had not allowed herself to vent or experience. Her body became rigid as Jessie fought for control, fought not to give in.

Kate held her as tightly as she dared, trying to remember the injured body, wanting only to draw her inside, wanting to rub away all that had happened, wanting to heal her mind, heal her soul.

"No, Jess," she whispered. "Please don't hold it back. Please don't do that. Let it go, baby. Let it go."

The wrenching cry was painful as everything broke loose in Jessie. The tears came, not restrained, but hard and deep, pulling loose with tearing sobs that shook her entire body, turning her inside out through her feelings, then back again slowly as she reached for the hurt she had not touched before.

Jessie leaned into the circle of Kate's arms, weak and shaken, her body convulsed in spasms from muscles strained from crying. She could feel wetness on her shoulder and knew Kate was crying, too.

Finally, it eased. There were more tears, but her body refused. Exhausted, Jessie held onto Kate's shoulders, her lips pressed tightly together against the pain that rose in waves from her belly. She looked wordlessly at Kate, wanting to talk to her, wanting to explain the tears. Then she realized that she did not have to speak. Kate's eyes were soft with under-standing and quiet.

Without undressing, the two women lay down across the bed, arms wrapped firmly around each other. Jessie quickly, almost instantly, drifted into a deep dreamless sleep, while Kate held her fiercely close and rubbed her back gently.

14

"NOW THAT IS WHAT I CALL a good meal, Valerie," Moon said as she rose from the table and started stacking dishes.

Val laughed. "Lord, Moon, no one has called me that in years. It sounds so strange."

I'll bet. I remember Bob calling you Valerie. Valerie, he would say in that authoritative voice of his, *Valerie, I think you should...* and then he would proceed to tell you what and how to do everything."

"It was pretty awful, wasn't it?"

Moon grinned at her. "Well, I did often wonder how you put up with him, especially when I saw how mad he made you."

Laura took the dishes from Moon's hand and placed them in the sink. "We were so bad in those days, Val. After one of those meetings where Bob did all the talking, corrected you in everything you ventured to say, told you everything you were supposed to do, Moon and I would go home and lay in bed, thinking all sorts of things we'd like to do to him."

"Like what?" Val asked, her interest piqued.

"Oh, things like tying his beard in a thousand little knots. Or kidnapping him and putting him in a room where he was told everything to do and exactly how he had to do it. Or gagging him so he couldn't talk for at least a week."

"And those were the nice fantasies," Moon added with a deep laugh.

"Nicer than mine," Val said with a nod. "I must have thought about castrating him at least a dozen times a week."

"He was so obviously gay, Val. I wonder whatever became of him?" Laura mused, running hot water over the dishes.

"I have no idea, but I hope he didn't find another woman to hide behind."

"Come out, come out," Moon sang as she shouldered Laura aside and reached for the sponge to wash the dishes. "I wonder how many men bully women in order to hide their lust for other men?"

"That would make a fascinating study, Moon," Laura said, pouring herself another cup of coffee.

"Wouldn't it though?"

The silence was comfortable in the warm kitchen. Moon washed dishes, and Val dried them and put them away. Laura lit a cigarette, ignoring Moon's look of protest. The dishes finished, Moon leaned over her and gave her a resounding kiss on the mouth.

"I love you in spite of your awful habits."

"That's good to know," Laura grinned, continuing to smoke.

"So how is Jessie doing?" Moon asked Val, who was hanging the dish towel on the door handle of the refrigerator.

Val picked up her coffee cup and refilled it. "She seems to be doing a little better. Not so jumpy as she was. The trial is only a month away, and I've sort of been expecting her to say something about it but she hasn't."

"I expect she's pretty nervous, whether or not she's saying anything."

"I agree," Val answered. "She got a letter in the mail last week, obviously from the same men. It was another threat telling her she had had her last warning."

Moon whistled softly. "How did she handle that?"

"I'm not completely sure how she's dealing with the threat itself. She's scared something is going to happen to one of us."

"Have she and Kate even begun to get it together?" Laura asked.

"That's the interesting thing. The night Jessie got the threatening note, Kate came to her room. Jessie was in a state, very freaked out and very angry, and she let loose at Kate, telling her that they were either going to have to deal with it, or she wanted Kate to get out and leave her alone."

"It, meaning the note, or it, meaning Jessie and Kate?" Moon interjected the question.

"It, meaning Jessie and Kate. She didn't tell Kate about the note that night. Well, it seems Kate got really pissed, too, because Kate thought Jessie assumed Kate didn't know what it was like to be raped and afraid and Kate let fly at Jessie."

"Whew. Sounds like a mess."

"Sure could've been," Val agreed, "but it wasn't. Kate finally told Jessie why she had been so closed up the whole time Jessie was in the hospital."

"Why?" Laura wanted to know.

"Kate was a battered child, but she was also an incest victim, raped repeatedly by her older brother for several years. Seems she even had a baby by him. Kate was having a hard time with all that in addition to trying to deal with the fact that her lover had almost been killed and raped. Moon is right: it is a mess. But from what Jessie told me, everything came out that night, and they are talking it through. Slowly, she said. Neither of them really knows exactly what to say or do to help the other, but Jess said she feels like just knowing is pretty powerful to them right now."

"I'm glad to hear it," Moon said quietly. "They could give each other a lot of support."

"Is Jessie still planning to come back to work on Monday?"

Val glanced at Laura. "As far as I know. We talked a little about that. She is scared to death to go to the shop. Too many associations there for her. It's perfectly understandable, but she wants to go anyway. She showed me that last note. I know she's worried that the men may show up at work. We talked a little about security, and she seemed relieved to know someone else was thinking about it, too. I don't think she ought to be left alone for a while, at least not until after this damned trial is over."

"Jessie's pretty independent. How does she feel about having one of us trailing around after her?"

"Right now, I think she wants it. I don't blame her. If it were me, I wouldn't want to be left alone. She knows that once it looks like things have really cooled off, we'll stop. I'm feeling pretty protective of her, and of myself, too. It doesn't seem at all unlikely that those men would try to get to her through one of us."

"Well, this way we can all look out for one another," Moon said with finality. "I'm not too old to enjoy the possibility of kicking a few asses myself."

Val laughed. She had seen Moon 'kick asses' before, years ago. "How old are you, Moon?"

"Forty-seven and proud of every second," Moon answered with satisfaction.

"You should be. I'll be forty next month," Val said.

Moon leaned over the table and patted Val's hand. "Just you wait."

JESSIE WIPED THE INK from her hands with a dirty rag and dropped it on top of a paper box. She lit her third cigarette of the day, sat down on the stool, and stared at the press as she smoked.

She had been back at work for almost two weeks, and she was finally beginning to stop jumping at every sound. Maybe the men would not return. Maybe. Laura, quietly and without mentioning the reason behind it, had started carrying the trash out to the dumpster every night, making the daily trip that Jessie had usually made in the past. Both of them unobtrusively checked the lock on the back door several times a day. Jessie often found herself staring at the lock, filled with a sudden panic that would temporarily immobilize her, leaving her body stiff with fear, her breathing short and ragged. After noticing this reaction, Laura had taken to announcing the source of sudden noises, the dropping of a package of paper, the slamming of a door or drawer, the characteristic tapping of her metal ruler on the side of the light table.

Jessie could hear Laura locking up the front office. It was after six, time to go home. Jessie took off her denim printer's apron and draped it over the press. She no longer stayed late hours working alone. She knew Val or Denny or Kate would be waiting outside to drive her home and that Laura would walk her to the car before heading off to her own.

Jessie was already feeling restrained in her movements. She was rarely alone, except when sleeping, a fact that she both welcomed and resented at the same time. She craved isolation, and she feared it.

Jessie rode home with Kate in silence, her mind elsewhere, her body tired from standing over the press almost all day. She was comfortable with Kate's presence as she watched passing sights without really seeing anything. There were Christmas decorations everywhere, and she blanked them out. The season depressed and angered her, making her feel even more the outsider for her rejection of it.

Shaking her head, Jessie turned her thoughts to what she wanted to do when she got home. Evenings at home now were given to all the things she had had no time for in the past—things such as writing, playing her guitar, talking with Val and Denny, planning the newsletter, even cooking, something Jessie dearly loved but had not done in a long time because of work and meetings. Val and Denny were wonderful to cook for because they were so open to trying new foods and got very excited over Jessie's experimentations. Kate preferred tried-and-true dishes and was frequently skeptical when Jessie suggested variations.

Kate stopped the car in the driveway. The house was dark. She reached for Jessie's hand and squeezed it lightly. "Can I come in for a while?"

Jessie glanced at the dark windows and nodded. "I wish you would. It doesn't look like anyone else is at home yet."

"Want me to stay until Val or Denny gets here?"

"Yes." Jessie was silent for a moment, and then she sighed. "I feel silly sometimes always wanting to have someone around. And yet, I want to be alone, too."

"I don't think it's silly, Jess."

Jessie smiled an acknowledgment and got out of the car. Kate followed closely and waited on the top step while Jessie unlocked the door. She watched the motion of Jessie's wide shoulders as she pulled the mail from the box and bent to pick up the newspaper. Then Kate looked away, trying to ignore the warm ache in her lower stomach. It had been almost two months since they had made love. But it was completely up to Jessie she reminded herself. Completely. She did not have the right to make that demand.

Kate stood by the small, cluttered desk in Jessie's room, glancing at the pile of papers balanced precariously next to the old typewriter. She could hear water running in the bathroom and the sounds of Jessie brushing her teeth.

"Are you writing again?" she called out. Jessie stepped into the room. "I'm trying to."

"What are you working on?"

"Nothing very coherent. Lots of thoughts. Nothing that quite fits together. Mostly, I've been keeping a journal and going back through some of the stuff I wrote several years ago. But the journal is especially nice because things don't have to fit together there."

"That's true."

Jessie pulled off her sweater and tossed it on the bed. She caught Kate looking at her as she unbuttoned her shirt. Crossing the room, she pulled Kate close and kissed her cheek.

"I love you, Kate."

There was a long silence. Kate was stunned by the words. She pulled back so she could see Jessie's face. "You've never told me that before."

"I know." Jessie's voice was quiet. "Did you just decide?"

"No," Jessie answered, rubbing her face against Kate's collar. "I've known it for a while."

"Why didn't you tell me?"

"I wanted to know what it meant when I said it."

"What does it mean?" Kate asked softly. She stroked Jessie's back then reached under the shirt to feel her ribs under her fingertips. She kissed Jessie's ear and waited, willing herself to be still and quiet.

"I was very idealistic, Kate," Jessie answered finally. "I wanted you to share that idealism with me and was pretty upset when I found out you didn't, and probably wouldn't. And then you were my first real lover, the first woman I had ever been to bed with. I wanted to care about you, love you, but I didn't want to be too involved. And I didn't want to be in love. I wanted to avoid that huge emotional upheaval almost every woman I've ever talked to said she had over and with her first lover. I wanted us to be radically different from everyone else, find completely new ways of being together."

"So are we just like everyone else?"

"No," Jessie said as she shook her head, "but I think we're only now beginning to find the new ways. Perhaps because of what's happened recently. You're my friend, Kate, my best friend."

"I'm glad. We almost weren't friends at all."

"I know. But everyone has their limitations. I'm just glad that wasn't one of yours."

Kate again leaned back so she could see Jessie's face. "You don't believe in forevers, do you?"

"I just hope for them. I am enough of an idealist to hope that they exist."

Kate felt relieved. Jessie had always been demonstratively loving and caring but had never been verbally expressive at all. Kate had often wondered exactly what Jessie was feeling but had never had the courage to ask. She trusted the overt physical signs as much as she dared rather than risk hearing truths she wasn't prepared to hear.

"Well then," Kate said with a grin, "if you don't believe in forevers, how long do you think we're good for? Any projections?"

Jessie rolled her dark eyes towards the ceiling, a glint of humor on her face. "For at least the next few hours."

Only Jessie's quick movement prevented Kate from nipping her ear. Laughing, she pulled Jessie tightly against her, nuzzling her neck playfully.

Jessie felt the sudden change in Kate. She felt the slight flutter in the other woman's stomach, the small tightening of her fingers, the deeper breathing. A momentary chill spread through Jessie. Kate wanted her. She didn't know if she could let Kate touch her, caress her. How could she tell Kate that?

She rubbed the small of Kate's back, circling wider to touch shoulder blades, hips, pressing Kate gently closer. Then Jessie felt her own ripple of wanting and the stab of fear. It was too soon, too soon for her. Kate drew back and looked at her, as though she had felt it, too.

There was an unusual stillness in Kate as she waited, a stillness Jessie could almost touch. She trailed her hands lightly up Kate's belly, pausing to feel the familiar curve of breasts against her palms, then down over the slight ridges of ribs, to pull once more at Kate's hips. She could feel Kate tremble as she leaned closer to Jessie, her body softening under Jessie's fingers. Jessie stroked her, remembering the fierceness of their lovemaking, the give and take that left them both breathless and exhausted afterwards. It did not ease the knot in her stomach when she felt Kate's hands moving on her back.

Shyly, they undressed and lay down together on the bed. Kate was silent and restrained, watching the expressions on Jessie's face as the younger woman leaned over her, her hand stroking lightly, insistently, uncertainty flickering in her eyes from time to time. Finally, Kate closed her own eyes and concentrated only on the growing urgency in her body, the heavy ache in her thighs. Jessie's hand slid into her softly, lightly coaxing her out, slowly, carefully drawing her to the crest, holding her there, then cupping her tightly as the waves broke and Kate cried out, her hand over Jessie's, pressing her fingers closer and holding them until she stopped shaking.

Jessie sighed softly as she leaned down and kissed Kate. Kate's grip was firm as she pulled Jessie close to her and whispered, her mouth against Jessie's ear, "I want to make love to you, too."

Jessie was still, her face resting on Kate's shoulder. She felt the fear, the twist of panic, the sudden move that could bring it all back, the weight of a body that would make her feel cold grass beneath her, the movement of a hand turning into a fist. She felt Kate's hand softly stroking her back, the touches light, careful. Jessie shook her head gently, no.

"I need more time, Kate. I don't think I'm ready for that yet. I'm sorry ..."

Kate hushed her with a finger pressed softly against her mouth. "Don't be sorry. It's okay."

Kate was conscious of every movement she made, of every motion of hand and body. She wanted to press herself into Jessie's flesh and remove the hurt when she pulled away, like removing the mold from the newly cast form, fresh, untouched. Instead, she rubbed Jessie's back, shifting her position slightly so their bodies fit together. As she felt Jessie relax into sleep, Kate pulled the blankets over them, carefully reached for the lamp, and turned out the light.

15

"LOOK, WHY DON'T I JUST PICK UP the copy proofs and bring them to you later? I'll be over that way, and I'm already closer to the shop than you are . . . No, I'm not particularly thrilled about it but it's the simplest arrangement, and it won't take but just a few minutes . . . That's fine, Val. I have to get off now. I still have to take a shower, and I don't want to be late for the beginning of the film . . . That one is towards the end of the film festival. I'll pick up a schedule for you while I'm there . . . Okay. Bye." Laura replaced the receiver in the cradle with a little more force than was necessary to break the connection. She hated to talk on the telephone anyway, but was especially impatient when she was trying to get out of the house. Muttering to herself, she stood up and headed towards the bathroom. She was going to be late. And she was slightly grumpy that she had hooked herself into an extra chore. Damn, she thought as she leaned into the shower and turned on the hot water. Waiting for the steam, she glanced into the mirror.

"Damn," she complained to her reflection who nodded back sympathetically.

The streets were crowded with parked cars, and Laura had to circle the block twice to find an empty space. Even the parking area at the shop was full. Her muttering intensified as she fought to fit her car into a space made almost too small by the vehicle behind. Moon sat passively in the passenger seat, knowing from past experience that saying nothing was vastly more important at a moment like this than having any sort of alternative suggestion. She also knew Laura was completely exasperated with the Afro Film Festival because of the emphasis on African men and the male traditions. She maintained her silence, only occasionally giving Laura long looks from the corner of her eye.

"I'll be right back," Laura said shortly, as she removed the keys from the ignition.

"Afraid I'm gonna steal the car?" Moon asked mildly.

"No!" Laura's tone was one of exasperation. "It's just that I'm so used to . . . Oh, forget it." She got out of the car and slammed the door. Moon watched as Laura stood tapping her foot, waiting for the traffic to clear so she could cross the street.

Jaywalking, Moon thought, remembering being arrested on that very trumped up charge during a demonstration in Mississippi. Ridiculous as it had been, Moon had never jaywalked again, crossing instead at marked intersections and always with the lights. "I do learn, oh yes, I do," she said softly to herself. Then she settled back in the seat to wait.

She could see the shop from where she sat in the car.

Lights were on inside.

"That's odd," she mused aloud. "Laura is going to be some kind of pissed off if she finds one of the other women there to pick up those page proofs." Moon watched the building, humming tunelessly to herself. Something about it bothered her. Just a feeling. Like something wasn't just quite right.

LAURA APPROACHED the building slowly. No one was supposed to be there, she thought angrily. That was the whole reason for her coming to the shop. She started to insert the key into the lock, but a small alarm went off inside her head. Maybe she should just check first. Peek in the side window. Quietly, she went around the building.

Moon had spotted her and was already pulling herself out of the car when Laura skidded to a stop beside the door.

"There are three men in there!" she said breathlessly. "What are they doing?"

"They've got a whole lot of paper piled in the middle of the floor. It looks like they're going to set fire to the place. They have cans of solvent sitting next to the paper."

Moon was reaching into the back floorboard of the car. "Call the cops," she said as she stood upright, an ax handle in her hand.

"What are you going to do?" Laura gasped.

Moon grinned at her. "Just gonna keep an eye on things until the cops get here is all. Go on and call them. And call Jessie, too," she said over her shoulder, starting to cross the street.

Laura watched her, indecision all over her face. "Girl!" she said to herself, then ran down the street to the telephone booth.

"LET'S DO IT AND GET OUT OF HERE!" Edgar said angrily. "We can't hang around this place all night."

"All right, all right. Just pour this solvent all over the paper and scatter it around on the equipment too. Hank, you got matches?"

Hank nodded. "I've got plenty of matches. Let's go, boys!"

MOON WATCHED QUIETLY through the window, staying back as far as she could. There was no way to go inside and stop them without the risk of being seriously hurt. She hefted the ax handle from her left hand to her right. But just wait until they came through the door, she thought. A small smile crossed her mouth as she remembered the face of the Kluxer who had ripped off his hood so he could aim better at her that night. She remembered the way the bullet had felt when it slammed into her shoulder, knocking her to the ground with a force she had never felt before. Yeah, she remembered how bad it had hurt before she passed out. Just wait until they came out the door. Her grip on the handle tightened with anticipation.

She heard the sound of the siren. Obviously the men inside heard it, too. Their movements picked up speed as they scattered the flammable chemical around the room. They all lit matches and tossed them onto the pile of paper. It caught almost immediately.

"Let's get out of here!" Moon heard one of them say. She glanced in once more to make sure she knew which door they would use as an exit and then, smiling, she grabbed the ax handle with both hands and crouched down.

Moon heard Laura behind her and did not look back when Laura touched her shoulder. "It's me, Moon."

"Ssshhhh! Give me room, honey. Give me room!" Moon whispered.

Laura moved back a step, glancing around for something to use as a weapon should she need one. There was nothing. She crouched, waiting.

The door to the shop flew open, and a tall man charged out, the flames back-lighting him so Moon's aim was perfect. She swung the ax handle. It cracked into the man's ribs with a jolting thump. The man screamed with pain and fell to the ground, drawn up and out cold. Probably broke 'em all, Moon thought with satisfaction. Drawing back, she waited for the other two. But no one came out.

The fire was spreading rapidly. Soon the whole room would be in flames. Edgar looked at Hank, terror spreading all over his face.

"We gotta get out of here!"

"Go!"

"You crazy? Someone just keeled Tom over like he was a goddam matchstick!"

Hank shoved him towards the door. "You want to burn to death, you idiot? Get out of here!" Hank pushed him through the open door, hoping Edgar would draw the attention of whoever was out there so that he could make a run for it. He watched as Edgar landed on top of Tom, out like a light. Who the hell was out there? Hank broke into a sweat, undecided. The heat from the fire seared his face when he turned back towards the room. But he didn't want his skull fractured either. He could hear the wail of the police siren as it drew close to the building. He had to get out before they got there. If they saw him ... The flames were pushing him towards the door. He backed away from them. No choice.

"Hey!" he shouted. "Hey! I'm coming out! Don't hit me! I'm coming out! I'm not armed or anything, I swear! But I have to come out!"

A loud laugh answered him. Then, "You'd better crawl, mister. You'd better crawl out of there."

Hank stared through the doorway, straining to see who was there. "I'm not crawling!"

"Then burn, fella. Your life is not worth a damned thing to me."

Something singed his elbow. With a shout of fear and rage, Hank jerked off his jacket and threw it on the floor, aware that the sleeve of his shirt was smoking. "I'm coming out!" he shouted in desperation. He dropped to his hands and knees. "I'm crawling out!"

Even on his hands and knees, Hank was out of the building in a matter of seconds. He leapt over Tom and Edgar who lay, unmoving, on the ground. Still in forward motion, over which he had little control, Hank felt someone grab his shirt collar and haul him to his feet. Then he felt cold metal through his shirt as he was pushed roughly over the hood of a car and searched. Handcuffs dug painfully into his wrists, and he was shoved through an open door. It was a police car and, thank god, it wasn't on fire. Hank looked up to see a massive woman standing by the door, a huge grin on her face. She held a stick of some sort in her hands. She leaned forward and studied him for a moment.

"You know, I'm almost sorry you didn't come out of there standing on your feet. It would've given me the greatest of pleasure to help you join your friends." Then she laughed and walked away in the company of a serious-looking young officer.

Hank began to tremble. He was cold. And he was scared. He could go to jail for a long time for arson. At the very least, they would kick him off the force. Trying to get hold of himself, he began mentally running down his list of contacts. Someone could help him. Someone. He had to get his story straight, make it look like it was all Tom and Edgar. Think, he told himself silently. *Think!*

JESSIE STUDIED THE RUINS. That was already how she mentally thought of the business. It was still smoking, even though the fire had been put out twelve hours ago. The insurance claims adjuster was supposed to meet her there at ten o'clock. She had a few minutes left to wait.

There was a detached calm to her as she walked slowly around the building. Maybe if the police department had called a fire unit when they received the emergency call, maybe then the place could have been saved. If, if, if. If wouldn't buy her a thing. It would take a while to get a settlement. What would she do now? What would Laura do? The business was a total loss. Between the fire itself and the water damage nothing could be salvaged. She poked at the smoking rubble with the toe of her shoe. She had cried last night. No tears today. Today, she needed to think.

Kate stayed a discreet distance away, unwilling to let Jessie out of her sight. She remembered the expression on

Jessie's face when they had arrived the night before only a few seconds after the fire department, the look as Jessie helplessly watched the fire, the look of utter horror and terror as Jessie saw the faces of the men who had done this damage. Kate had thought Jessie was going to faint and had grabbed her fearfully. All Jessie could get out was "those men, those men," over and over until Kate finally understood: they were the men who had beaten and raped her. At that, Kate and Val had taken Jessie to the car to wait.

The police had insisted that Moon and Laura come to the station with them so they could give statements. Two of the men who started the fire had to be taken to the hospital. The other had shot looks of complete hatred at them through the window of the police car. Jessie had also gone to the police station, although the officers had little to say to her once they established her identity other than that they were sorry, and that they had the men in custody with positive identification and eyewitnesses to their actually dropping the matches. Kate had stayed with Jessie while they waited for several long hours for Laura and Moon to finish giving their statements.

Then they had gone home. Jessie had not slept. She was too numb to sleep, too numb to talk. Kate had finally dropped off from sheer exhaustion on the sofa while Jessie sat in the chair smoking and drinking beer.

Laura's car pulled up, and she and Moon got out. Laura looked worried. They stood beside Kate, and the three of them watched Jessie silently for a moment.

"Is she okay?" Laura asked.

"I think so," Kate answered. "How are you holding up?"

"Tired, child. I am tired. This is bad enough. I can't even imagine what it must feel like for this to be happening to Jessie on top of everything else that's already gone down."

"It's not easy for you either," Kate said. "No," Laura agreed. "It definitely is not."

"Maybe the claim won't take too long," Moon offered. "Then you two can get set up again."

"That's what I'm hoping." Laura did not look convinced.

"I am so glad the police caught those three guys last night. They were the same three men who beat up and raped Jessie. And one of them is a cop."

Moon looked hard at Kate. "Really?"

"Yeah."

"If I had known that," Moon said softly, "I would've hit them even harder. And I sure would've nailed that last one, too."

The look on Kate's face was puzzled. "What are you talking about?"

Laura smiled, nudging Moon with her elbow. "This one got to play out one of her lifelong fantasies last night. She got to pole-ax two of those three men."

"Pole-ax? I don't get it."

"Simple. I waited outside the door with an ax handle. I got the first guy right in the ribs. I got the second guy right over the top of the head. And I made the third guy crawl out on all fours to keep me from popping him, too. And woman, it felt soooo good."

"You're the one who laid them out?"

None of them had heard Jessie's approach. She stared at Moon, the beginnings of a delighted smile playing across her face. "You did that, all by yourself?"

"With unlimited pleasure."

"Moon, you absolutely amaze me sometimes. Why don't you let me buy you and Laura a drink tonight?"

"You got it. Well, I think that's your man over there. He's got the looks of an insurance guy."

Jessie and Laura both grinned as they turned and walked towards a young man in a grey overcoat. Moon glanced at Kate.

"Let's wait in the car. It's freezing out here."

16

THE ROOM WAS CROWDED and conversation was animated as Jessie pushed her way through to the kitchen. Val had said she wanted a good party for the solstice, and it looked like she was getting her wish. Kate was operating the tap on the beer keg and gestured to Jessie, asking if she wanted a refill. Jessie shook her head. She had been drinking entirely too much over the past four months. She needed to cut down.

Jessie was enjoying herself in spite of her earlier doubts about being in a party mood. The thought of so many women crowding her home had been disturbing at first. But she had loosened up as the evening progressed, talking with many women she rarely saw anywhere other than parties. And even though she still didn't quite feel fit enough to dance, it was very pleasant to watch everyone else.

Jessie found an ashtray and worked her way back through the crowd into the living room. Leaning against the stair railing, she smoked and indulged the moment of isolation in the middle of the crowd. She remembered the other parties she had come to in this house. And she felt like an entirely different woman.

Kate's mouth was warm on her ear. "Want to dance with me?"

Someone had put a slow record on the stereo, a pace Jessie felt she could handle. She smiled at Kate.

"Sure," she answered.

They found an unoccupied corner and moved slowly together, enjoying the closing feeling, the gentle touching of their bodies. Jessie pulled Kate closer to her, letting her lead as she leaned into her, content to close her eyes and follow. It was odd to Jessie that they danced together so well. They rarely went dancing and when they did, it was at the bar, where disco music pulsated.

Jessie concentrated on the rhythm of Kate's body, the slow sway and slight dip, the feeling of Kate's breasts against her own. It was only when they danced that Jessie was ever really aware that they were almost exactly the same height. Jessie relaxed, letting the sensual closeness seep into her, feeling her body warm and begin to open to Kate. She did not open her eyes, afraid that the feeling would go away if she acknowledged the surroundings. It seemed like a long time since she had felt like this.

Kate felt the change, too. She breathed lightly into Jessie's ear, holding her close, her hands pressed firmly against the small of Jessie's back. She wanted to whisk her away to some private corner. But instead she danced, barely moving, all her attention locked onto the woman she held against her.

The sudden shift to hard-driving disco music momentarily stunned them both, abruptly breaking the mood between them. Jessie stepped back with a rueful grin.

"I think I need to put a little distance between me and this music for a while," she said.

Kate glanced uncertainly at the door. "I would suggest a walk, but it's awfully cold out there."

"I was thinking I would just go up to my room for a little while." Jessie practically had to shout to be heard over the music. She wondered how long the neighbors would be willing to put up with the noise before starting to complain.

"Oh," was all Kate said. "You could come with me."

Kate grinned. "I would like to."

Jessie grabbed her hand and they went up the stairs hastily, both vibrating from the noise neither was used to or particularly cared for. It was not completely quiet in Jessie's room, but the decibel level was lowered considerably when she closed the door. Jessie carefully locked it behind her and smiled at Kate.

"I've already tried to come up here once before, and there were two women in here obviously also seeking privacy."

"Bet they weren't happy to see you."

Jessie laughed and pointed at the rumpled bed. "I don't think they even noticed me."

Kate laughed, too, as she dropped onto the foot of the bed. "This is much better. The noise was getting to me."

"I liked dancing with you. I wouldn't have minded if they had played another slow song."

Kate looked at Jessie, very much aware that they were talking to one another like women just getting to know each other, almost like they were seeing each other for the first time. It felt odd, but it was not completely unexpected. It was also obvious to Kate that Jessie was feeling somewhat shy and uncertain.

Very slowly, without touching her with her hands, Kate kissed Jessie. Kate felt the tension in her own body, but she held it firmly at bay, knowing that if Jessie sensed it, she might pull away. Finally, she lifted her hands to Jessie's shoulders, then ran them lightly down her arms, softly crossing the palms of Jessie's hands. Kate moved more firmly into the kiss, and she rested her hands on Jessie's thighs, unmoving for a long moment. She slowly began to unbutton the younger woman's shirt, pausing to touch soft flesh as her fingers moved upward.

The tremors that ran through Jessie were only partly desire. She fought the momentary surges of fear, wanting Kate and afraid at the same time. She tried to rationalize the fear away. But it wouldn't leave.

As they lay back on the bed, Kate leaned over Jessie and kissed her eyelids. "What do you want me to do?" she whispered. "Go very slow. And keep your hands where I can see them."

"I love you, Jessie."

Jessie's eyes opened, and she looked at Kate. "Touch me."

Kate had never been so aware of every movement, every gesture, as she was then. When she eased Jessie's clothes off, she saw that her hands were trembling. She did as she was asked; she moved slowly, gently, carefully keeping her hands where Jessie could see them. When she finally slipped to her knees on the floor and pressed her mouth against Jessie, she reached up Jessie's body to cup her breasts. Then she slowly savored the taste and the smell of her, fighting the urge to cry.

JESSIE WAITED FOR HER breathing to return to normal, her fingers still locked in Kate's hair, Kate's face against her thigh. She tugged lightly at Kate's hair, urging her upward, but Kate didn't move. Then Jessie felt tears against her leg, and she sat up abruptly, pulling Kate's face up so she could see her.

"What is it? What's wrong?"

"Nothing's wrong," Kate managed to say. "I didn't think you would ever want me to love you again."

Jessie wrapped her arms around Kate and rocked her slowly.

"I wasn't sure you would ever want to," she whispered.

ONE OF THE YOUNG graduate student interns was waiting for Kate as she entered the office and immediately dropped into the chair. Five hours of sleep. Her eyes felt swollen and gritty.

Betsy waited silently, just inside the door, wanting Kate to notice her before she spoke. It was a habit that grated on Kate's nerves. She sighed softly.

"What is it, Betsy?"

"A woman came in here early this morning with two children. She's in the living room. The kids are still asleep, I think. All she would tell me was her first name and the names of the two kids and that she has to stay here. She says she can't leave this building or he, presumably her husband, might see her. No. She said he might kill her. She won't answer any questions. I thought maybe you could get more out of her since I'm not having any luck."

Kate almost groaned from tiredness. She had come in hoping almost desperately for a quiet, uneventful day, and wanting there to be someone who could take her place for a few days. She rose and retrieved the white index card from Betsy's hand without a glance at what was written on it.

"I wish these women who come here would realize that we have responsibilities and procedures and that they can't come in and expect us to change everything just for them. I mean, we're supposed to keep records. It's necessary to have records. We can't change everything to make one woman happy."

Kate stared at her. "I can't believe you said that."

"Women like her are a lot of trouble. They just plain make trouble for everyone. I have a job to do, and she's not making it easy for me to do it. I tried to tell her that but she . . ."

Kate looked at the card. On it, Betsy had written, Name: Beth. 2 male children, app. 6 and 8 yrs. old. Names: Mark and Timmy. Client refused to give any additional info. Withdrawn and uncooperative.

Kate glanced at her as she ripped the card in half and headed towards the door. "You have a lot to learn."

"But . . ." Betsy sputtered.

"I'll talk to you later," Kate snapped as she left the room.

KATE LEANED BACK in the armchair and studied the small woman seated on the sofa. One child sat beside her, a sullen expression on his face. The other boy, obviously younger, sat on the floor playing with a small car.

The woman had not told her much other than she was running away from an extremely violent husband who beat her up frequently and that he had been arrested for something the woman would not reveal.

"Beth, I'm assuming you live here in Durham. Is that true?" Beth eyed her nervously.

"What difference does it make?"

"You say your husband beat you up, that he's in jail right now, but that he might be out soon. You also say you're afraid he might kill you if he finds you. The reason I asked was because I'm wondering if you think there's a chance he might find out where this shelter is located and come here looking for you. We have several women in the area who have opened their homes for us to use as hideaways for other women who are critically endangered until we can make arrangements to get them out of this area. If you feel your husband might come here looking for you, I can . . ."

"No," Beth interrupted. "I want to stay here. I couldn't go to a complete stranger's home."

Kate knew not to push. "That's fine. It's completely your decision to make, however you feel the most comfortable. Let me tell you a little bit about the shelter. Usually, women stay here for not more than ten days. By then, we normally have had the time to make arrangements for them to go elsewhere, or they leave on their own. There are three women living here now. One of them also has a son so your boys will have some company for a while." Kate shifted her position slightly. "There's food in the kitchen, and you can prepare your own meals. There's no one to do the cooking or the cleaning up, so we ask that you do the dishes and put things away after you finish. There's also a washing machine. There's no dryer, but there is a line out back. The telephone is for local calls only. If you need to make a long-distance call, you'll have to see one of the staff members."

"I don't know anyone long distance," Beth said softly.

"Okay. The only other thing I can think to tell you has to do with leaving the shelter. We ask that you do not leave. But if you must, then please tell us that you are leaving, where you are going, and when you expect to return. That way we'll know whether or not we should be worried if you aren't back in what we consider to be a reasonable amount of time."

"Not so very many rules," Beth commented. "We don't need rules."

Beth stared at her for a moment. "Ha ... my husband," she corrected herself quickly, "he had a rule for everything ... And he was always changing them without telling me."

"Well, we don't do that here. I'll show you to your rooms. There's a radio and television upstairs, but you'll need to work out the use of them with the other women. We don't get involved in any disputes between women who are staying here unless it's absolutely impossible for you to settle it yourselves. You can sleep as late as you like, stay up as late as you like, eat whenever you like. One other thing. Since the kitchen is downstairs, you'll probably be downstairs fairly frequently. Refuge is staffed at all times, mostly with volunteers. The door stays locked. Please do not open it for anyone, most especially not for men. Some women's lives may depend on your following this rule. If anyone comes to the door, call a staff member immediately. This rule is the one we are rigid about. It's for everyone's safety. Okay?"

Beth nodded. Kate rose from the chair and led Beth and her sons to the stairway.

BETH UNPACKED HER SUITCASE, carefully arranging her clothes in the drawer. Underwear was meticulously folded and placed in the order in which Beth put them on. Two sweaters went into the next drawer. Hesitating, Beth stared at the third and fourth drawers. She had always only had two for herself, the bottom two. Hank hated to have to bend down for his clothes. She didn't really have enough to warrant using a third drawer. Then, with a quick gesture, she pulled the drawer open and placed her nightgown and a sweater side by side. She closed it gently and glanced around her as though half expecting someone to question or reprove her.

Timmy sat on the edge of Beth's bed, his face drawn into a scowl as he swung his legs back and forth and stared at the floor. Beth tried to ignore him, hoping he would go back into the next room and unpack without having to be reminded.

"I don't want to stay here," he said finally, his eyes defiant as he glared at his mother.

"I know you don't."

"Then why do I have to?" he demanded.

Beth sighed as she glanced at him. She continued to put clothes on hangers and place them in the tiny closet. "Because we have no other place to go, Timmy."

Mark looked up from his play in the corner. "It's nice here. I like it."

Timmy looked at him disdainfully. "Ah, you don't know nothing. You're just a kid."

"Anything," Beth corrected him absently.

"I hate it when you tell me how to talk," he shot back.

Beth glanced at him again, hearing the baiting tone of his voice, knowing Timmy was spoiling for a fight. "We are going to stay here for a few days. There's no other place," she said.

"There is, too. There's home."

Mark looked at his mother in alarm. "I don't want to go home."

Timmy jumped off the bed and stood over his younger brother, hands on hips. "We got a home and that's where we're supposed to be."

"I've already explained this to you, Timmy. There's no reason to get into it again."

"Is my daddy in jail? Was that woman down there saying the truth?"

Beth nodded. "Yes. Your daddy is in jail. He did a very bad thing, and they put him in jail."

"But you said he would be out soon. Maybe even today," he persisted.

"That's right."

"Then we should be home when he gets there. Dad's gonna be real mad if he gets home and we aren't there."

"I'll bet he will be," Beth said softly, "but he would be just as mad if we were. Your dad is mad all the time, Timmy. It doesn't matter what we do for him. There's nothing I can do about it."

Timmy's eyes danced as he contemplated Beth, obviously enjoying the moment. "You'll be in a lot of trouble if he gets there, and there's no supper, and the house is dark, and we're gone. He'll be madder than ever then. He'll come looking for us."

Beth turned back to him. "Timmy, I asked you to unpack your things and put them away. Do that now, please."

"Don't you tell me what to do!" he shouted angrily.

"And don't you raise your voice to me, young man! Get in there and do what I told you!"

"You wouldn't do that if my daddy was here," he said, glowering at her.

Beth took a step towards him then stopped abruptly. "No, I probably wouldn't. But he's not here and I am. Do what I told you to do. Now, Timmy Parrish. And not another word."

Timmy stalked past her and went into the adjoining room, slamming the door behind him. Beth sat down on the edge of the bed, her body leaning forward, her hands over her face.

She could feel herself trembling as she rocked slowly to and fro. Then she felt a small hand on her arm.

"Are you crying, Mom?" Mark asked.

"No, honey. I'm not crying. I just don't like to fight with your brother. I don't like to fight with anyone."

"Mom? Will you hold me?"

Beth looked at him. "Are you scared?" Mark nodded. "A little."

"So am I," she sighed. Beth reached out and pulled him onto her lap, wrapping her arms around him and holding him close, her chin resting on the top of his head. He curled in her arms, almost like he had done when he was a baby. If only she had been able to raise them alone, maybe things would be different with Timmy. He had once been like Mark, soft and gentle, sweet as daybreak. Then Hank got hold of him. Beth kissed Mark's hair and set him on his feet.

"You'd better go help your brother unpack the suitcase. It's not fair for him to have to do it all."

"Okay." Mark turned and walked towards the other room, his steps slow. Beth could hear the two boys talking after Mark closed the door. Then the talk escalated into shouts. Beth rose to her feet. She wished just one night would pass without the two of them having a fight about something. She waited for a moment, hoping they would settle it without her becoming involved.

" ... always get what you want ... not fair!"

"I'm the oldest ... top bunk ..."

" ... not fair! I want it!"

" ... do what I say, you little ..."

Beth could hear the sounds of the scuffle, and she turned towards the door. As she opened it, she gasped. Timmy had Mark pinned against the wall and was holding him by the collar, his fist raised in the air. He looked just like Hank, his young face twisted into an ugly, killing scowl. Hearing Beth enter, Timmy released his younger brother abruptly, giving him a warning look as Mark scampered away out of reach.

"It's okay, Mom. I'm gonna have the top bunk, aren't I, Mark?"

Mark raised a tearful face to his mother. "Do I have to let him, Mom?"

"Tonight. You can have it tomorrow night."

Mark nodded and turned away, his body slumped from her betrayal. Beth left the room. As she began to close the door, she heard Timmy's voice.

"I don't care what she says. The top bunk is mine. You try to get up there and I'll break your neck. You hear me?"

Beth closed the door. She could not listen to any more of what Timmy was saying. She was afraid she might grab him and . . . She didn't know what she might do.

Sitting down on the bed, she felt her hands tremble. "He's just like Hank," she whispered to herself.

17

HANK STOOD ON THE SIDEWALK and stared at the dark house. No wonder he hadn't been able to get Beth on the telephone. The bus ride from the police station had been terrible. Only niggers and white trash rode those damned buses.

Searching through his pockets, Hank finally located his key. There'd better be a good reason for why she wasn't home, he thought grimly to himself. Four days, four lousy days he'd spent in jail and not a word from her. His wife, for god's sake, hadn't even come to see him, hadn't even come to help get him released. None of the other officers would look at him or talk to him. If it hadn't been for his friends, he might still be there. Hank thrust the door open and stepped inside, fumbling for a light switch.

"Beth!" he yelled, kicking the door closed. No one was there. He turned on lights as he went through the house. Everything was neat and clean. No note. Nothing. Maybe she had just gone to her mother's for a while.

Hank peered into the kitchen. The dishes were washed and put away. Only one cup sat in the spotless sink. He walked down the hall. The boys' rooms were empty, the beds made.

Puzzled, Hank went into the bedroom he shared with Beth. It was also neat and clean, like she expected to be back any moment. Suddenly suspicious, Hank opened the closet door. Beth's clothes were gone. Cursing loudly, he yanked open drawers. Empty. He charged into Timmy's room. Gone. Beth had left and had taken the kids. Momentarily stunned, Hank sat on the edge of his oldest son's bed and stared at the floor. Where would she have gone?

He went back to the kitchen and took a beer from the refrigerator. Lighting a cigarette, he tried to think. She wouldn't have gone to her mother's house. It would be too easy for him to find her there. She had no friends, no place to hide out. Where could she have gone?

Hank drank steadily for nearly an hour, his mind plunging from Beth to his own plight. He could deal with Beth later. And he would deal with her, he thought, his eyes narrowing. She had some fucking nerve trying to leave him. She would never leave him. If anybody walked around here, he would be the one doing the walking.

He stubbed out his cigarette into the rapidly filling ashtray. That goddamned Jessie Pyne had come to the police station the day after they had busted him for the fire and had gotten him on the beating and rape thing, too. Got Tom and Edgar. From what Hank had been able to gather, whoever that broad with the ax handle had been had really done a number on Tom, broke nine ribs clean as a whistle. Edgar was okay, just a concussion. Hank was glad they were in the hospital. It was easier for him to think and plan with them out of the way.

Hank ran through the options. They had them clean on the fire. Eyewitnesses and everything. But the other ... that was Jessie Pyne's word against theirs. Quickly, Hank went through his mental list of friends and allies. He could set it up with some of his buddies to get them all covered for the night they had surprised that little cunt outside her shop. They would swear on a stack of bibles that Hank had been with them all evening. Hank smiled. That's what friends were for. And besides, some of them owed him. He had saved their asses often enough. He would have to think about the arson charge later. That one was harder. He had no ideas. He would just stick to his story that he had seen the two men inside and had gone in to investigate. Hell, cops stood by each other. It would work. It had to.

Hank was scared. It made him angry because he wasn't used to being scared. His wife had run off on him. He was suspended from the force. His stomach rumbled with hunger. She should be here to make dinner. When he finally got his hands on her, he would teach her a lesson she would never forget. If she thought he had been tough before, just let her see how really tough he could be. He jerked open the refrigerator and took out coldcuts. Snorting with disgust, he made a sandwich and wolfed it down hastily. A sandwich for supper! No matter what a man had done, he deserved a hot meal when he came home.

Hank turned off the lights and went back to the bedroom. He had phone calls to make, and he needed some sleep. He hadn't slept much in four days. It was hard to sleep in the lock-up. Too much noise and too many interruptions. Stripping down to his underwear, Hank sat on the edge of the bed and reached for the telephone. A slip of paper caught his eye. Still in the process of dialing, he picked it up. It was torn from the newspaper. SHELTER FOR BATTERED WOMEN OPEN IN DURHAM.

Hank replaced the receiver as he scanned the article quickly. . . . the location of the shelter is not being revealed . . . arrangements have been made . . . law enforcement officials will provide information about and transport to the shelter any woman and/or child who needs a place to stay until . . . Maybe that's where she went, Hank thought to himself. A smile crossed his face as he picked up the telephone and dialed.

"Sergeant Bill Davis, please," he said. As he waited, Hank lit a cigarette and grinned. Thought she'd get away, did she? "Bill? Hank Parrish . . . Yeah, a bit of trouble but I'm not too worried about it . . . I appreciate that a lot. Listen, I need some information. My old lady took a walk while I was locked up, and I think she might have gone to that new shelter for women. Can you give me that address? I want to go down there and talk to her . . . That's great. Sure, I'll wait. Thanks, Bill."

JESSIE TURNED UP THE COLLAR of her coat and shoved her gloved hands deep in her pocket. The wind off the ocean was icy. The sea was grey-green with winter and an approaching storm, and she and Kate had the entire beach to themselves.

The wind made it hard for them to talk so they walked silently, their shoulders touching, until they came back to the cutoff back to the motel. There were not shells to gather; the roughness of the surf pounded them nearly to dust before they ever reached the shore.

Jessie shed the layers of clothes, the heat of the room oppressive after the cold outside. Kate stood by the stove, dicing vegetables for stew. The tiny efficiency apartment had been incredibly cheap to rent in December, but Jessie was willing to bet the price tripled when tourist season arrived.

"Can I help?" she asked as she crossed the room.

"Nope," Kate answered with a shake of her head. "It won't take but a few minutes. Then we just have to let it cook for a while."

Jessie sat down at the table, propping her feet in the chair opposite her.

"It feels good to be away for a while," she said.

"I know," Kate agreed, wiping her hands on a paper towel as she reached for the carrots and onions.

"Why don't you let me cut up the onions?" Kate grinned. "Okay."

Jessie sat upright and began to peel. The onions were strong. Within seconds, she could feel the build-up of tears in her eyes. "I'm glad you suggested this."

"So am I. I wasn't sure I could get someone to cover for me, especially after Betsy left the shelter in such a huff. We can't afford to lose people, but I'm glad she left."

"Why?" Jessie asked, wiping her eyes gingerly on the flannel sleeve of her shirt.

"Her attitude. She was so caught up in the bureaucracy of the shelter that she didn't see the women as human beings. They were people to be catalogued, and she got pretty hot if they didn't cooperate with her paperwork. She seemed very judgmental about the women, sometimes almost like she thought they had gotten what they deserved, like she didn't always believe them. She never said that outright, but there was just something about her attitude that conveyed it. Anyway, after that last woman came to the shelter and Betsy labeled her 'uncooperative' on her card, I lost my temper. It was obvious that the woman was terrified and worried that her husband might try to kill her if he found her. It seemed completely understandable to me that she wouldn't want to give out much information about herself. She had no reason to consider us trustworthy. We're perfect strangers to her."

"Why did Betsy think she was being uncooperative?" Jessie sniffed, her nose beginning to run from the onions.

"Because all she would give us was her first name and the first names of her two boys. Nothing more. Absolutely nothing. I guess it messed up Betsy's system of order and paperwork. It's true that we do have to keep records. But identities are not part of those records. Actually, we have to keep statistics, and we can gather those without knowing a single name. I was never quite able to get that across to Betsy."

Jessie rose and added the pile of chopped onions to the simmering stew. She was hungry, wanting dinner to be ready instantly. Peering inside the refrigerator, she took out the cheese and began slicing it. Putting it on a plate and adding crackers, she opened two beers, then set everything on the table. Kate washed her hands and sat down next to Jessie, reaching hungrily for the food.

"This was a good idea. I don't think I could just wait for the stew to cook. It'll take at least a couple of hours."

Jessie grinned at her as she ate. Kate's appetite never ceased to amaze her.

She sat quietly beside Kate, comfortable with the small talk and the silence. Things felt more natural, more normal, between them now. It was a relief to Jessie. She didn't feel like she was always fighting a battle. She sipped her beer and relaxed. Coming to the beach was a good idea. They both needed the rest, and they needed time alone together, away from interruptions and responsibilities.

"Are you still wanting just a part-time job?" Kate asked. Jessie nodded, "Yeah. I may have to take something full time though. The college students have most of the part-time jobs already."

"If the insurance company would just get it together and pay off."

Jessie smiled. "That would help. Laura and I are still trying to decide if we want to attempt to set up the business again. It was wearing us both out completely. Laura likes the temporary typesetting jobs she's gotten, says it leaves her with enough free time to feel like a human being. So I don't know what we'll do. I think we're sort of waiting until after the trial, to see what happens."

Kate was silent for a moment. "You had nightmares again last night."

"I know."

"Do you remember what you dream?" Jessie nodded. "Yes."

"They'll go away eventually, Jessie."

"Did yours?"

"Pretty much. I still have them once in a while but not often."

"How long?" Jessie watched her face. Kate looked at her. "A long time."

"I thought so."

"But I never talked to anyone about what happened to me," Kate said. "I've often wondered if the dreams would've gone away sooner if I could've talked about it all."

"I called Carol Sloane last week. I have an appointment with her for next Tuesday."

"I thought you didn't want to see a therapist," Kate said, surprised.

"I didn't. But I need some help that I don't think I can get from friends. I ran into Leslie the other day, and she asked how I was. When I said fine, she asked if I wasn't furious? I realized that I have felt almost no anger. So I called Carol. I walk around feeling like I want to cry all the time. I get uneasy talking to my friends constantly. I get tired of hearing me say the same things over and over."

"Well, I'm glad you called her."

"I think I am, too. I'll let you know after I've seen her a couple of times."

Jessie's expression was reflective. Kate watched her for a moment, then asked quietly, "What is it, Jess?"

"One of the reasons I hesitated calling Carol at first," Jessie said slowly, "was because she is a straight woman. I was worried that I couldn't talk to her about this."

"Why would that matter?"

"I know it shouldn't matter. I guess it does because those men knew they were raping a lesbian. They made sure I knew that. That was a big part of it for them. Except for one guy."

Jessie rose and went to the stove, stirring the pot of stew. Kate watched her, trying to phrase her next question carefully. Jessie still had not told her exactly what had happened. She had gotten what information she had from Val.

"What about that one guy?"

Jessie leaned against the stove and folded her arms over her chest, a frown furrowing her face. "A lot of what happened is still foggy to me. I remember lying there on the ground. I was hurting so much, I just wanted them to get it over with and go away. I don't think I had considered that they might kill me. I'm not sure it even mattered at that point. One of the men, the one called Hank, I don't think he actually raped me. It might have been my imagination, or maybe the pain level was already so high I just couldn't feel anymore. But I could almost swear he was faking it."

"Does that make you feel he was less guilty?"

Jessie shook her head immediately. "No way. I feel the same about him as I do about the other two. If he didn't actually rape me, I know he would have if he could have gotten it up. And if my perception of what happened is indeed accurate, he went through a pretty elaborate hoax to convince the other guys that he was in on it."

"Did he hit you?"

"No. One guy did all the hitting. Tom. He was the one who got his ribs broken by Moon. I have to admit that I never thought I would enjoy, even a little, seeing another human being hurt. But I didn't mind a bit when they carried those two off on stretchers."

"If Laura and Moon hadn't been there, they might've gotten away completely."

"Probably. But there's a huge part of me that really wishes I had been the one holding the ax handle when they came through the door."

Kate nodded. "I can understand that. I'm really glad you decided to go down and swear out warrants on all of them for what they did to you."

"Well, the cops weren't completely convinced, especially since that guy Hank turned out to be a cop himself. The hospital records are probably the only thing that will ever get it to court."

"You know," Kate mused quietly, "I overheard the new woman at the shelter tell one of the other women that her husband beat her with the buckle-end of a leather belt in addition to using his fists."

"And they wonder why women sometimes kill their husbands." With a snort, Jessie turned back to the pot of stew. Kate watched her, her mind dwelling on the small, nervous woman who was now living in the shelter.

"She won't really talk much to anyone," Kate said. "I mean Beth, the new woman. She keeps to herself, stays with her kids mostly. One of those boys, the younger one, is really a sweetie. The other one, Timmy, gives me chills. Unreasonable as it may sound, I don't turn my back on him when he's around."

"Trust your instincts," Jessie said as she reached over Kate for her cigarettes. "Who knows what sort of life he's led or what he's seen? He might just be scared to death, but I don't think being cautious around him is paranoid."

"The little one, Mark, came into the office yesterday and wanted to know if he could look at the books. I showed him a carton of kids books we got in a while ago and haven't had time to put on the shelves. He got out a stack and curled up in the chair in the corner and read for hours. I almost didn't know he was there. He and his brother are completely different."

"But how will they grow up?"

"I know," Kate sighed, "But I can keep hoping that somewhere along the line, women will be able to change their sons, that there can be a different kind of man."

"Not in our lifetimes."

"Maybe not. But women still give birth to sons, and there's nothing anyone can do about it except try to help affect that change from the moment they come into the world."

"Maybe," Jessie said, only half-believing or wanting to understand.

"JESSIE, I HAVE A GREAT IDEA." Kate sat on the edge of the bed, holding a steaming cup of coffee in her hands. Jessie groaned and opened one eye.

"I'm asleep," she mumbled, pulling the covers over her head.

"No, you're not. I just woke you up. I have an idea about a temporary job for you." Kate pulled the covers down so she could see Jessie's face. "Aren't you even going to listen?"

"How long have you been up?" Jessie asked in a whisper. "About an hour."

"Well, I haven't. I'm not awake. I haven't even had any coffee yet."

Kate pressed the cup into Jessie hands. "Here. Take this one. I can get more."

Jessie forced herself to sit upright, balancing the coffee precariously as she tried to shove a pillow behind her back. It was chilly in the room. She pulled the covers up under her chin and sipped the hot liquid from the cup. Kate returned with her own coffee and sat down once again.

"Want to hear my idea?" she asked. "Sure," Jessie muttered into her cup.

"We just got a building fund at the shelter, for repairs and things like that. There's enough money in it to pay someone for part-time temporary work to get things fixed around the place. It's not a whole lot, a few hundred dollars, but there's enough work and enough money to keep you busy for a while."

"I'm not a carpenter, Kate."

"We don't need a carpenter. We need someone who knows how to do things practically and cheaply. You know that. Part of that money may have to go for materials, too, not just for labor. Maybe by the time you finished at the shelter, the insurance money will have come through for you and Laura. Well, what do you think?"

Jessie looked at her. "I think I see potential for an endless number of problems."

"Why?" Kate asked, her voice puzzled.

Jessie climbed out of bed and began to put on her clothes, fully awake much more quickly than was usual for her. "The main reason is that we are lovers."

"I don't understand what that has to do with anything. This is a business arrangement."

"Come on, Kate. Think about it. I would, in effect, be working for you. You would be my boss, for crying out loud. It wouldn't work. I'm not saying I'm not touched that you thought this up with me in mind but I don't think . . ."

"There's got to be a way we can think up somehow to make this work."

Jessie only half-listened to Kate's jumbled sentence. "Well, I can't think of a way right offhand."

"I don't like thinking that the fact we're lovers should influence this."

"Maybe it would be a little easier for you to understand if you were at the receiving end rather than being the one to make the offer. It gives me the shakes just to think about it." Jessie pulled the grey top to her sweat suit over her head, still shivering a little. "Well, it's only a suggestion right now anyway. I don't administer the building fund."

"Who does?"

"Carla. After all, she's donating it."

"So I wouldn't be working for you? I would be working for her?"

"I think so."

Jessie considered it for a moment. Doing off jobs at the shelter was a much more enjoyable thought than going back into a male-controlled printing business, even briefly. "I might consider working for Carla. Provided," she added in a definite tone of voice, "you kept strictly out of it and that we did not discuss it outside the shelter."

Kate grinned delightedly. "Deal! I'll talk to Carla as soon as we get back."

18

KATE CIRCLED THE PLAYGROUND, one hand shielding her eyes from the sun as she peered at the children milling around the swings. No sign of him. She hadn't the vaguest idea where he could have gone. Beth had been no help, saying she didn't think Timmy knew his way around at all. He could be anywhere. Probably trying to find his way home.

"Lost someone, Kate?"

"Betsy!" Kate said, surprised to see her.

"I was just on my way to talk with you, Kate."

"Good. I'm looking for one of Beth's boys. I could use a little help."

"Timmy?"

"That's the one." Kate was exasperated. "Did he run away?"

"He sure did. We don't have any idea where he could be so we're just sort of combing the area hoping we'll spot him."

"I'll keep an eye out, too."

Kate looked at her. "Thanks, Betsy."

Kate watched the younger woman as Betsy strolled off. The new semester had begun. Maybe that's why Betsy looked so tired. Damn him, Kate thought angrily. She had better things to do than freeze to death looking for a nasty-tempered little boy. The trial started tomorrow. Turning, she headed back across the playground. Maybe someone had found him already.

Betsy spotted him near the restrooms. Casually, she pulled her cap lower so he couldn't see her face and then slowly ambled in his direction.

Timmy sat on the ground. He was tired. He didn't know which way to go to get home. He could ask a policeman; they were supposed to help if you were lost. But if his daddy was in trouble and in jail, maybe he shouldn't talk to a policeman. And those women from that place were all looking for him. He'd seen them, all right. He watched the large city buses go by. He wondered if he got on and told the driver he was lost if the driver would take him home? But buses cost money, didn't they? He felt his pockets. No money. Not even a penny. But maybe if he was lost . . . Maybe if he cried and everything. He wasn't far from crying anyway.

"Hi, Timmy."

The voice in his ear almost scared him to death. He tried to get up, but his legs just wouldn't work. Then a firm hand caught his shoulder and held him still.

"I know you ran away. I know you hate that place. But your mom is probably worried sick, and you have to go back. Now you can either walk with me, or I can carry you. Your choice."

He looked up at Betsy. "My mom doesn't miss me. She has Mark."

"Mark isn't you."

"She loves him best anyway."

"Why do you think that?"

"I can tell." His voice was defiant, but his eyes were uncertain.

"How?" Betsy sat down beside him, seeming relaxed as she broke off a blade of grass and shoved it into her mouth. But she was watching him very carefully, ready to grab him if he tried to bolt away.

"The way she treats him. She's always hugging him and kissing him. She's always nice to him. She's never nice to me."

"Are you ever nice to her?"

Timmy stared at her and began to frown. "I want to go home. I want to go home to my dad. He loves me best. He said so. He says Mark is a sissy and Mom spoils him. Dad says I'm a man, tough like him." His look dared Betsy to challenge him.

Betsy shook her head. "Even men need to be loved and hugged sometimes, Timmy."

"Not my dad," he boasted. "He's the toughest. He don't need that sissy stuff. I don't want to be like Mark. Dad says that if I'm like Mark, I'll grow up to be a faggot."

Betsy blinked, her composure momentarily challenged. Her eyes narrowed as she contemplated the boy beside her. "Do you know what a faggot is?"

"Not exactly. But I do know it's almost as bad as being a nigger! And nobody wants to be a nigger. Or a faggot," he added quickly.

"Where on earth did you learn to talk like that?" Betsy asked incredulously.

"My dad. He says . . ."

Betsy stood up abruptly. "I think I've heard all about your dad that I can stand. Do you also know that your dad beats up your mom? What do you think about that?"

Timmy glared up at her. "Dad says . . ."

"That's it. Let's go." Betsy grabbed his arm and hauled him to his feet. "March, young man. And not another word out of you."

BETSY LOCKED THE DOOR behind her and watched Timmy run up the stairs, taking the steps two at a time. Kate touched Betsy's shoulder briefly. "Thank you. Where did you find him?"

"Outside the restrooms on the other side of the park. After talking to him, I really feel sorry for Beth."

"Why is that?"

"The kid's old man is obviously one of the worst examples of a bigoted human being who ever walked the earth, and that little boy worships the ground he walks on. 'My dad says' this and 'my dad says' that. I couldn't believe what I was hearing. His father told him that if he let his mother hold him or hug him that he would grow up to be a faggot." Betsy followed Kate into the office and accepted the cup of coffee Kate handed to her. "When I asked him what a faggot was, he didn't know, but he said his dad had told him it was almost as bad as being a nigger. Can you believe that?"

"I can believe almost anything. I'm glad you found him."

"This time. But how are you going to keep him here?"

"A locksmith is coming tomorrow. We're going to have a deadbolt lock put on the door that has to be opened with a key. We should have done that a long time ago."

Betsy sat down and sipped her coffee. "That sounds like a good idea. All you have to do now is keep him in until the locksmith gets here."

Kate smiled wryly. "And that should keep us all quite busy for the next twenty-four hours."

It was quiet in the tiny office as Betsy drank her coffee and Kate smoked, staring through the window. Betsy sat her cup down on the desk and watched Kate for a moment.

"Kate, what would you say if I told you that I want to come back to Refuge to finish up my internship?"

Kate met her gaze evenly. "I guess I would ask you why."

"I want to be here."

"That's not enough, Betsy. You know that. These women come here, needing desperately to trust someone. They have to know we are on their side, that we believe them, that we don't hold them responsible for what has happened to them regardless of circumstances. This place is usually a last resort for women. They don't come here if they have any sort of alternative. The women are more important than any records or forms or statistics."

Betsy leaned forward. "Kate, I know that, in my head at least. But we are raised not to believe it. We are told over and over to doubt ourselves, our perceptions. We are taught to hate each other, to compete with each other, and always, always, to consider each other liars. A lot of that has to be unlearned. I know when I doubt another woman that a large part of the doubt comes from that conditioning."

"But the women at Refuge are not at a place in their lives where they can educate you, Betsy."

"I don't expect them to. But I've got a lot to learn, and un-learn, and some of that process can happen by just being here and listening."

Kate was still dubious. "I don't know . . ."

"Can we just try it? I don't even mind a probationary pe-riod." Kate laughed. "Well, I certainly do. I object a lot to that word. Betsy, you can come back, if that's what you really want to do. But . . ."

Betsy held up her hand. "I know what that but is, Kate. You don't even have to say it."

"Okay. When will you be here?"

"When do you need me?"

"How about tomorrow? Jessie is supposed to testify at the KKK trial, and I really want to be there."

"How is she doing?"

"Scared to death."

"I'll be here."

Kate smiled at her. Tomorrow was going to be a long day.

JESSIE SAT AS QUIETLY as she could. She felt out of place in the large room, crowded by people, wearing a pantsuit that made her feel ridiculous. Her hands drummed nervously on her knee. Kate reached over and squeezed her wrist reassur-ingly. Jessie gave her a desperate look. She just wanted to get it over with.

"The state calls Jessie Pyne."

Jessie jumped when she heard her name. Kate's smile of encouragement was anything but encouraging. Kate looked sick.

Jessie started to stand up but the defense attorney rose to his feet. "Your honor, the defense requests that Jessie Pyne be excused on the grounds of extreme prejudice."

"Approach the bench," the judge said wearily, glancing at his watch. The attorney and the assistant district attorney leaned their heads close to the judge's, and all Jessie could hear were whispers. She sat down, her stomach rolling from tension.

"What is going on up there?" she whispered to Kate. "I don't know. But they have a copy of the newsletter."

The judge was indeed looking at a copy of the newsletter Jessie helped put out. She groaned audibly and wondered if they would let her leave the courtroom if she threw up. There was obviously an animated discussion going on up there, complete with hand gestures and emphatic nods of various heads. Finally, the lawyers went back to their respective places, with the defense attorney's face a study in fury. He shot Jessie a dirty look and sat down. The judge nodded to the assistant D.A.

"Call your witness."

"The state calls Jessie Pyne."

Jessie rose and walked down the short aisle.

"SO, WHAT WAS IT LIKE?" Moon demanded as soon as Jessie sat down. She took a sip from the drink Moon had ordered for her and made a face.

"What is this?"

"Take a few more sips. Then you won't care as much. Come on, Jessie. Denny and I were the only ones who couldn't be there. Tell us what happened."

Denny nodded, her glasses slipping down to the end of her nose. "Talk, Jess."

"It was terrible. I don't ever want to have to do that again."

Moon shot her a look of total exasperation. "That tells us a whole lot. Give us details, girl. The nitty-gritty. The gore. I want a blow-by-blow accounting here."

The other women at the table laughed at Moon's antics. Jessie took another sip of the drink. It was true; it didn't taste as bad now as when she first started.

"They called me, and then the defense attorney tried to have me dismissed because I was 'extremely prejudiced,' as he put it. They had this little conference with the judge, during which the guy gave the judge a copy of the newsletter to look at. But the judge said to call me anyway. Then as soon as I got up there the defense attorney asked that I be dismissed on some other grounds. I don't remember what they were. So they had another conference during which I got a lot of dirty looks. Then the judge told the jury that they were to ignore Martin's objections and told the D.A. to proceed. As soon as Parks started to ask me questions, Martin interrupted again, saying the defense needed a recess for two hours. The judge granted it."

"Yuck, Jessie," Denny said, frowning. "Sounds awful."

"It got worse. We came back after lunch, and I went back up there. Martin objected to almost every question Parks asked me. It seemed like he was trying to play on the jury. But hell, I don't know. I know nothing about law or courtrooms. But he was after my ass. I didn't realize how bad until he started to cross-examine me. He pulled every dirty trick in the book. He brought up my association with Communist coalitions. He brought up my being arrested for civil disobedience in DC. He brought up my being a lesbian, a perversion he called it. Every time he did it, Parks would object, and the judge would have it stricken from the record and told the jury to disregard it. But you could tell by the looks on their faces that they weren't about to forget one word of it."

"It was as if he were trying to prove that no matter what a bad sort his client was, Jessie was worse," Kate commented.

"He did a pretty good job of it, too."

Laura swirled her drink around in the glass. "I'll tell you what kind of lawyer he is. He's the kind that wins. If I had done something bad and I wanted to get off at all costs, he's just the sort of guy I would hire. He's dirty, unethical, and crafty—and he wins."

"Then it's over for you?" Denny asked. "That's all you have to do?"

"There's a chance I may be recalled, but it's slim. I don't want to go back. It was bad. The absolute worst thing for me is that I really think the jury will let those men go. I can't tell you exactly why I feel that way. Just the looks on their faces. They felt sorry for him, and the rest of them, too, and they hated me."

TOM SAT IN THE CHAIR, his feet propped on the coffee table.

He moved very slowly, obviously still in a great deal of pain. "So what did you come over here to tell me?" he asked.

Hank rubbed his hands together. "Charlie, Dave, and Jim are all prepared to swear in court that we were with them the night Jessie Pyne was beaten up and raped. We're covered on that one. There's no way she'll make those charges stick."

Tom eyed him. "What about the other?"

"The arson thing?"

Tom nodded coldly. "That's the one."

"I'm still working on it."

Tom leaned forward, his face white from the pain the movement cost him. "You'd better work real hard, Hank, old boy. You'd better get us out of this one."

"I didn't get us into it all by myself," he shot back defensively.

"It was your bright idea to torch the place."

"And you were all for it," Hank replied angrily.

Tom leaned back, pressing his arm to his ribs. "Well, fearless leader, you'd better come up with a real good plan for this one. You'd better get us off. Because if you don't, I'll kill you. And don't you forget that for a minute."

19

JESSIE CHECKED THE ANGLE of the cabinet door to see if it was level. It wasn't. She had put the hinges on in the wrong place. Again. Exasperated, she took the door off and laid it across the kitchen table. She had never done any repair work like this before. Why Kate had thought Jessie knew all about it was beyond her. She could build shelves, bookcases, do a pretty decent job repairing windows and frames. But she had never hung any kind of door before, not even on a cabinet.

Jessie was so caught up in measuring, she didn't hear Beth come into the kitchen. Beth hesitated in the doorway, surprised by the tools spread out all over the room.

"Excuse me," she said.

Jessie looked up. "Oh, hi. I'm just trying to fix this door. Let me know if I'm in your way and I'll move my stuff."

"I thought I might be getting in your way if I came in," Beth said softly.

"No. Come on and do whatever you need to do. I'm trying to figure out how to get this door on straight. I'm not very good at this."

Beth opened the refrigerator and took out a loaf of bread. "You look like you know what you're doing."

Jessie winked at her and grinned. "That's half the secret. I'm supposed to look like I know, even when I don't. Actually, I'm not a carpenter or a cabinetmaker. Some things I do well but I missed doors somewhere along the way." Jessie put the door back on and began to tighten down the screws, bracing the door with her elbow. She watched Beth from the corner of her eye as Beth spread peanut butter on slices of bread and then reached for jelly.

"Lunch for your kids?"

Beth nodded. "Yes. I don't feel like arguing about nutrition today. They're watching cartoons on TV, and they're quiet, and they aren't fighting. If peanut butter and jelly sandwiches will keep them that way, then peanut butter and jelly is what they will get." Smiling at Jessie, she left the room with the two saucers in her hands.

Jessie stepped down from the chair and surveyed the door. "It's straight," she muttered delightedly. She opened and closed it several times. "It's by god straight. What do you know?"

"It looks very nice for someone who says she doesn't know what she's doing." Beth had come back in and was putting away the jelly. Jessie smiled at her.

"Thank you. I was about to make some tea. Would you like some?"

A look of gratitude briefly crossed Beth's plain face. "I would love some. If it's not too much trouble."

"No trouble." Jessie set the kettle on the stove and turned on the burner. Then she began to pick up her tools, humming quietly as she loaded them back into the cardboard box that served as a tool chest. Beth sat down at the table, watching her silently. "You treat everyone around here so normally. Isn't that hard for you?"

Jessie looked at her, puzzled. "Why should it be hard? You are normal. So are the other women. It's just your circumstances and your men that aren't normal."

"The other women talk a lot about what their husbands and boyfriends do to them."

"You don't talk about it?"

Beth shook her head. "No. I'm not proud of it."

"I doubt they are either. But it's nothing to be ashamed of. You never asked for it, no matter what you did or didn't do. It's not your fault."

Beth stared at her hands. "That's hard for me to believe," she said, her tone of voice wistful. "I kept thinking, for years and years, that if I just did things better, if I were smarter, that he wouldn't hit me anymore, that he would be nice. I knew it was my fault. Other women kept their husbands happy. I never saw them with bruises or acting scared. But Ha . . . my husband was never happy."

"Maybe he was just mean," Jessie said softly as she poured boiling water into the cups. "What kind of tea do you want? I recommend the Earl Grey, with honey."

"That sounds nice," Beth answered with a smile. No one had ever made tea for her before.

"I think it's hard for women to believe that it's not their fault. But it's not." Jessie set the cups on the table and drew up a chair. "Would it bother you very much if I smoked?"

Beth looked startled, unused to being consulted. "No. Go ahead. My husband smoked. He smoked a lot. A lot bothers me."

"I used to smoke a lot, but I cut down when I was in the hospital. Almost stopped completely. But it's a hard habit to break."

"Why were you in the hospital?" Beth asked as she waited for the tea to cool a bit.

Jessie lit the cigarette and exhaled slowly. "A group of men beat me up and raped me," she said finally, looking directly at Beth.

"Oh lord," Beth whispered. "I'm sorry."

"So was I," Jessie answered briefly. "What is your name? I'm Beth."

"Jessie. Jessie Pyne."

Jessie was startled by Beth's reaction. The woman drew back, her face drained of color, and stared at her as though afraid.

"I . . . I saw your picture . . . in the newspaper. Several months ago. You were . . . helping a black woman, a black woman who was hurt."

Jessie watched her closely. "She died. Were you at that march?"

"No. No, I . . . Hank, I mean, my husband would never allow me to . . . I've got to go check on the children." She left the room, almost running. Jessie stared after her. Hank? Her husband's name was Hank? It couldn't be the same man. Hank wasn't that uncommon a name. She sipped her tea slowly and finished her cigarette. Then she rose to her feet. She hesitated for a moment, wondering what to do with Beth's cup. Then, with a shrug, she poured the cold tea down the sink and washed the two cups, leaving them in the drainer.

She heard the scream of brakes being released and looked out the window. There was Jake with the load of wood he had promised. She saw him wave from the cab of the semi when he spotted her face at the window. Better go outside and show him where to drop the load. No telling where he might leave it otherwise. Forgetting Beth momentarily, Jessie went out the back door.

KATE STUCK HER HEAD OUT and shouted to be heard over the chainsaw. "Jessie? Jessie!"

Jessie looked up and slowed the saw to idle. "Yeah?"

"I have to go to the store. The locksmith still hasn't shown up, and there are no other staff people here. If he comes while I'm gone, will you show him what needs to be done?"

"Sure," Jessie yelled.

Kate blew her a kiss and disappeared. Jessie wiped the wood chips from her goggles and revved up the saw.

TIMMY HUFFED DOWN THE STAIRS, stomping loudly. "I won't do it," he shouted upwards. "I won't wash dishes! Only girls wash dishes!" He stormed into the kitchen and put the plates on the counter by the sink. His dad would have a fit if he ever caught him washing dishes. His mom was trying to make a sissy out of him. Well, she wouldn't do it, not to him. Mark was sure a sissy, crying over everything. He raised a fuss over that little black eye Timmy had given him. But he warned that sneak. If Mark tried to get into the upper bunk, he would pop him one. He didn't even hit him that hard, for crying out loud. You would have thought he bopped him with a baseball bat or something.

Timmy shuffled into the living room, his hands in the pockets of his sagging jeans. His mom had tried to make him put on a belt, but he was tired of her always telling him what to do. It sure was a bother, though, to have to keep pulling his pants up all the time.

The face at the window in the door scared him at first. Then he looked closer. Excitement welled up in the boy, and he ran to the door, struggling with the lock. He threw the door open and threw himself into his father's arms.

"Dad! I knew you would come!"

Hank hugged the boy briefly and then set him on his feet, stooping in front of him so they were eye level.

"Is your mom here?"

Timmy nodded. "Yeah, she's upstairs. Boy, is she ever ..."

"Ssshhhh. Don't make so much noise."

"Oh yeah. You're not supposed to be in here, are you?"

"Says who?" Hank growled.

"Not me," Timmy answered with a happy smile. "Are we going home now, Daddy?"

"Damned right. All of us. Where your mother got the big idea to waltz out with the two of you is beyond me. But I'll take care of her big ideas once and for all when we get home. Now you go upstairs and get your things together. And you tell your mother I want her down here right now."

"I heard you, Hank." Beth stood on the steps, her eyes wide with fright. "You're not supposed to be here. Get out."

Hank blinked in surprise. Then his eyes narrowed in anger. "You don't tell me what to do! Pack your things, and let's get out of this place."

Beth stopped Timmy as he tried to race up the stairs past her. "We're staying, Hank. I'm not coming home, and I won't let the children come back either."

"Let go of me!" Timmy tried to break Beth's grip on his shirt. "No! You are staying right here. I want you to see just what kind of man your daddy really is. Be still, Timmy!"

"Come down from there, Beth," Hank said softly.

"You're not going to hurt me anymore. I won't let you."

"Be reasonable, Beth," Hank smiled at her, carefully keeping an eye on the other doors to make sure no one else entered without his knowledge. "I never did anything you didn't bring on yourself. Come home and act like a wife should act, and I promise I'll never hit you again. It's all your fault. You know that, don't you?"

"None of it is my fault."

Hank took a step towards her, and Beth backed up the stairs. "Don't come up here, Hank. I'm not alone."

Hank laughed. "If you think I'm scared of the other broads here, you sure are stupid. You hear that, Timmy? Your mom thinks I'm scared of a bunch of women."

Timmy laughed uncertainly, looking from his father to his mother who had not loosened her grip on his shirt. "You're in enough trouble already, Hank. Don't make it any worse."

"I'm not in half the trouble you're gonna be in if you don't let go of my son and come down here right now!"

"It wasn't enough you hit me. You had to beat on the kids. And then you had to pick a woman out to beat up and rape. Then you had to set fire to her business. Where do you stop? Where do you draw the line?" For a moment, Beth thought she might throw up; her fear was so churning inside her. But she clung to the banister and to her son, making herself hold her ground.

Suddenly, Timmy twisted and lunged down the stairs. Beth grabbed for him but Hank was faster, jerking the boy into the living room and grabbing her arm. Beth lost her balance as he hauled her down the steps. Hank threw her on the sofa and stood over her, breathing hard.

"Let's hear some more of that tough talk!"

Beth kicked without thinking, narrowly missing his groin. She wouldn't, she couldn't let him beat her up again. If he did it again, she would go crazy. She would lose her mind.

Hank jumped back, more amazed than hurt. He laughed and grabbed her by the front of her blouse, and drew back his hand. "I'll beat the living hell out of you for that!" He slapped her, then slapped her again, his face contorted with fury. Timmy stood frozen in the corner.

Hank didn't see Jessie enter the room, the ax and the maul in her hands. She stood in the doorway, unable to move for a long moment. Then she got a good look at the man's face.

Without thinking, she gave in to the surge of fury. She swung the maul with a shriek. Hank caught the motion from the corner of his eye, released Beth, and jumped back as the maul swung by inches from his face. The blade buried itself in the wall with a loud thump and crack of plaster. Hank backed away, tripping over a hassock as he tried to get some distance between himself and the woman coming at him with an ax. On one knee, he looked around desperately for something with which to defend himself. He grabbed the poker from beside the fireplace. Jessie swung the ax and knocked it from his hands, the shock of metal on metal numbing Hank's arm to the shoulder.

Hank could have sworn he heard the blade whistle as she swung the ax again and again, never missing him by more than two or three inches. Hank crawled backwards across the floor, looking for escape. But Jessie had him pinned in a corner, swinging the ax back and forth in front of his face, across his groin, close to his chest. Every time she swung, she yelled. The sound drove itself into Hank.

"Beth!" he screamed desperately. "Beth, get her away from me! Get her away!"

Beth sat on the sofa where he had dropped her, mesmerized by what was happening in front of her. Horrified, she still didn't move.

"Dad? Daddy?" Timmy's voice was soft as he watched. "Get her away from me!" Hank was in tears, his face a pasty white as he tried to press his back through the wall. "Somebody do something! She's gonna kill me! Please! Oh god!" His voice broke off as he cried, his body drawn into a knot on the floor.

Jessie stood over him, feeling nothing. "Get in the closet. Crawl into that closet and close the door behind you."

Hank uncurled himself and shot into the closet, watching Jessie every minute. He was convinced she would sink the ax into him the moment he turned his back. When the door closed, Jessie flipped the lock and dropped the ax onto the floor, unable to hold it any longer. Her hands shook, and her mouth was dry. She hadn't noticed she was crying.

Kate stood at the edge of the room, her mouth open, two bags of groceries clutched to her chest. Finally she spoke, her voice a rasp. "Jessie . . . are you all right?"

Kate looked around the room, seeing the maul sticking out of the wall. Jessie nodded slowly as she walked towards Beth, her steps as unsteady as a drunk's. "Beth, are you all right?"

Jessie knelt in front of her, putting her hands on Beth's thin shoulders. "Are you okay? Did he hurt you?"

"I'm fine," Beth said, her voice cracking. Jessie held onto her, feeling faint.

Then Beth started to laugh. Leaning forward, arms crossed over her belly, she laid her head on Jessie's shoulder and laughed. Kate had still not moved. Jessie continued to hold Beth, a bewildered expression on her face. Finally, Beth straightened up and looked at Jessie.

"You . . ." she gasped, still laughing. "You made him crawl into that closet. You made him . . . if you only knew how many times I wanted to see him have to crawl, how many times I wanted to see him have to ask someone for something . . . if you only knew how long I had wanted him to ask me to help him . . . If you only knew." Beth ended in a whisper, and her laughter slowly changed into tears. Jessie pulled her close and rocked her back and forth while Kate watched. "If you only knew. If you only knew. If you only . . ."

20

JESSIE SAT DOWN AT THE DESK and leaned her head against the back of the chair. The police had come. Hank was locked away in jail once more. Beth was upstairs with the boys. Timmy seemed like a changed child, numbed from the experience and completely subdued.

Kate brought in a cup of tea and pressed it into Jessie's hands. Then she lit a cigarette and gave it to her. "You were truly amazing," she said softly.

Jessie looked at her tiredly. "I didn't even know what I was doing, Kate. I just reacted."

"You may very well have saved Beth's life."

"I'm just glad it's over."

Kate took Jessie's hand and held it, her finger tracing the pattern of veins under the pale skin. "I called a friend of mine in Asheville, a friend who told me a long time ago that she wanted to help in any way she could. I asked her if Beth and the children could come there for a few weeks, until things get sorted out here and Beth can decide what she wants to do. Jane said yes. The boys should love the farm. Beth will have some peace and quiet. I think she needs it. And I don't think there's any way her husband can find out where she is. There won't be any records kept."

"I'm glad to hear that. She needs to be a long way away from here."

"I just told her about it. She cried. I think she's packing up right now. I'll put her on a bus this afternoon."

"Good. She needs to know the whole world isn't like the one she's had to live in all these years. I wish I had a farm to go to right now."

"What do you need other than a farm right now?" Kate asked softly.

"Right now?" Jessie looked up at her with a small smile. "I need about fifteen hours of sleep. But I'm too tense to lie down."

"How are you feeling about what happened?"

"Scared. I think I could've killed him if he had come at me."

"He would've deserved it," Kate said vehemently.

Jessie glanced at her cup. "But I wouldn't have. It's scary for me to know I wasn't thinking, just reacting."

"You were thinking. Otherwise, you probably would have killed him. It seemed pretty clear that you were in full control of that ax."

"Maybe." Jessie looked up at her, a grin spreading over her face. "Did you see the expression on that cop's face when he found out I had used the ax? And when he saw the maul buried in the wall? Lizzie Borden!"

Kate laughed. "I think he felt safer with Hank than with you."

"He sure gave me hell for it though."

"Well, you just used what was at hand. I'm proud of you, Jess. You fought back. That's something I have always fantasized about doing. It feels good to know it can really be done."

Kate ran her fingers through Jessie's tousled hair, then rose from her stooped position. "Are you going to be all right by yourself for a while? I have to get Beth ready for the bus. I think I can probably get Betsy to take her to the bus station."

"I'll be fine," Jessie answered.

"Okay. The locksmith should be finishing up soon. After that, you could just sack out here on the sofa if you'd like."

"How's the little boy doing?" Jessie asked.

"Timmy?" Kate shrugged. "I'm not sure. He thought his dad was the toughest man who ever lived, worshipped him. This has been quite a shock to the kid, I think. Beth was going to try to get him to take a nap before we left for the bus. She said she didn't know what else to do for him right now. He's not talking to anyone. Or at least, he wasn't a little while ago."

"How does she seem to be doing?" Jessie persisted. Kate reached out and stroked her hair. "She seems to be doing fine. A little numb, but she acts like she feels safe for the first time. There's a spark in her I haven't seen before."

"Good." Jessie closed her eyes, suddenly exhausted. Over and over, she replayed the scene in her mind; she had known exactly what she was doing. She hadn't wanted to hurt Hank, only make him feel the same helpless terror she had felt. She had wanted to frighten him, cower him, humiliate him. She had done that. Jessie smiled up at Kate as Kate touched her cheek and turned to leave the room.

Jessie stood quietly in the living room, studying the hole in the wall she had made with the eight-pound maul. A large chunk of plaster was missing, and a crack ran almost to the ceiling. She would have to fix that. She touched the hole, almost not believing she could have done it. She looked at her hand. In the palm, pale but visible, were crescent-shaped scars made by her fingernails. Jessie stretched her fingers, feeling them flex easily for the first time in months.

BETH SAW JESSIE as she carried her suitcases down the stairs and put them by the door. She stepped up as close as she dared, her gaze fixed on the hole in the wall.

"Jessie?"

Jessie turned, a smile breaking across her face. "How are you?"

"Good. I'm good. I was hoping I would see you before I left. I want to say thank you."

Jessie shifted uncomfortably. "I wish you wouldn't. I did it mostly for me. I'm sorry he had to be your husband. I'm sorry for both of us."

Beth sat down in a chair and stared at the backs of her hands. "I know what Hank and his friends did to you. Kate told me the whole story. I knew something was going on. I only wish I had known how to stop them. But I was afraid, afraid of what he would do to me if I interfered."

"It wasn't your fault. Chances are you wouldn't have been able to do a thing anyway."

"I will come back and testify if my statement isn't enough."

"I appreciate that. I hope you won't have to."

"Me, too." They sat quietly together, enjoying the silence in the room. Finally, Beth spoke again. "I guess I'll never figure him out. I guess I'll never understand what makes a man like him hate so much."

Jessie looked at her. "I know."

JESSIE MUST HAVE DOZED sitting in the chair. When she opened her eyes, the room was dark and there was a hard pounding on the door. Lifting the shade cautiously, she peered out. Moon, Laura, Val, and Denny stood on the porch.

Jessie unlocked the door, relief surging through her. She wondered briefly how long it would take her to calm down completely.

Moon grabbed Jessie and swung her around the room. "What a woman! What a woman!"

Jessie let herself go limp in Moon's arms, knowing it was useless to struggle until Moon decided to put her down. Finally, Moon set her down with a jarring thump and turned

Jessie to face her, a tight grip on Jessie's shoulders. "You are something else. I wish I could have been here!"

"You can do better than that. You can take me out for dinner and a drink. Then take me home and tuck me in bed. I am tired and hungry."

"You got it," Moon agreed enthusiastically.

A voice close behind Jessie startled her. "Jess," Kate said. "It sounds good to have Moon treat you to dinner and a drink, but I would like to stake a claim on the tucking into bed part."

Jessie could feel the flush starting on her chest. She turned with a moan, hoping it wouldn't turn into a full-fledged blush. But the others saw the creeping red and shouted laughter across the room. Finally, Laura was able to speak. "The insurance check came through today, Jessie."

Jessie looked at her carefully. "What do you want to do?"

"Well, we should talk tomorrow, I guess."

"All right," Jessie agreed.

"Jessie," Laura said reflectively, "have you ever considered owning a bar?"

Jessie stared at her in disbelief. "I don't know the first thing about bars."

"There's one for sale," Laura said, a wicked grin spreading across her face. "Just think about it, okay?"

Jessie shook her head and laughed. "Okay. Let's get out of here, please?"

Kate closed the door and locked it behind them. It was cold outside. Jessie zipped her jacket and turned up the collar, slowing down to wait for Kate.

"Y'know, Jess, I don't think we should fix the wall." Jessie glanced at Kate. "No?"

Kate grinned. "Nope. I think we should leave it just the way it is."

BETSY HANDED BETH the tickets and a twenty-dollar bill. Beth had already slipped the small bag of food into Mark's knapsack. Carefully herding the children in front of her, she checked their suitcases at the baggage area, then found seats for the two boys in the waiting room.

"Stay right here and don't move," she said as she headed towards the snack shop. She bought cartons of milk and some cookies. Then she pushed through the crowd, hoping the children were where she left them. As she worked her way through the people milling about the ticket counter, she noticed a newspaper rack. Inserting a quarter, she removed the top paper and allowed the door to snap shut.

Beth handed the milk to the boys and sat down beside them. "Can we really ride horses, Mom?" Mark asked excitedly. "That's what Kate said. But you'll have to listen to Jane and do what she tells you so you can learn the right way."

Beth glanced at the two boys. Mark looked eager, ready for what he saw as an adventure. Timmy stared quietly at the wall, his expression far away. Beth sighed. It would take time, a lot of time. She crossed her legs, ankle on knee, and leaned back. It would be better this way, no matter what happened. Settling herself more comfortably into the plastic chair, she smiled.

Then, she opened her newspaper and began to read.

Afterword

CLENCHED FISTS, BURNING CROSSES AND CRIS SOUTH'S
SOUTHERN LESBIAN FEMINISM

▼

CLENCHED FISTS, BURNING CROSSES is a novel very much *of* its time—the fierce entanglement of antiracism, liberation, and the Women in Print movement that characterized Southern lesbian feminism—and a novel *ahead* of its time. Its themes and critiques speak to our current moment of #metoo, #blacklivesmatter, and intersectional feminism.

Cris South grew into this literary and activist moment from a working-class background that was unusual in women's liberation. Her story and Southern lesbian feminist organizations and publications laid the foundation for this important novel of the Radical South.

South was born in Charlotte, North Carolina, in 1950. Her family was conservative and working class. She married a man and had a son; after she began to understand herself as a lesbian and left her marriage, she lost custody. Soon after, she was deeply involved in activism in the 1970s, which included feminist and gay and lesbian activism. She explained in an interview:

> I had just come out and got more and more involved in the movements that were so strong in those days. I did a lot of work in antinuke, antiracism, while struggling with my own having grown up as a working-class woman with very racist family. They couldn't understand me at all. I struggled with being a lesbian mom who had her child taken away from her and yet doing the work I knew I had to do in the community. The '70s and early '80s were some of the most fascinating political times for the lesbian, gay racial communities, because so much was going on—the whole Greensboro lunch counter sit-in launched the antiracism movement in North Carolina. And my father was very opposed to it.[1]

For South, growing up in a racist family meant that unlearning racism was the work of a lifetime. She found colleagues and partners in this journey through women's liberation and the women in print movements.

South met Catherine Nicholson, co-founder of *Sinister Wisdom*, a multicultural lesbian literary and art journal, and they became close friends, along with Harriet Ellenberger, Nicholson's partner. The friendship exposed South to a broad network of lesbian feminists in the American South and beyond. At women's conferences, South met feminists such as Adrienne Rich, Cherríe Moraga, and Gloria Anzaldúa—all women with national profiles. She said, "I can remember being at a writing conference, all of us drinking beer and smoking cigarettes and talking politics with Cherríe and Gloria and a bunch of other women that were in a writer's group." Lesbian feminist networks (and notably, all three of these well-known feminists were lesbians) opened up a new world of activism and ideas to a woman who had spent all her life, up until that point, in Charlotte, North Carolina.

This is not to say that feminist relationships were easy. In South's experience, working-class women were a rarity in the women's movement: "It was one thing to be a working-class dyke in those days. Then, there seemed to be really two real classes, and one was working class. And one was the highly educated master's and PhD crowd who taught in colleges and everything. I was a working-class dyke who was very intimidated by people with things after their names. I started hanging out with many, many different kinds of women that I had not experienced before." South found that experience both challenging and transformative. Her friendship with writer Dorothy Allison was grounded in their shared experience of class in the women's movement: "Dorothy's trippy, and she's one of the most wonderful human beings that ever walked on two legs," she told me. "But we were both Southern working-class lesbians. And we bonded around that. Dorothy and I became really close friends. We talked a lot. We bonded around sexual freedom and sexual expression, around working class—a lot about class and writing." That friendship with Allison continued through breakups and cross-country moves.

South's life changed dramatically when she decided to move to Durham, a midsize North Carolina city and home to Duke University, where she met Mab Segrest, Minnie Bruce Pratt, and others, all of whom were part of the Feminary collective. Pratt encouraged South to claim her right to a voice, despite being intimidated by PhD students and university professors. "Minnie Bruce was instrumental in helping me," South said, "because she thought I had something to say. And it was worth it."

This transformation was facilitated by Feminary, a feminist collective that rebranded the local women's studies newspaper into a feminist journal of the same name.

The name of the group (and the journal) came from a term Monique Wittig coined in her experimental lesbian novel *Les Guerilleres* to describe the books that women in the novel carried around their necks as a sign of liberation. The name's French feminist origin was surprising, as Feminary was unapologetically grounded in Southern identity. The founders' mission statement made this explicit in the inaugural issue of the magazine: "As Southerners, as lesbians, and as women, we need to explore with others how our lives fit into a region about which we have great ambivalences—to share our anger and our love."[2]

They also emphasized storytelling, the importance of antiracist work, and "feminist and lesbian organizing in a region whose women suffer greatly in their lack of political power." They concluded with an evangelical zeal: "We want to know who we are. We want to change women's lives."

Feminary quickly became a central meeting place for far-flung members of the Southern lesbian-feminist tribe. Class and race analyses were central to their work; Southern patriarchy was the problem, and broad coalitions against that hegemony were seen as the only solution. *Feminary* made excavating the radical South central to its embrace of a multicultural lesbian feminism. It was framed as a distinctively Southern, antiracist publishing forum, one that purposefully included women of color. The journal emphasized the voices of African Americans, all of whom had roots in the South, and also sought out Native American and Hispanic voices. It aimed to create new ways of remembering and defining, new maps, and new conceptions of the South. From 1978 to 1982, *Feminary* served to queer and remap the South.

For Cris South, Feminary was an egalitarian experience; there was no pulling of institutional rank. The original members—Helen Langa, Pratt, Eleanor Holland, Segrest, and South—challenged each other, divided work equally, and provided a safe environment to learn and liberate themselves from their racist upbringing: "Each one of us would take an issue, and we would head up that issue and everybody would work on it. But there was one person coordinating, which turned out to be one of the smarter things we did." This meant that the perspective of each member was valued and fore-grounded. It also meant that members could challenge one another and learn from each member's distinct perspective.

Egalitarian relationships were always the ideal in feminist collectives; the reality usually fell short. According to South, Feminary worked very hard to make this ideal their reality. And as they received feedback from readers, the collective continued to evolve with its definition of the South and "Southernness," in its inclusion of diversity on the board, and in its constant state of learning and responsiveness. As a result, the work featured in *Feminary* remains both relevant and groundbreaking today.

Despite this extraordinary work, *Feminary* lasted only three years; it was the vanguard of a multicultural lesbian feminist South. As was the case for so many feminist periodicals, the lack of capital led to its demise. South explained:

> Doing *Feminary* was very, very hard. We didn't really
> have a home for it. For a while, Eleanor [Holland] was
> going over to a little print shop ... after working hours
> and printing on their printing presses. Then we got a
> little printing press, and we moved it into the YWCA in
> Durham, but it was in a side room that was unheated.
> We would have to set up heaters and try to thaw out the
> ink. And Eleanor and I were the only ones that knew
> how to run the presses. And there was so little money;
> it was hard. We were doing the best we could.

Their egalitarianism stopped with the practical realities of printing and the lack of financial support. Ultimately, *Feminary* moved to the West Coast with the hopes of better funding, but only one issue was published before it folded permanently, joining the fate of so many other pioneering feminist periodicals.

Despite its brief tenure, however, *Feminary* planted seeds that flowered over the next decade. The conversations it engendered and the intersectional feminist analysis it championed resulted in a number of important books, including Mab Segrest's *Memoir of a Race Traitor* and Minnie Bruce Pratt's *Rebellion*, but its first fruit was South's 1984 novel, *Clenched Fists, Burning Crosses*.

Clenched Fists, Burning Crosses

South told me that the idea for the novel came from something that happened to her after she attended an anti-Klan march:

> I was wearing the button that I was going to wear at the rally had I gone. It said, "Stop the KKK." I lived way out in the country in northern Orange County [North Carolina], and north of Hillsborough. And I went into a little country store. There were a couple of guys sitting at the woodstove over in the corner. I went up to the counter and John stands here and he says, "Stop the KKK?" And the guys at the woodstove turn around and focus all their attention on me. He said, "Don't you live up there at Newt Tucker's place?" They may as well have drawn a map, everybody [then] knew where I lived.

After that incident, someone showed up at her remote cabin, where she lived alone:

> A car pulled up in my driveway and sat there with their headlights on the house. Scared me to death.

> Newt came, and when he found out what's going on, he handed me his rifle. And I was not pro-gun, but these guys scared me. And they came back. And this time I walked out the door with the gun just resting across my arm. I didn't aim it at him. I just stood there. We just stared each other down. They backed their car up and left. I almost fainted. I was that scared. And they never came back.

South remembered that feeling of terror and used the novel to explore her worst fears—especially that something would happen to her dog while she was away.

South's fears were not unfounded. South had attended the "Death to the Klan" march in Greensboro in November 1979 when five of the organizers, the militant Communist Workers Party, were murdered by the Klan. The alleged perpetrators were subsequently tried and acquitted.[3] South connected the Klan and the work she was doing at a battered women's shelter at the time and decided to explore the relationship between racism, homophobia, misogyny, and violence. In the novel, one of the members of the Klan is a domestic abuser as well.

The novel's epigraph comes from poet and activist Pat Parker's essay "Revolution: It's Not Neat or Pretty or Quick," in which she places the Klan within a feminist critique of a patriarchal society. South frames her novel within a critique of contemporary culture, a critique that refuses to consider the Klan an aberration: Instead, for South, the Klan is emblematic of a racist patriarchy that everyone experiences. *Clenched Fists, Burning Crosses* insists that we understand the link between racism and homophobia and how violence, including domestic abuse and rape, protects that system. And it models the kinds of coalitions necessary to combat that oppressive system.

At the novel's core is Jessie Pyne, a newly out lesbian trying to come to terms with her sexual identity and her responsibilities as an activist, ally, lover, and friend. Her sexual coming out—when she has sex with a woman for the first time—is inseparable from her political coming out. When the novel opens, she has had an argument with her business partner, Laura, because Jessie dismissed a newspaper report about the Klan as "silly." Laura teaches her some suppressed Southern history about the role of the Klan in a larger racist heteropatriarchy:

> Let me give you a little piece of reality to think about. In the early 1900s, my grandfather and grandmother bought fifteen acres of land in northern Georgia. They were farmers. The Klan paid them a visit. They burned my grandfather's house to the ground and rode through all the crops. Two years later, because my grandparents wouldn't leave, they came back. They burned the place again. They tore up the crops. But this time, they beat my grandfather and left him a cripple for life. He was a young man with a wife and five kids. They had to move into town and my grandmother had to do maid's work to support the family. Some local white men visited my grandfather and told him that they had heard there was some mischief brewing, but they hadn't taken it seriously. Mischief! Then those good-intentioned white men offered to buy granddaddy's land from him. They bought it for twenty-five cents on the dollar. (18)

Laura suggests that there is a seamless system of economic disparity in the South constructed through violence—that is, the shock troops (the KKK) do the terrorizing and the rich planter class scoops up the rewards. And Jessie soon learns that white people who break with white supremacy also face similar forms of racial terror—for example, in the scene where the gas station attendant points out her "Stop the KKK" button and when Jessie finds herself under surveillance.

Before Jessie's own ordeal begins, however, South makes sure we see the link between racial and sexual terror. Just a short time after the gas station scene, Jessie's landlady, Dorothy, tells her a story about her aunt, who has been institutionalized by her husband, illustrating how this system targets women, especially poor women. The title of the book is explained in this passage:

"We was there to pay a visit to my aunt. She'd been there goin' on eight years, and I reckon she was crazy. Least that's what they said. I remember it like it was yesterday. Her lyin' there, not sayin' a word to nobody. . . . But she kept her hands clenched into fists with her thumbs inside like this," Dorothy demonstrated with her own hands, "and her fingers clenched down tight over her thumbs. Been like that the whole eight years. Nobody could open that woman's hands. It like to made me sick to look at her, sick to my heart and soul. She was a pretty woman 'fore she got put in there. But her skin was as white as pastry flour, and her eyes didn't seem to have no color to 'em.

"And her hands, Jessie, I wisht you could seen her hands. Her thumbnails had done growed clean through her hands and was stickin' out the other side. The nails of her other fingers had growed into the meat, too. Nurses said they had tried to open her hands and cut them nails but they couldn't do no good with 'em. Finally, they just gave up tryin'. I guess a woman clench her fists long enough, ain't nothing nobody can do about it. Reckon it could happen to any of us."

"They grew through her hands?" Jessie asked incredulously, not wanting to believe the story. Mrs. Carpenter glanced at her, sensing the disbelief.

"That's what I'm tellin' you, aint it? Woman, I seen it with my own eyes! And she let a man do it to her!" (39)

This grotesque image sticks with the reader, as it sticks with Jessie throughout the course of the novel. Here, South reframes the common association of a clenched fist. Usually, it is depicted as a symbol of power, defiance, and pride, the fist right before a punch is thrown. South, by contrast, portrays the clenched fist as a symbol of disempowerment, of frustration, of defeat, of—in Langston Hughes's words—a dream deferred. A woman trapped under the surveillance of the state clenches her fist until it is useless.

By placing this anecdote so close to Laura's history lesson, South reminds us that poor white women were also targets of Southern patriarchal violence, punished brutally for stepping out of line. The violent rape that Beth, the wife of a racist police officer, suffers is an example of this institutional control. For white women of a certain class, the revelation that rape is an essential tool of Southern patriarchy was surprising. It was a shock for many white Southern lesbian feminists to learn just how fragile that protection was. When white women challenged patriarchal authority, rape was often used against them; in Jessie's (the "N**ger lover's") case, she did not deserve respect. Many Southern lesbian feminists first came to political activism through the civil rights movement and anti-Klan activism, and the use of sex as a weapon against them was consistent and brutal.

Jessie would soon experience this escalation herself. When she witnesses a murder at an anti-Klan demonstration, she becomes a direct target. Her home is trashed, her dog is hanged, and splashed in red paint on the walls in her home are the words "ni**er lover" and "queer." The harassment culminates midway through the novel in Jessie's grisly gang rape—an act of political terrorism intimately connected to the murder that prompted it.

South's description of the brutal rape in the novel makes it clear that sexual violence is logically tied to other forms of violence; that rape is a tool of terror, along with beatings and lynchings. A Klansman beats Jessie outside her print shop: "She didn't see the fist coming. She felt it instead, bony and unyielding against the side of her face. The blow slammed her back and shoulders into the dumpster. . . . Tom jerked her to him, his breath warm on her cheek. 'You're not talking so big now, are you? Go on. Fight back. I like that.' All clarity vanished as he hit her again" (96). The punch leads, inexorably, to another one; and his strange sadistic sexual language quickly becomes a sadistic group rape.

The detail of the initial attack is hard to read; the narrative seemingly blacks out and dissociates during the rape, as the protagonist does. The men believe they have done her a favor by "just" raping her. The assumptions of rape culture are explicit: all women need to be taught their place, and they secretly enjoy being brutalized. That Jessie survives and triumphs over her attackers by the end of the novel does not erase the violent reality of this disciplinary rape.

This brutal assault occurs about midway through the novel. Most of our culture's stories of rape end with the assault—"victims" are assumed to be irrevocably broken. South's novel, by contrast, makes us consider how Jessie both survives and recovers from this assault, and how Beth decides to escape the system of terror that exists in her marriage. Jessie suffers, haunted by recurring images of clenched fists, a symbol of her own sense of powerlessness and helplessness: "Sometimes lately I catch myself clenching my fists so tightly that I cut the skin on my hands. I dream about being like that woman, my fists always tight and useless, and my not being able to open them anymore" (124).

As she struggles with her own rage, grief, and shame Jessie discovers that no one in her circle is unaffected by sexual violence. Kate, Jessie's lover, was beaten by her father and raped by her brother; her best friend's lover was gang raped; Laura, her Black business partner, was beaten; and Laura's white lover, Moon, was shot and left for dead by the Klan in

Mississippi in the 1960s. And the violence is not limited to her lesbian feminist circle; one of the rapists, Hank, a police officer and a Klan member, abuses his own wife, Beth, beating and raping her viciously.

The novel asks the question: How does one survive sexual and racial terror? South shows us that it is friendship, community, and resistance. South provides a nuanced portrait of the diverse women in feminist groups, their connection in the American South to civil rights and antiracist work, and the ways everyone has to grow and challenge preconceptions. Laura is one key source of friendship, but so too is Jessie's girlfriend, Kate, who survived her own violent childhood and must reckon with it as well. Jessie's larger friend group also provides models of survival and resistance. They cannot prevent terrible things from happening, but they can support, encourage, and shelter. Val finds Jessie after her rape, takes her into her own apartment, and takes care of her. Her friends never leave her alone, in the hospital or at Val's apartment.

That friend network also provides models of resistance, organizing, and activism. Moon, a civil rights worker who meets Laura in Jackson, Mississippi, shows Jessie how to fight back. This is shown in a scene when Moon and Laura discover Klan members in the printing shop, call the police, and prevent the Klansmen's escape from them. *How* they do so is telling; Moon waits outside the printing shop with an ax handle. All three Klan members are apprehended by the police, allowing Jessie to later identify her rapists, who are then charged. When Jessie overhears the conversation about Moon's acts of retaliation, she shows signs hope for the first time since her assault:

> Laura smiled, nudging Moon with her elbow. "This one got to play out one of her lifelong fantasies last night. She got to pole-ax two of those three men."
> "Pole-ax? I don't get it."

"Simple. I waited outside the door with an ax handle. I got the first guy right in the ribs. I got the second guy right over the top of his head. And I made the third guy crawl out on all fours to keep me from popping him, too. And woman, it felt soooo good."

"You're the one who laid them out?"

None of them had heard Jessie's approach. She stared at Moon, the beginnings of a delighted smile playing across her face. "You did that, all by yourself?"

"With unlimited pleasure." (170)

As much as this group of activist friends reject guns and machismo at rallies, they are not pacifists; they believe in putting up a fight. Jessie takes this lesson to heart at the end of the novel.

Kate runs a battered women's shelter, and this allows for the final cowardly member of the trio, Hank, to face his own reckoning. Hank's wife escapes to the shelter, having finally found the courage to leave her husband. A fellow police officer tells Hank where the shelter is (despite knowing that Hank has been arrested for arson and that his wife has left him), and when he appears, Jessie protects Beth, sinking a maul into the wall just inches from Hank's face, leaving him whimpering in the corner as she swings an ax at him over and over again, just barely missing him each time. "'Get her away from me!'" Hank says. "Hank was in tears, his face a pasty white as he tried to press his back through the wall. 'Somebody do something! She's gonna kill me! Please! Oh god!' His voice broke off as he cried, his body drawn into a knot on the floor. Jess stood over him, feeling nothing. 'Get in the closet. Crawl into that closet and close the door behind you'" (210). Very few survivors of rape get the chance to confront and shame their attackers. Jessie's mastery of this scene of potential violence—her "Lizzie Borden" moment—is a profound kind of wish fulfillment. That Jessie, newly emerged from the closet and punished viciously for it, forces her rapist into a closet is deeply satisfying.

It is also a moment in which Beth and Jessie, both survivors of Hank's violence, find kinship. In this scene, Beth says to Jessie, "You made him *crawl* into that closet. You made him.... If you only knew how many times I wanted to see him have to crawl, how many times I wanted to see him have to ask someone for something" (211).

The pairing of Beth and Jessie becomes clear in this final scene, and Beth's testimony against her husband makes it possible for Jessie to hold those men accountable for what they did to her.

Clenched Fists, Burning Crosses is a novel unflinching in its depiction of the violence of the Southern system—its racism, sexism, and homophobia, and the vicious interpellations that allow the system to function. But it is also, paradoxically, a hopeful novel, one that insists on the power of queer folks to survive, resist, and thrive in spite of the forces arrayed against them. The final scene of Jessie's celebration with her lesbian feminist community emphasizes their resolve: Southern lesbian feminists will not be intimidated, and they will not be driven out of their communities.

How the Novel Came Into Print

The publication history of *Clenched Fists, Burning Crosses* is a study in intersectional feminism. South worked full-time in print shops, so finding the time to write this novel was a challenge. She received $100 from an anonymous donor, which helped give her time to write. Another patron was Tia Cross of the Cross pens fortune, who also donated time and money to the cause. Both Cross and *Landykes of the South* coeditor Merrill Mushroom read drafts of the novel. And, in the final push to finish the book, South and Mab Segrest stayed in a borrowed beach house during the winter and wrote for a month. South explained: "A friend of our parents had an old mobile home down there, and I would get up every morning and go out and watch the sunrise. This was in November, so it's cold as hell in North Carolina beaches. Then I would sit cross-legged on the bed with the typewriter on pillows in front of me and work. Then Mab and I would meet in the middle of the trailer for lunch. And I spent that month finishing the book. It was a long process and arduous process." At first, she said, she wasn't sure how to end it. "Part of me wanted the Ku Klux Klan to learn their lessons," she said, "and realized that probably wasn't going to happen. I mean, they do occasionally. So that's what I did with it." She also wasn't sure where to send the novel: "There still wasn't a lot of books like this. You could get lesbian eroticism. You could get books of political stuff like what Adrienne Rich and people like that were turning out. You could get books of poetry, but you weren't getting much political fiction. So it was a unique book for its time."

South's connections in lesbian feminist circles helped her get the novel published. She began talking with Naiad Press, which, cofounded by the irascible Barbara Grier, was the self-proclaimed "biggest lesbian press in the world." But as Naiad shifted its focus to lesbian romance and genre fiction, South realized Naiad's publishing goals didn't mesh with hers. It was also important to South that the cover reflect the content and not look like the typical Naiad Press covers, which were notorious in lesbian circles for "trashy" aesthetics and low-quality printing.

South soon sent the manuscript to Nancy Bereano at Crossing Press, who had published several other Southern lesbian feminists. (Bereano would go on to found the legendary Firebrand Press.) At Crossing, Bereano published important work but did not have the authority or budget to promote her books. South explained:

Crossing wasn't really willing to put any money behind their authors. What they wanted me to do was use my own money and go out and promote the book and sell the book. I was working class. I was working in print shops. I didn't have money to travel to DC and Richmond and all those places to do readings and sell books. So it didn't get promoted very well. And [Bereano] wasn't able to do much. Plus, they wanted her to stop publishing stuff like my books and start editing cookbooks. [Crossing] wanted cookbooks, and that's why she ended up leaving them.

South said that working with Bereano was a good experience; the only thing she didn't like was the title Crossing chose. She wanted it to be simply "Clenched Fists." The book received one good review in the *New York Times* and then the book, as she put it, "fizzled." It has not been in print since—until now.

Aftermaths: Antiracist Activism

In the 1990s, fellow Feminary members Minnie Bruce Pratt and Mab Segrest continued in the tradition that South defined in *Clenched Fists, Burning Crosses*. Segrest worked as an anti-Klan activist; her 1995 *Memoir of a Race Traitor* became a touchstone for contemporary antiracist activism. Pratt had an equally important cultural impact with her collection of essays, *Rebellion*, which brought many of her *Feminary* articles together with contemporary work. Yet her insistence that history provided multiple models of radical transformation fuels her own essays.

As for Cris South, she traveled many miles after publishing the novel: California, where she worked at a lesbian cafe in Berkeley; Hawaii, where she lived with her now-wife's family; and Palm Springs, where she now lives with her wife—they've been together for twenty-eight years. She loves Palm Springs, which is queer-friendly and "we don't have to hide at all," she told me. She also said she would like to write a sequel to *Clenched Fists, Burning Crosses*.

WE ARE DELIGHTED to bring this important Southern novel back in print as part of our Radical Souths series, and we invite you to think about its continued relevance in our current political moment. One of the most important messages of the novel, for South, is that she had to unlearn racism because she was the product of a racist upbringing. She valued the chance to be with people who challenged her to grow and to work through her own fear to deconstruct that racism. "We are all racist," she said, and we have to get there with other folks to learn and not be threatened by those challenges.

Notes

1. Cris South, interview by author, May 15, 2024. Subsequent quotations from Cris South are from this interview and have been edited for clarity.

2. *Feminary: A Feminist Journal for the South, Emphasizing the Lesbian Vision* 10, no. 1 (1979): 4.

3. Mab Segrest wrote about this incident extensively in *Memoir of a Race Traitor* (1994).

www.ingramcontent.com/pod-product-compliance
Lightning Source LLC
Chambersburg PA
CBHW030819020726
47499CB00006B/1993